Cowboy

ALSO BY SARA DAVIDSON

Loose Change
Real Property
Friends of the Opposite Sex
Rock Hudson: His Story

COWBOY

Sara Davidson

Cliff Street Books
An Imprint of HarperCollinsPublishers

A hardcover edition of this book was published in 1999 by Cliff Street Books, an imprint of HarperCollins Publishers.

HarperCollins books may be purchased for educational, business, or sales promotional use. For information please write: Special Markets Department, HarperCollins Publishers Inc., 10 East 53rd Street, New York, NY 10022.

First paperback edition published 2000.

Knot illustration and design by Emilie Smith

The Library of Congress has catalogued the hardcover edition as follows:

Davidson, Sara.
　　Cowboy / Sara Davidson. —1st ed.
　　　p.　cm.
　　　ISBN 0-06-019326-3
　　　I. Title.
　　PS3554.A92586C69　1999
　　813'.54—dc21　　　　　　　　　　　　　　　　　　　　　98-30753

ISBN 0-06-093135-3 (pbk.)

00 01 02 03 04 ❖/RRD 10 9 8 7 6 5 4 3 2 1

ACKNOWLEDGMENTS

I want to thank Ken Topolsky, my TV partner, who suggested I call this book: *Even Cowboys Get the Jews*.

Thanks to Tom Robbins, who responded, "If the hero likes to smoke dope and complain a lot, you could call it: *Whine, Stoned Cowboy*."

But things were not always so jolly. There was a time when I had a first draft that did not work, no agent, no publisher, and no friend who could suggest how I might fix the draft. I would not have been able to come from that bleak time to this without the faith and help of key people: Jo-Ann Mapson, one of my favorite writers, who saw the book when I couldn't; Dennis Palumbo, who understands how to walk the writer's path; Caradoc King, my British agent, who came back into my life with unfailing enthusiasm after a gap of twenty years and led me to Joy Harris, my new agent and friend, who offered the counsel that started me writing again.

I'm grateful to longtime companions: Kathy Goodman, Dan

Wakefield, Karen Sperling, Andrew Weil, and Winnie Rosen, who encouraged me, as did Betsy Carter, Robin Schiff, Matthew Burke, Angela Rinaldi, and Beth Sullivan. I thank my family, Terry, Gary, and Summer Jennings and Alice Davidson for their unwavering support, and Nina Zimbelman, who helped me stay on track with myself. A special thanks to Diane Reverand, my editor, for her guidance and exquisite sensitivity. Finally, I thank my extraordinary and talented children, Andrew and Rachel Strauss. Bless you all.

AUTHOR'S NOTE

This book is based on a true story—a love affair I've had with the character whom I call Zack. For reasons of privacy, however, I have placed this story in a fictional context. I've created imaginary characters for the heroine's extended family, including Jeff, Rose, Veronica and the children, Sophie and Gabriel. No relationship should be inferred between these characters in the book and any living persons, nor should incidents about them be taken as fact.

The story is set during a period when I worked as a writer on the television show *Dr. Quinn, Medicine Woman*. I have used real incidents and the actual names of some of the prominent people on the production: Jane Seymour, Joe Lando, James Keach, Beth Sullivan, Jim Knobeloch, Jeanne Davis, Josef Anderson, Toni P., Toni G., Julie Henderson, Bryan Petty, Bobby Roth and Ozzie Smith. All other characters described in connection with *Dr. Quinn* are fictional.

—S.D.

INTRODUCTION

Alfred Kinsey once said, in writing about men, that there was no clear boundary between heterosexuals and homosexuals but a continuum of sexual preference, with men who are exclusively heterosexual at one end and men who are exclusively homosexual at the other, and most falling somewhere along the spectrum. "The world is not to be divided into sheep and goats," Kinsey wrote. "It is a fundamental of taxonomy that nature rarely deals with discrete categories. Only the human mind invents categories and tries to force facts into pigeon holes. The living world is a continuum in all its aspects."

This strikes me as piercingly apt when applied to the categories of fiction and nonfiction, novel and memoir. At one end of the spectrum are works that are entirely imagined, and at the other end, works that purport to be fact. Most, however, are a blend of fact and imagination, and yet a line has been drawn to separate one from the other.

I have long worked in what I perceive as the slippery slope between the two poles, the terrain where we find such entities as the nonfiction novel and the imagined autobiography. In *Loose Change*, published as nonfiction, I wrote about real people and historical events, yet I used fictional techniques—inventing dialogue, rearranging time, and combining scenes for dramatic purpose. In *Friends of the Opposite Sex*, a novel, I also wrote about real events and people but imagined more and altered the details and names.

When I began this book, I thought I was writing a novel. It was told in the voice of a woman named Caroline, but it was inspired by something that happened to me: a romance that had no future. From the first, the affair was ludicrous, impossible, laughable, something my friends would roll their eyes about and say, "Sara, you're brave." Zack was a cowboy who'd barely finished high school and lived in the desert where he practiced the nineteenth-century craft of braiding rawhide into bridles. I was a writer of books and television shows with degrees from Berkeley and Columbia. We walked, or I should say, leaped into the affair knowing that it had no future and we went on from moment to moment because we needed it and we were absolutely sure that in a short time we would look at each other and have nothing to say and that would be that.

Yet it has endured. The affair had a future that is now the present, and it has taught me things I did not know about love, the body, and the heart and the way we link ourselves to people who may not be politically or socially or in any way correct.

After I'd written three hundred pages, though, I could see the novel was not coming to life. I tried to fix it, change the point of view, restructure it, drop it, bury it under piles of other more pressing and economically rewarding work, but it kept knocking, demanding its turn. I would wake at five in the morning with a black knot of fear in my chest and a wish for my life to be over so I would not have to struggle with this book.

Then it came to me to write the story in my own voice, as I remembered it, which is not the same as the way it occurred. I tried to convey the experience as strongly as I could, and to that end, I began to add elements and imagine things I could not have known by any other means. To protect the privacy of my children and ex-husbands, I created fictional characters to stand in their stead and speak and act in ways they hadn't. What has resulted is a book that defies categories—a hybrid—and if that sounds like an elaborate dodge, what I can say is that I'm telling you this story in the best and perhaps the only way I can.

1

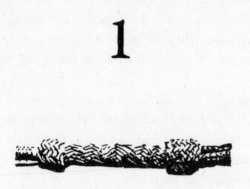

I've always loved cowboys. The way they look has a great deal to do with it. The sight of the Marlboro man on a billboard can give me a jolt of longing as I drive through traffic on my way to work. I imagine that the way some men respond to the sight of a woman in seamed stockings and garter belt is the way I feel when I see a man in chaps. The rough leather directs the eye up the legs to the place where the leather stops, just below the groin. The tight-fitting jeans, the boots with spurs, even the hat with its rakish, playful shape contribute to an image that I find deeply appealing.

It's an image that suggests ruggedness and wildness, cockiness, a sense of fun, and an intimate power over animals. Until the summer of 1993, however, I did not associate this image with a fine-tuned intelligence. I did not expect a cowboy to be articulate and well-read, I expected him to possess a crude, right-wing dumbness, so that for a woman with a certain education, a romance with a cowboy would be a misalliance.

I was intrigued, then, when I heard about cowboy poets. I was writing and producing a Western TV series, *Dr. Quinn, Medicine Woman*, when one of the wranglers on the set showed me a poster for a cowboy poetry and music festival in Elko, Nevada.

The wrangler, Earl McCoy, had puffy jowls and a stomach that pooched out over his belt, but the cowboys on the poster were lean, muscular, perched on a fence rail with their Stetsons tipped down over their foreheads.

"These men write poetry?"

"Hell, yes," Earl said. "Good poetry."

"Where is Elko, Nevada?"

"About four hours east of Reno." That was four hours east of not much.

He gave me tapes of them singing and reciting their poems, and after listening to them, I knew I had to go. I talked my friend Jeanne Davis, a colleague on the show, into coming with me, and arranged to write an article about the festival so that if it proved a disaster, I wouldn't be wasting a weekend. The other producers on the show joked that I was going to Elko "to get laid by cowboys," and, of course, there was a seed of truth in this. I had an instinct something might happen in Elko but I did not put much stock in that instinct; I didn't pack any form of birth control.

Two weeks later, I stood in my closet trying to decide what to wear. Jeans, obviously, but I had Calvin Klein jeans, I would look like a city slicker but that was unavoidable. I washed my hair and let it dry, fluffing it with my fingers. My hair was curly and when I was younger I'd spent painful hours trying to tame it, blow it dry, straighten it with an iron, or wind it on giant rollers with Dippity-Do, but now I left it natural.

Everything in my grooming routine was honed for efficiency and speed. I wore no makeup. I smoothed on skin moisturizer with sunblock, pulled on the jeans and a teal-colored shirt from Banana Republic and Italian shoe-boots and I was ready to walk out the door.

I drove my daughter, Sophie, who was eleven, and my son, Gabriel, ten, to their dad's house, opening the back of the station wagon to let Sophie out with her cat, Butterball. She was wearing a brown tank top, brown corduroy jeans, and brown nail polish with gold polka dots.

"Why can't I come with you?" she said.

"You know why. It's your weekend with Dad."

"If it's all right with him, can I come?"

I hugged her. "I'll be back Sunday night. I'll bring you a present."

Gabriel was dragging his skateboard out of the car, along with a bagful of CDs. "Can I have money instead of a present?"

"No."

"I'll take a present then." He leaned forward and kissed my cheek. "Love you, Mom."

"I love you too." I watched them walk to the door and waited for it to open. "Don't forget your reading!"

When I pulled up to Jeanne's house, she was waiting on the sidewalk with two large tote bags. She'd once been a flight attendant and I knew that in those tote bags was everything we could possibly need: a travel alarm clock, three boxes of Band-Aids in three different sizes, containers of healthy Sun Chips, regular and barbecue flavor, herbal tea bags, and an electric coil to heat water for the tea.

"Why are we doing this?" I said.

"It'll be a hoot," she said, buckling her seat belt.

"We have no idea what we're going to find."

She switched on the radio to KZLA, the country-music station, to set the mood. "Earl goes every year."

"Earl's strange."

Heads turned as we walked through the airport in Nevada to pick up our rental car. Jeanne was five feet ten, with that long, dazzling, bright blonde hair you find on women in Sweden, and I was equally tall with dark hair and neither of us wore a bra. We did not look as if we came from Elko.

We drove across town, passing the Red Lion Motel, which had two giant plastic steers in front, the Commercial Hotel, which had a white king polar bear rearing up over the door, numerous feed stores, and Brenda's Wedding Chapel, where you could get married with no blood test and no waiting.

When we arrived at the Elko Fairgrounds, however, we saw that the bleachers we'd expected to be filled with cowboys were packed instead with families—tourists wearing Bermuda shorts and carrying Big Gulp drinks. On the stage, a group of geriatric cowboys were singing "Tumbling Tumbleweed," and one broke into yodeling. Jeanne looked at me. "We're having an American experience."

We left the stands and walked through an exhibit shed where people were selling cowboy crafts and gear. We bought tooled leather belts and silver necklaces, looked at handmade boots and saddles, and were nearing the end of the exhibit when a man called to me.

"*New York Times*," he said, reading the badge I'd pinned on my shirt. "What's that?"

I turned and looked at him. He was wearing a tan Stetson and dark aviator glasses, and had brown curly hair that tumbled to his collar. Did he really not know?

"A newspaper."

"Oh. I thought it was a mathematical problem."

I looked at Jeanne and rolled my eyes.

"What do you do for the newspaper?" he asked.

"I write."

He nodded. "Figures. You've got those beady eyes."

"Beady?"

Jeanne said, "Don't you mean piercing?"

"That too," he said.

I turned away, saying softly to Jeanne, "This guy's a jerk." She took a closer look. "I don't know. He may be deep."

"Would you like to see my work?" he asked. He showed us bridles and reins he had made out of rawhide, which he cured himself and braided into intricate designs. To my uneducated eye, they looked like all the other rawhide items I'd seen on display, but one of his pieces caught my attention. It was a comical piece, which I would later come to look on as conceptual art: a fly-swatter, with three shocks of hair from the tails of three different horses—sorrel, palomino, black—fastened together with rawhide knots and beautiful pieces of old reatas. "Works good too," he said, flicking it against a post, making a sharp, swishing sound.

He handed it to me, and I fingered the fine-woven knots encircling the switches of hair. "How much is it?" He thought a moment. "Two hundred dollars." I smiled and put it back on the table.

"There's two weeks' worth of work in that," he said.

"I'm sure that's true."

"It's fabulous," Jeanne said.

"You ladies stop back again. My name's Zack."

"I'm Sara. This is Jeanne."

He touched the brim of his hat to us, and we walked on.

◆

The next morning, Jeanne and I tried to change our plane reservations to leave Elko early, but that was not possible. We decided to skip the fiddling workshop, the cowboy a cappella singing, and the open-mike poetry session, and drove up into the Ruby Mountains to hike. The mountains were covered with snowfields, although it was June. Water was running everywhere, and we could hear it purling over rocks, squirting down creeks, and shooting into waterfalls that flowed right over the hiking trails.

We stopped to eat at the Pine Lodge, where, beside us in our booth, was a diorama: a stuffed mountain lion crouched on a rock, poised to pounce on a stuffed white-tailed deer. We ordered the Sunday buffet—chicken-fried steak, barbecued beans, hash browns, ham, bacon, and biscuits with sausage gravy—an orgy of grease that put us in a state of shock.

By the time we returned to the Elko Fairgrounds, the moon was rising and the mood had changed. There were many more cowboys now—"buckaroos" from Nevada and Idaho—and they did not look like the cowboys on our set. They had long, thin mustaches that stood out from their faces and curled up in sharp, waxed points. They were wearing shocking-pink and purple scarves around their necks, tall hats with horsehair stampede strings that dangled down their backs, and freshly ironed Wranglers tucked into knee-high boots.

In the dance hall, the cowboy singer, Ian Tyson, was performing one of his hits from the sixties, "Some Day Soon." Tyson's voice—honey golden, laced with sadness—cast a spell over the hall and people flowed onto the dance floor to do the two-step. I was working my way across the room when I saw

Zack. Months later, he would tell me that when he watched me coming toward him, he thought, "Trouble on the hoof. Keep your head down, maybe she won't see you." Then he was on his feet.

"Hey there." He pointed a finger at me.

"How're you doing?" I said.

"Oh, I'm sort of in shock."

"Why?"

He was wearing a pale-blue shirt with black Western stitching and jeans tucked into baby-blue boots. "I'm not used to going anywhere outside of Casa Grande."

"Where's that?"

"Arizona. Down south, by Mexico."

He asked me to dance. Ian Tyson was singing about the girl whose rodeo cowboy was driving in tonight from California. Zack was not wearing his sunglasses and as we danced, he kept his green eyes on me, direct and unblinking. His eyes were an intense green that's rarely seen outside the cat kingdom, and he stared longer than was socially acceptable. I stared right back; who the hell did he think he was? His face was attractive, though, all straight lines like the faces in Greek statues except for a nub in the nose where it surely had been broken. But he was a yokel, an insolent yokel. When the song ended, I excused myself, hoping to discourage further contact, and spent the rest of the night interviewing poets and singers while Jeanne, I noticed, sat with Zack on the steps outside, drinking beer from long-necked bottles.

When I was ready to leave, I beckoned her.

"Do me a favor?" she said. "Say good night to Zack. He's been asking about you. He's got quite a crush—"

"I know, I'm avoiding him. I'm sorry if you were stuck."

"No, I was having a good time talking—" Jeanne stopped. Zack was walking toward us.

"We're just leaving," I said.

"Can I walk you to your car?"

"You don't have to. It's close."

He took hold of my arm below the shoulder. "Then come with me, just a minute. I want to show you something."

I looked at Jeanne, who gestured with her head. "Go on. I'll meet you at the car."

As I walked with Zack toward the craft shed, he told me he was living in a trailer on a cutting-horse ranch with his son, who was twenty.

"How old are you?" I asked.

"Thirty-nine."

"Do you know how old I am?"

"No, ma'am. That's none of my business."

I laughed. "Older than you."

"You've vintaged well."

He switched on the lights in the shed and we walked back to his stall. He picked up the flyswatter and held it out. "I want you to have this."

"Thank you, but I couldn't accept that." I didn't want to be indebted.

"How 'bout we trade?"

"For what?"

"Something you wrote?"

I offered to send him one of my articles, but that didn't seem a fair trade for the flyswatter. He said he would make me a belt in exchange. "Let me measure." He took a string of rawhide, looped it around my waist, and cut it with his knife. I wrote down my address for him, but not my phone number. He did not have a phone, he told me as he walked me to the car. "I'm not rich. I drive a sixty-eight Chevy truck."

"That's none of my business," I said.

He laughed and put his arm around my shoulder.

We found Jeanne perched on the hood of the rental car, singing "Jingle Jangle Jingle" with a group of men in cowboy hats. Zack began massaging my shoulders. His fingers were unusually large, solid, strong.

"You have good hands," I said, turning my head so our eyes met.

"Humbly speaking," he said, "I have magic hands."

A week later, I received in the mail a handwritten letter and a key chain Zack had made of rawhide, with my name braided on it and a leather key dangling from the ring. "Oh, my dear God, all I do is dream of you," he wrote. "My fears are many, but I humbly offer you my key. I am unable to say for sure where it fits, or if it works anymore at all. I guess that's the chance you'll have to take. God have mercy on us both."

I shuddered as I read the letter, not merely because of its Gothic emotionalism but because every third word was misspelled. When I showed it to Jeanne, she held it up and said, "You realize, the only thing standing between you and this man is Spellcheck!"

I put the letter and key chain away, intending never to reply. I focused my attention on writing and preparing to shoot an episode of *Dr. Quinn*, in which her first love, long believed dead, suddenly reappears in town just as she's about to marry someone else. On the weekends when I had my children, I took them to their soccer games and dance lessons and for bike rides by the ocean. When they were at their dad's, I went out with a record producer named Terrence. He was sharp and witty, he had a mane of silver hair and drove a Porsche Carrera, but I was having trouble feeling any emotional connection and was worried the deficiency was in me. He was pressing me to make love and I thought, Maybe it will break the ice, but when we climbed into his antique iron bed, the stubble on his face cut my skin. No matter what he tried, I was numb, dry, dead. "This isn't working," I said.

He looked puzzled.

"I'm sorry." I tried to joke. "If I was a guy, I'd be limp."

"This has never happened."

"I know, it's never happened to me either. But it's not your fault, believe me. It's . . . my problem. Let me catch a cab home."

"No, I'll take you." We drove to my house in silence and the next day, I found a fax on the floor of my study that I didn't want to touch. The paper was curled; it seemed to give off a radioactive glow. It was a letter excoriating me for my character flaws, advising me I was one of those Jewish women "who has great difficulty surrendering, except to inconsequential men," and ending, "Have a productive life, Sara."

I was depressed in the days that followed, not because of Terrence but because I'd failed, in the years since I'd been divorced, to form an attachment with a man that lasted longer than a few months. I swung between reconciling myself to the fact that I lacked the talent, the gene, the gift—not everyone gets it, not everyone can ski—and feeling compelled to go out and give it one more try. I actually sympathized with Elizabeth Taylor when she said, on the eve of her eighth marriage, "I want to do it right."

Under the sway of this compulsion, I'd taken an ad in the personals, which is how I'd met Terrence. Many of my friends—although few admitted it—had experimented with the personals. It was like a secret vice. People used fake names (I used my daughter's) and had to suffer the occasional embarrassment when someone they knew or worked with answered their ad. I composed my lines and submitted them to the *L.A. Weekly*, which supposedly catered to the creative community. "Tall, slender, successful writer, 44, divorced, two kids, seeks partner with quick mind, slow hand." I was forty-nine but everyone lied in the personals.

Men who wanted to respond could call a 900 number and listen to a recording I'd made. The *L.A. Weekly* allotted you a minute and a half to describe yourself and what you were seeking. The object was to sound enticing, appealing, and yet discourage deadbeats and weirdos. "I work hard," I said, "and when I'm not working, I love listening to all kinds of music, dancing, books, great conversation, comedy, nature, and being outdoors." I wanted to meet a man, I said, "who has a passion for what he does, who's respected in his field, self-supporting, and who's also playful and game for adventure." If men liked my tape, they could leave a recorded message for me with their phone number.

I spent weeks listening to the disembodied voices of bizarre, eccentric, lost, and, in a few cases, dazzlingly promising men. Terrence told me on the phone that he'd been married to a well-known singer, his kids were grown, and he liked to hike and cook and discover young, unknown musicians whose work he could produce. I also talked on the phone with a screenwriter whose parents were Brazilian and who'd gone to Harvard and been a correspondent in El Salvador and liked salsa dancing. But the promise and intrigue had evaporated shortly after our first actual date. (In the case of the Brazilian screenwriter, *he* had the limp dick.) It seemed the way of the nineties: You meet in the personals and break up by fax.

At loose ends, I spotted the box with the key chain from Zack. I opened it and fingered the leather key. I sent him a note I thought was noncommittal and a copy of the article I'd written about Elko. Later he would tell me, "For you to put a stamp on an envelope was enough encouragement for me." He sat down and cut out black leather for a belt, laced it with rawhide, and mailed it. The belt was elegant, unique, and fit perfectly. I called to thank him—he'd given me a number where I could leave a message—but the woman who answered the phone said he wasn't there.

A week later, he called from a pay phone on the highway outside Casa Grande. "What are you doing?" he asked. I said I was writing an episode based on the life of the naturalist John Muir. He talked about the horses he was training and the yearling buck deer he'd just seen in the desert in the middle of hunting season. "I came around a thicket and there he was, standing stone still. He was so beautiful, so wild, and so afraid." When we hung up, I felt a warmth that was surprising.

A few weeks later, he moved to a place in Phoenix that had a phone, and our calls became longer and more frequent. We talked about our children; Zack had married at eighteen and had two daughters and a son by the time he was twenty-one. The second child, Nathan, was born with a rare disease, Hallermann-Streiff syndrome, which gave him physical deformities and eyesight so poor he was legally blind, although he loved to draw and won art contests. When Zack had divorced, his wife had moved out and taken the two girls, but he'd kept his son with him and was helping him go to college. "He's special," Zack said. "I think he's beautiful."

The next time we spoke, Zack said he'd called the airlines to see how much it would cost to fly to Los Angeles. I took the roam phone into my bedroom and lay down. I was still not sure of Zack's intentions. Things were strange in the nineties: I'd met men who flirted and pursued me and then declined to make love. He told me he'd heard a song that morning that reminded him of me, "First Kiss."

"What do you think about kissing?" I asked.

"Oh, I like it a lot. I like kisses that go on for two or three . . . "

He paused, and I thought he was going to say, "hours."

". . . days."

I invited him to visit over Labor Day. My children would be staying with their father and we would have three days.

"So I should bring my toothbrush?" Zack said.

"If you want to brush your teeth." Then I grew nervous: it had been months since we'd met in Elko, and we'd spent no more than an hour together. The next morning I went tearing into Jeanne's office at the writers' trailer and asked to see the photos she'd taken in Elko. "Is he tall? I can't remember."

"Yeah, he is." She fished the pictures out of her desk and I stared at one that another cowboy had taken of the three of us.

"He's not that tall," I said.

"Well, he's standing next to us and he's slumped."

The day before his flight, Zack called and said, "I feel like a high school kid, fixin' to go on his first date. Could I ask you something, without offending you?"

"I don't know."

"Let's see." He took a breath. "Is this research?"

"You?"

"Yes, ma'am."

"No, sir."

"Thank you. I had to ask."

2

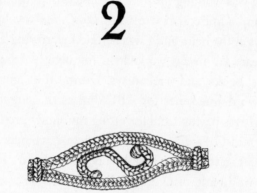

What have I done? What the hell have I done? For three years I'd been trolling, lonely, aching, going to parties, asking friends to look through their Rolodexes for available men. Now this cowboy. It was absurd. Crazy. I'd taken a wacky left turn that was going to lead straight to a dead end. I felt implausibly happy, though, the Tuesday morning after Labor Day, as I drove up the Pacific Coast Highway, passing the lagoon where swarms of pelicans were flying low and stabbing at the ocean with their odd, droopy beaks, coming up with fish. At Malibu Canyon, I turned inland and the landscape changed abruptly from seacoast to golden foothills covered with manzanita and live oaks. There were many mornings, making this drive, when I felt infused with luck: I was being paid well to drive through this beautiful countryside and spend my hours writing a TV Western. And then there were days when I felt gray and dispirited and the pelicans were wasted on me.

If I felt gray, it was because, for the first time in twenty-two years, I was working for someone else—Beth Sullivan. I loved Beth and admired her work, but *Dr. Quinn* was her creation, she was at the helm and I was behind her, rowing. For twenty-two years I'd always worked on my own, writing magazine articles, books, and screenplays. During the eighties, I'd created two drama series for ABC, but as the nineties began, I found I was having trouble getting my shows produced. I was in the midst of a divorce and signed an agreement that was to prove a catastrophe. I bought my ex-husband's share of the house we'd built, using all my liquid assets, because I wanted to keep the children stable while we were adjusting to the divorce and joint custody. I thought I'd wait a year and then, when I felt stronger, I'd sell the house and move to something more affordable. But this was a fatal mistake. Less than thirty days after I signed the agreement, the California real estate market collapsed and my house dropped 40 percent from the price I'd just paid my ex-husband. Two weeks later, on my birthday—the actual day—my editor called from New York to tell me that the first draft of the book I'd just submitted, a memoir about baby boomers as parents, was not what she wanted and she was canceling the contract.

I was blind-sided. I had no income in sight now, a huge mortgage payment, all my money tied up in the house and no possibility of selling it because no one was buying anything. For months I did not sleep, I lay in bed, twitching and turning as if I were on a spit, making popping sounds as my juices splattered on the fire.

Friends suggested I take a job on someone else's show. As it happened, I had just met Beth at an event peculiar to Hollywood. A group called the Creative Coalition was holding political awareness-raising meetings to inform people in show business about such key issues as health care. The object, as I understood it, was to educate the stars so they could take stands and speak intelligently on talk shows. I went to the meeting at the home of the actor Richard Masur because I thought I might meet some interesting men. I don't know why Beth came, but I doubt that it was to hear the exceedingly boring lecture on the Canadian single-payer plan.

We met at the food table and before we'd finished spooning angel-hair pasta with sun-dried tomatoes onto our plates, we'd exchanged phone numbers. Beth was smart, strong, loved to laugh, and fought like a tigress for what she believed in. Blonde and earthy, she had a zest for life in all its aspects. We began taking walks and having dinners and talked about collaborating on a future project. We were both, at the time, writing pilots for CBS, but we knew the odds were against us. The network had commissioned more than sixty scripts and only a few would make it to the air. When the fall schedule was announced, my pilot was sent to the trash heap along with fifty-five others, but Beth's was ordered for production.

I was standing at the stove, browning onions to make turkey chili, when Beth called to ask if I'd come work on *Dr. Quinn.* This was the offer I'd been hoping for, but I felt squeezing pains in my chest. Good-bye, I thought, to setting my own hours, picking my own projects, taking the kids for a bike ride or to the library after school.

"The money won't be terrific," she said, "but if we stay on the air I can get you more."

"It's not the money," I said. "It's . . . my life."

She gave a throaty laugh. "Oh, well, I don't have a life anyway."

"I'm afraid I won't see my kids."

Beth was silent. "We could work that out."

I poured tomato sauce into the onion mixture and stirred it. "Where are you shooting?"

"Agoura. The Paramount Ranch. It's a half-hour drive."

The noose tightened. Agoura was not a half hour, it was more like an hour, each way.

"How about this," she said. "Come in from ten to four. Do the rest of your writing at home."

"Are you serious? You think that would work?" Most staff writers stayed at the set until eight or nine, sometimes midnight.

"Sure. As long as you get the work done. What do I care?"

I felt relieved, giddy. This was a deal no one else in television would have offered and I grabbed it.

"What happened with the cowboy? Did he show up?" Jeanne called. She was standing on the steps of the writers' trailer when I drove up the morning after Labor Day.

"Yes. I'm sorry, we meant to call you."

She hurried down the metal stairs. "How was it?"

I took my briefcase out of the backseat. "Great."

She gave a triumphant laugh, "Ha-ha!" and put her arm through mine. "You didn't have trouble finding things to talk about?"

"Not at all."

"I knew he was deep."

"Wise."

"Very wise. How was the sex?"

"Disaster at first, but he's a quick study."

She gave another "Ha-ha!"

"We owe you a lot. But Jeanne, it's impossible."

"Come on, things like this don't come along every day. And Phoenix isn't that far."

"That's the least of it."

Zack had almost not made it off the plane. I was standing at gate nineteen of Southwest Airlines, wearing a pink cotton shirt that I thought was flattering tucked into the best-fitting jeans I owned, watching the passengers swarm off the plane from Phoenix. Would he be wearing the tan Stetson? Yes, to feel secure. Was I at the right gate? The passengers were thinning out now and then the flow stopped. Did he miss the plane? Change his mind? The flight attendants were coming out, pulling their wheel-away bags behind them. I stopped one and asked, "Did all the passengers get off?" She turned and stared down the corridor to the plane. "No, there's one more."

Zack rounded the corner and walked out, slow, deliberate, wearing the Stetson, black boots with red lightning bolts, and a leather bag slung over his shoulder. He pointed a finger at me, the way he had in Elko. He looked smaller and his face was more weathered and creased than I'd remembered. My heart sank. How would I get through the weekend?

We walked toward each other, reached out to hug, and I averted my face. His lips grazed my cheek. He put his arm around my waist and kept it there, tight, as we started out of the terminal.

"Were you thinking of taking the plane back to Phoenix?"

"I considered it." He looked at me sideways. "How're you doing?"

I told him that in the hour before coming to the airport, I'd managed to yell at my son for not being ready on time and at my daughter for spilling a can of Campbell's chicken noodle soup on the floor. We'd all been agitated and upset when I dropped them at their dad's.

"Kids pick up when you're nervous," Zack said. "They've got radar. And if you're in a hurry, they'll do anything to stall you."

"I feel bad. I hate leaving them like that."

"Call 'em up and apologize. I've already apologized to all my kids for my failures." He pulled me closer and, strangely, I felt better.

I drove from the airport to the beach, thinking we'd watch the sunset and get reacquainted in person before I brought him to my house. I'd packed beach chairs, a blanket, and Dom Perignon in a cooler in the back of the car, a silver-blue, six-year-old Mercedes station wagon on whose floor you could find kid detritus—hair ties, Band-Aids, potato chip crumbs.

"Nice vehicle," Zack said.

He carried the chairs and cooler down to the water and we settled on the sand. I struggled with the cork. He reached for the bottle. "I'm good at taking things apart," he said. He put his thumbs on either side, slowly eased the cork forward, and it popped. "Whoa! I never had champagne before." How could that be?

We began to relax. The sky turned rosy and heated as he kept filling our plastic cups with Dom Perignon. I cannot tell you what we talked about or at what point he kissed me, but it was slow, sensual, easy. No bristles were cutting my skin. He slid off his beach chair, pulled me down with him and we rolled around on the sand until it was dark and too chilly to stay.

I drove to my home, a two-story modern house on a street lined with palm trees that listed in the direction of the ocean. As I showed Zack through the rooms, all painted white with large windows, he seemed like a creature alighted from a far-away planet. "It's sorta different," he said, looking up at the glass blocks. He walked about gingerly until he found a corner for himself on the balcony where he could sit and smoke a cigarette. He turned and smiled.

"Why are you smiling?"

"I'm plumb pleased—this is going so well."

He unzipped his leather bag and took out a piece of butter-colored elk skin, rolled up and tied with a latigo string. He began unfastening it, and I knew what was inside: the flyswat-ter. "I've been looking for a home for it," he said. "I've been waiting a long time."

I heated up the gourmet treats I'd gathered for dinner—penne with Italian sausage, focaccia, and baby-lettuce salad with goat cheese and balsamic vinaigrette—poor choices, it turned out. He thought Italian food was "foreign," anything green was suspicious, and "I won't have nothing to do with cheese from a goat." He liked the Dom Perignon, though. "Can we crack open another bottle?"

"I don't have one." I explained that it didn't come in six-packs. But I did have some Merlot, which we carried into the living room where we stretched out on the couch and contin-ued kissing. He was exploring, teasing, taking soundings, and it was exquisitely arousing, like the kissing I remembered from when I was sixteen, parked in the hills with my first boyfriend in his Chevy Impala with the cicadas singing and the scent of jasmine in the night air.

"I'm curious," I said. "Do cowboys use condoms?"

"Yes, ma'am. I came prepared. I watch Oprah Winfrey."

I laughed, but told him I was not quite ready for that kind of intimacy. "Would you mind sleeping in the guest room?"

"That'd be fine." We walked upstairs, said good night, but he did not sleep in the guest room. He began herding me, slowly, steadily, toward the bedroom, and then we were on the sheets and he was moving so roughly and urgently that it was painful and I wanted it to be over. He sighed and curled against me to sleep. What a disappointment, I thought. But he was so sensuous and skillful at kissing. Maybe he doesn't know about female anatomy, maybe he doesn't have the basic information.

I lay awake, listening to him breathing, oblivious, and considered whether to talk with him about this. Twenty years after the women's liberation movement, I still found it awkward and dicey to broach the subject with a new man. The summer before, I'd had a romance with the president of a network who was getting divorced and called me for his first date. We'd gone to Berkeley around the same time and shared a passion for the novels of Thomas Hardy. He took me to a performance by Eric Bogosian, then to dinner at the Ivy. When I was trying to decide between the Chilean sea bass and the roast sirloin with garlic mashed potatoes, he said, "Order both." But his rendition of making love, I discovered, was ten minutes. I was able, by the most indirect means—coaxing, hinting, teasing—to get him to stretch it out to thirty. I didn't have the nerve to speak to him directly because

I had fantasies about the future and he was elusive. I was afraid he'd be insulted, intimidated, get jumpy, and bolt. (Which he did anyway; he went back to his wife.) But with Zack, I had nothing to lose. There was no future; we had three days, and if this was what our lovemaking was going to be, I'd just as soon drive him back to the airport.

In the morning, while he was drinking coffee, I asked if he'd enjoyed himself.

"Oh, I mean to tell you. It was great. I trust it was tolerable for you?"

I smiled. "The kissing was wonderful, but after that, you kind of lost me, and . . . if you like, I could show you things . . . ways you could bring me along with you." I watched his face for signals that he was offended or hurt, but his eyes lit with interest. Later he would tell me, "I'd never had a woman talk to me like that. I *definitely* was in California. I was not just gonna get laid, I was gonna get educated. I thought, You want to show me something I don't know about? Have at it."

It was as I had suspected: he had married, at eighteen, a woman who was inexperienced and shy. In the following years, he'd had numerous one-night affairs but no woman had shown or told him much about her sexuality. We walked back upstairs to the bedroom and I didn't mumble or stammer as I might have with the network president. It was: look, this is where, here's what happens. And you don't have to sprint for the finish line, the fun is in the detours.

That's about all I had to say. He took to it like the proverbial duck to water, the bird to air, the puppy to a garden where there are morsels hidden below ferns and under hillocks and he's been given license to dig. One of the frustrations of trying to talk to a man about sex is that you can show him what pleases you and learn what excites him but you can't teach someone to be sensual, to be imaginative, unless he's predisposed, and Zack was. He seized the information I'd given him and ran with it, making me gasp for breath, discovering zones and inventing variations I had not dreamed of. And I've been around the pool.

"I know folks don't like to be compared to animals," Zack said, "but your feet are like horses' hooves."

We were lying on the bed, on my Laura Ashley quilt of green vines and purple roses, and he was carefully, artfully cutting my toenails. Then he used an emery board to file and shape them. I had accidentally broken one of my fingernails opening a drawer, and he had offered to cut it. But he had not been able to stop there. He had gone on to trim all the fingernails on both hands and then moved down to my feet.

"The hoof is made of the same material as your toenail. It's dead, it doesn't hurt when you cut it, but if you cut too far, it hurts and bleeds. So you gotta be real careful."

Zack said he had gone to farrier school for six weeks, "so I could learn to shoe my own horses. But I wasn't cut out for it. A good farrier can do a horse in forty-five minutes, but no matter how I rushed and tried to cut corners, it took me about two hours."

He stopped to peer, appraisingly, at the toenail he was filing. Then he smiled. "But the shoes I did were sculpted. And they were balanced."

I watched him work on my feet, with loving precision, and I thought about the cowboys portrayed in popular stories and songs: the charming devil who rides away, who flirts and betrays, who never stays home and is always alone, "even with someone he loves." I thought, also, of the cowboys Pam Houston describes in her collection, *Cowboys Are My Weakness*. I'd read her stories, admiring her style and wit but growing increasingly irritated at the succession of cowboys with whom her heroine became involved: men who cheated, lied, did not listen, and could not be counted on. They went off on vacations with rival women and walked out on their girlfriends dying of cancer.

Yet here was Zack, the genuine article, and he was nothing like those cowboys. He spoke his feelings, showed his heart. With almost every other man I'd known, I'd had the sense that he was keeping himself behind a maze of corridors and walls, and I was constantly coaxing, digging, wooing the creature to come out. But with Zack, there seemed to be nothing between his eyes and mine.

I felt tremors of fear. Why this person? He's a being from another planet, he doesn't wear a watch or read a newspaper. He's never heard of *King Lear*. If a phrase comes to me from the play and I want to repeat it to him, I first have to explain who Shakespeare was and what *King Lear* was about and then tell him the phrase and what it means. I don't have the patience, I'll go out of my mind.

When we woke up the next morning, I wanted him to meet my children. In the three years since I'd been divorced, I had not let a man stay in the house with me while the children were there, but I wanted to test the waters.

I suppose I also wanted them to see me with a man who treated me as Zack did. He opened car doors and stood there patiently until I was comfortably settled, then buckled the seat belt around me. He insisted on carrying my packages, kissing my hand, holding chairs. At first, this had made me uneasy, not because of any feminist squeamishness at old-fashioned male courtliness—I enjoyed that. But the adoration and deference were things that usually sent me running.

When I told him I wanted to bring the children over, Zack put on a fresh, white shirt and clean, pressed jeans. He brushed his teeth and shaved, standing at my sink. It moved me to see the effort he was making. I slipped my arms around his waist and looked in the mirror. My childhood fantasy— my ambition, when I was eight—was to have my own horse. When my birthday arrived, I begged my parents to buy me one but my mother explained that it cost too much and we had nowhere to keep it. "We live in Los Angeles," she said. "We can't have a horse in the backyard."

"Then would you introduce me to a cowboy? A real cowboy?"

"Kids are important," Zack said. "They're part of the package. And they're going to be territorial about their mom."

I picked up the children from their dad's and as I drove them to my house, I told them a story Zack had just related about training a young horse. "Whenever I got on him," Zack had said, "he'd try to run away. I'd pull his head back, facing me, but he still kept charging forward. So I ran him into a wall. I knew that if I lived through it, he'd never run away on me again. And he didn't."

The children were shocked, fascinated. I finished the story as we pulled into the garage, and they walked, with wide eyes and no small amount of trepidation, into the house to meet him. He had spread some of his tools, leather, and rawhide on the table and started to show them how to braid a circular knot.

Sitting down on either side of him, they began twisting strands of leather around a dowel. Sophie finished her knot first and handed it to him. "Good work," Zack said. "And you're as pretty as your mother."

She wrinkled her forehead. "Are you kidding? I'm way prettier than Mom."

I laughed, I agreed. Sophie had long, white-blonde hair she'd inherited from her father, large brown eyes, and a body she'd inherited from me but which I no longer owned—all leggy and willowy.

"Can you, like, rope a cow?" she asked.

"Yes, ma'am."

She rose up quickly and ran to the garage.

Gabriel was working with great absorption, his head bent over the leather strings. Although he was a year younger than Sophie, he had more patience and a longer attention span. She was always in motion, like a hummingbird, never sitting so much as alighting at the edge of a chair as if she might fly up at any second. She'd been able to harness this energy in dance, and from the age of six, she'd been taking classes: ballet, jazz, hip-hop.

Gabriel's love was music. He played the drums and was starting a band with two other ten-year-olds. He wore his dark hair in a style popular with boys in West Los Angeles—a surf cut, long on top and shaved underneath. He liked to wear baggy shorts and a wallet with a chain that dangled from his pocket, and he never went anywhere without his skateboard.

"There," he said, holding up the knot, which was tighter and more symmetrical than Sophie's.

"You got the makings of a great braider, not that I'd wish that on you."

"What are we gonna do next?"

"I hadn't planned anything," Zack said. "My own kids never showed this much interest."

I brought out the flyswatter Zack had made and asked Gabriel where we should hang it.

He took it and studied the design. "My room."

"That's a present for your mother," Zack said.

"Can you make one for me?"

"I can make one *with* you."

"Now?"

"I don't have all the materials."

Sophie came running back with an old piece of clothesline rope. Zack fashioned it into a loop, twirled it in the air, once, twice, then shot his arm forward and the loop slipped over her head and he pulled it tight around her waist. She screamed. "I want to try that." Zack showed her how to hold the rope and swing it. Then she and Gabriel took turns trying to lasso lawn chairs, but I was growing restless. "Maybe," I said, "if we're nice to him, Zack will come back another time."

"Tomorrow?" Gabriel said.

"Not tomorrow," Zack said.

"Why not?"

"I just came for Labor Day."

"I declare tomorrow Labor Day."

Zack put his hands on Gabriel's shoulders. "I have to go back to Phoenix tomorrow, but your mom needs lookin' after and when I'm not here, that's your job. You hear?"

Gabriel nodded.

◆

"Ladies always say they want a cowboy, but they really want the rancher," Zack said. We were driving out to the Paramount Ranch where *Dr. Quinn* was shot, and he was explaining that a cowboy is a hired hand, a blue-collar laborer who works long hours for low wages and no benefits. "You've got no chance of ever earning enough to buy a ranch of your own. You're always gonna be takin' care of other people's cattle and horses."

Zack said that on the ranches and feedlots where he worked for fifteen years, the cowboys show up at four in the morning and work until five at night, six days a week, with no time off for vacations. "You bring your own food, even coffee."

"There's no chuck wagon?" I said.

"Hell no."

"What happens if you get sick?"

"You best not get sick." He said that if a cowboy breaks a rib or pulls a muscle, he'll doctor himself with animal remedies because he has no insurance. If he gets a toothache, he'll have the tooth pulled.

"Then why do people do this?"

He took off the dark aviator glasses. "The passion."

We pulled up to the entrance gate to the ranch, where a dozen tourists were trying to take pictures of the fake Western town. I waved to the guard, José.

"Working on the holiday?" he called.

"No, we're just going for a ride."

He motioned the tourists aside, unlocked the gate, and we drove through. Then he closed it behind us.

"This is it," I said as I drove down the center of the Western street lined with storefronts: the saloon, the telegraph office, Dr. Quinn's medical clinic. All the buildings were painted and distressed to look as if they'd been constructed in the 1860s. "It seems a whole lot bigger on TV," Zack said.

I drove up the hill to the remuda, a series of corrals made of aluminum panels in which we kept forty horses, most of them brown so they could be used interchangeably in scenes. I'd called Mike Riggins, the wrangler boss, and asked if we could borrow two. He'd told the guard who watched the horses on the weekend to saddle them for us, and they were tied to a railing when we pulled up.

Zack buckled on his spurs and walked over to inspect the horses. He tightened their cinches, adjusted the curb straps. He put one foot in the stirrup, rose straight up and swung the other leg over the horse in a single motion that was elegant. I hoisted and jerked myself into the saddle. He looked amused. "We'll practice mounting and dismounting later," he said.

I followed him as we rode across the ranch, picking up the trail for Malibu Creek State Park. His body was relaxed, he didn't move from the saddle as we trotted through a field of high grasses. Zack stopped. "Want to lope?"

I stared at the trail ahead. It ran straight down the hill into a gully and then climbed up the opposite cliff. "I was told you should never run horses downhill."

"That's right, you shouldn't." Zack winked, and as I watched, his horse gathered up his back legs and sprang and my horse followed. I held my breath: we were dropping straight down the face of the cliff in choppy, rough lunges. The horses seemed to plunge and brake, plunge and brake, and I grabbed the saddle horn and jammed my heels down as we hit the gully floor and went tearing up the opposite hill.

Zack stopped and turned to watch me. "You all right?"

I brought my horse to a halt and put my hand on my chest,

patting it, trying to stem the flow of adrenaline. "I want to do that again."

He laughed. "That's my girl." He swept his arm forward and we started climbing into the jagged red mountains of the state park.

"How's your horse?" I asked.

Zack gave a thin smile. "He's okay. But I like riding young horses, before anybody else gets on 'em. At my last job, I was in charge of starting two-year-olds. The more time I spent riding young horses, the more I got into the Zen of it."

I was intrigued that he knew nothing of Shakespeare and yet knew about Zen. "What do you mean, the Zen of it?"

"I'd close my eyes, keep my feet loose and relaxed, and just feel what they wanted to do—jump or spin—and go with them. After a while, they'd calm down and trust me. Then I could give them the slightest touch and they'd respond."

I felt he was doing the same with me. All he had to do was run a finger along the inside of my wrist and my body was alert. He put his horse alongside mine and we kissed while the horses rocked beneath us in a slow, steady rhythm. The sun was warm on our backs, and we undid each other's shirts and kept kissing for what seemed like miles. There was the fine smell of the horses and the sagebrush, and our hands on each other and the powerful animals, moving in unison, and it was the closest I'd come in many years to bliss.

For our last dinner, I fixed him a baked potato and steak, which he wanted cooked until it was dried out and gray despite my pleas to try it rare.

"All I want to do is ride horses, braid things, and make love to you," he said. "But you're two different people. When you're in your full dress, in your work mentality, like in Elko, you're scary. But I like that."

"Why am I scary?"

"Because you could demolish me with words, any time you wanted." He smiled. "But when you're alone with me, you're childlike and soft. I can have my way with you."

We had been alone, except for the children's visit, all weekend and we made love until it was time to leave for the airport. He forgot his leather tools and I had to drive back for them, then we got caught in traffic on the freeway and had to make our way on surface streets. "You're doing fine," he said, taking hold of my neck and rubbing it. I pulled up to the terminal with five minutes to spare. He opened the passenger door and stepped out. I said what I'd been holding back for three days. "I love you."

He looked startled, and leaned down so he could see in the window of the station wagon. "That's good, because I'm half in love with you myself."

"I know you love me."

"How do you know that?"

"I just know. It makes no sense at all."

He laughed, a wonderful deep laugh. "You're right, on both counts." He touched the brim of his tan Stetson, hitched up his bag, and walked to the gate.

3

I could feel the tension when I walked into the trailer. Beth said, "Hi there," but did not meet my eyes, nor did the others sitting at the conference table. Except for one lone male, Josef Anderson, we had an all-female staff: Beth, me, Jeanne, a researcher named Julie Henderson, and two young writers whom we called Toni P. and Toni G. Twice a month, Beth brought in a Korean manicurist, whom she was helping find work in this country, and the young woman moved from chair to chair, trimming cuticles and painting clear polish on our nails while we worked out stories.

Beth sat at the head of the table, wearing her uniform: a white T-shirt, faded jeans, white sneakers, and a baseball cap into which she tucked her blonde hair. She had her two large dogs, a black Lab and a silver weimaraner, curled at her feet, and she sipped from a sports bottle of water with vitamin C mixed in.

She held up a script I'd written called "The Race." "We've

got a lot of work to do here," she said. I tensed; I'd already written three drafts of "The Race" and thought it was locked. "It's too light," Beth said, "there's not enough substance. We need a better medical story and the B story has to be changed so Brian enters the pie-making contest to compete with his sister." I looked around the table; everyone was nodding agreement and I felt my muscles cramping, group by group. We started prep today and would be shooting in a week. Beth said the script was in such poor shape she'd decided not to use it for the season opener in September, as had been planned. She was replacing it with a script by Toni P. about the army causing a smallpox epidemic among the Cheyenne. I glanced at Toni P., who lowered her eyes but could scarcely contain her delight. Months later, however, when both episodes had been shot and sent to the network, CBS decided the smallpox show was too dark. "The Race" was reinstated as the season opener, and it became one of the most beloved and remembered shows.

Not by me. Looking back, I can see that the final shooting script was stronger and more interesting than the draft on the table that morning. But at the time, I did not feel we were improving the story. I felt that six people were flogging me with whips.

We went over the script page by page, word by word, starting with general notes. The show was an "homage" to—which meant I was lifting the plot from—*National Velvet*. Jane Seymour, playing Dr. Quinn, was going to dress up as a man to ride her horse in a race from which women were excluded. "At the end," Beth said, "let's not have her get disqualified. Let's have Loren hand her the prize money, and *then* she takes off her hat and shows them who she is."

"Okay," I said.

Toni G. jumped in: "Loren tries to grab the money back but she tosses it in the air. All the townspeople scramble to pick it up."

"I don't like that," I said.

"It's cool!" Toni said. She threw a stack of note cards in the air to demonstrate and they rained on the floor.

"It's corny, and I don't have a good feeling when someone throws money away and people rush after it like locusts."

"That's your hang-up," Toni said.

"It's not the point of the show. This race was not about money—"

Bryan, our production assistant, opened the sliding door. "Sara, your daughter's on line four."

"My daughter? Excuse me." I walked into my office and picked up the phone. "Sophie, what is it?" She was crying so hard I couldn't understand her. "Take a deep breath," I said. "Just tell me."

I heard a burst of laughter from the conference room.

"I got . . . kicked out of dance class," Sophie said.

"What for?"

"Can you come pick me up now, please?"

I told her I couldn't leave work but I'd call Veronica, our housekeeper from El Salvador, and have her drive to the dance studio. "What happened?"

"You won't be mad?" Her voice was small.

"No, I'll never be mad at you for telling the truth."

I heard Beth saying something about an "anticlimax."

Sophie blew her nose. "I lost control and . . . I called Alison—" She started to cry again. "I used foul language."

"Oh, Sophie, what did you say?"

Her voice was faint as a whisper. "Fucking bitch."

I paused. "You must have been really angry."

"She was telling everyone I shouldn't be Belle. I'm not good enough." Sophie's jazz-dance teacher, Carmen De Long, had given her the prize part of Belle in the school's performance of numbers from Disney's *Beauty and the Beast*. "Alison said I can't even do a double pirouette. That's not true! I told her, 'I don't appreciate that. Please stop telling lies,' but she just laughed at me. So I called her a . . . And she told Carmen. Now Carmen says I can't be Belle!"

I heard Beth's voice rising as she argued with Toni G. about whether Dr. Quinn should throw money or roses in the air.

"They're happy now," Sophie said. "I thought, when I got Belle, everyone would like me but they don't. They're glad I lost it. When are you coming home?"

"I'm afraid it won't be till after dinner."

"Mom!" Her voice broke.

"I'm sorry, there's an emergency and we've got to work late."

"I'm quitting dance."

Every fiber in me was straining to walk out of the trailer and get in the car.

"Sophie, I know that's how you feel right now. You want to run out of there and never go back."

"Has that ever happened to you?"

"Yes," I said. "But you've worked really hard and you shouldn't give up. Do you want me to call Carmen?"

She didn't answer.

"I'll talk to her. She knows how competitive the girls are, and I'm sure, if you make a sincere apology, she'll give you another chance."

"I already apologized," Sophie said.

"We'll work this out. Please, don't worry, it's going to be all right. I'll . . . call her from here."

For two straight days we labored over "The Race," restructuring the story, ordering in meals, not leaving the table except to use the bathroom, not leaving the ranch until ten at night. Then I had two days to rewrite the script from scratch. I took breaks to call the kids and to call Carmen, who agreed to let Sophie continue dancing the part of Belle "on probation." By the time I drove home, I felt beaten and wrung out. I walked softly into the children's rooms and stood by their beds, watching them sleep. Then I crawled into my own.

In those moments in the darkness, my mind turned to Zack. On the morning after Labor Day, I'd felt as if lightning had ratcheted through me and my cell chemistry was altered. I woke up yearning for him, trying to bring back the feel of his fingers on my torso and his body stretched along the length of mine. I wanted to call him right then but forced myself to wait, to see what he'd do.

As the week wore on, though, I was drawn so completely into the pressures and demands of work and children and keeping the house afloat that I began to lose the sense of him. The memory, the physicality was breaking up and dispersing, like the connection on a cell phone when it sputters and cuts out. It had been an exotic adventure, a one-shot event. I'd blurted "I love you." Momentary madness. By Friday night, when I finished the shooting script of "The Race" and sent it out to the cast and crew, Zack had faded into the mists. I tried to bring his face into focus and couldn't quite see him except in a general way.

He called Saturday morning from a pay phone. "Hello there, sweetheart. I just had to call and see if I dreamed you up or what." His voice was warm and deep; it made me think of newly sawed wood. He said he'd driven to a pay phone because in his house, he'd just had phone service installed that did not permit him to dial long distance so he wouldn't run up bills. As we talked, we were interrupted by a recorded female voice asking for money and the sound of coins dropping: *ding* for quarters, *ding ding* for dimes.

"Did you get my letter?" he asked. "I mailed it off a few days ago."

"No. What did it say?"

He laughed softly. "I been missing you. I'm not ready for this to end just yet."

"I'm not either."

"How 'bout I come see you again?"

I was silent a moment.

"You busy?" he said.

"Very."

"Well, I'll come see you for one night then. Just to hold you. You need someone to do that."

"Maybe," I said, "I should come visit you the next time."

He laughed again. "My house is sorta cluttered. The yard . . . well, it's overgrown."

"I don't like disorder," I said.

"I noticed."

"You probably have a dog, too."

"Mmm-hmm."

"Where does he sleep?"

"On the chair."

"The only thing I hate as much as disorder is dogs."

"You never had one?"

"Gabriel's been begging for one, but I told him, 'Sure, if you take care of it. I will not feed it, I will not walk it. If it runs away, I will not put up signs.'"

He whistled. "You're a hard woman."

"I've just never liked dogs. But we have parakeets and a cat and Sophie used to have mice."

"Now that's one thing I don't tolerate. Mice. Where I come from, we try to get rid of 'em."

"These were tame mice."

"My dog's tame. It's just me and Nathan that's not."

We agreed it would be best if Zack came to Los Angeles again, but there was the matter of the ticket. He said it might be a while before he had enough money to buy one. I offered to pay, but he refused.

"You flew here last time," I said. "It should be my turn." I called my travel agent and had her send him a ticket.

I rehearsed what I'd tell the kids. I asked friends and a child psychologist whom I'd consulted in the past and they suggested I keep it simple. I sat the kids down at the round wooden table in the kitchen. "Zack is coming back to visit."

"Yes!" Gabriel said.

"Can he bring a real rope, like, a lasso?" Sophie said.

"Can he sleep in my room?" Gabriel asked.

"He's going to sleep in my room."

Their mouths opened. I told them I had dated many men, "but Zack is the first I really care for who cares for me. He's kind, he's thoughtful—"

"Are you gonna make sex?" Gabriel asked.

Sophie said, "It's 'have sex,' stupid."

"Don't call your brother 'stupid.'"

"Are you?" Gabriel said.

"That's private."

They drove with me to the airport to pick him up. He was standing on the pedestrian island outside Southwest Airlines—we spotted the tan Stetson first—and as he walked toward us, boot heels clicking on the pavement, I was startled. I'd forgotten and I remembered: the insolent green eyes, the brown curly hair, the straight lines of his face except for the nub in the nose where it had been broken. I stepped out of the car. He dropped his leather bag and kissed me and I felt the kids staring through the car window. "Hey, baby," he whispered. He got in the driver's seat and nervously started handing out presents: an Apache teardrop necklace for Sophie, a bear's tooth on a rawhide cord for Gabriel, and lassos for both of them. "Cool! Thanks," Sophie said. Cars started honking and a bus rolled past us with a noxious blast of smoke. I told Zack we'd better get moving.

We drove straight to Clover Park, where Gabriel had a soccer game. We set up beach chairs on the strip of grass where the parents were clustered. Most of the parents were wearing shorts or jogging outfits, and they stared at Zack in his Stetson and jeans tucked into black boots with red lightning bolts. Zack reached for my hand, lifted it to his mouth, and kissed each finger. I smiled at the parents, who turned their heads away.

Sophie took out a pad and colored pencils and started sketching dancers. My ex-husband, Jeff, came walking across the field with his girlfriend, Rose. Jeff was an agent who represented actors and directors. Well built and fit, he wore his ash blond hair in a trendy buzz cut. Rose, a business affairs lawyer for Warner Brothers, was wearing purple leggings and a spandex sports bra. I introduced them to Zack, who stood up and shook Jeff's hand. "How do you do, sir." He tipped his hat to Rose. "Ma'am."

Rose looked amused, but I could tell Jeff was thrown by being called "sir." He turned to me. "We've got a business lunch after the game. There won't be any kids there. Could you keep them till about five?"

"Sure."

He shaded his eyes and stared at the field. "How come Gabriel's playing fullback? That's not his best position."

"The coach has a new strategy," I said. "During the first half, he's going to put the strongest players—the best ball handlers—on defense, so the other team can't score and gets frustrated and demoralized."

Jeff looked dubious. "That sounds pretty half-baked. I think you need a strong offense too."

"Gabriel's okay with it."

"Good." He smiled and walked with Rose to the outer edge of the parents' group where they set up their folding chairs.

The coach's strategy worked. During the second half, Gabriel was switched to forward and kicked two goals, one of which turned out to be the winning point. Zack and I took the kids to Fosters Freeze for ice cream to celebrate. Then we drove to the mall to buy socks and to Super Cuts, where they both had haircuts. For three years, I hadn't been with a man and my children at the same time, going through the ordinariness of a Saturday, and I was basking in it. The salon was noisy and chaotic, with music blasting from speakers: Tag Team singing, "Whoomp! There It Is!" Zack pulled me out the door and kissed me while Gabriel and Sophie were being shampooed. Then we went home and made lunch: bacon, lettuce, and tomato sandwiches on white toast with lots of mayonnaise. We licked the crumbs. "This is the best lunch we've ever had," Sophie said.

In the afternoon, Zack showed the kids how to team-rope, throwing their lassos around the head and feet of an imaginary calf they'd constructed out of a sawhorse and brooms. Gabriel wanted Zack to tie him up like a bandit. Zack tied him to a chair, then to a tree, and gagged him with his red bandanna. Every time Gabriel struggled free, he begged Zack to make it harder to escape, but after an hour, Gabriel was red-faced and overexcited. He leaped onto Zack and started pounding and kicking him. When Zack grabbed his hands and yanked him off, Gabriel burst into tears.

"You hurt me!"

"I didn't mean to," Zack said.

"Yes, you did!"

"I hope you'll forgive me."

Gabriel ran up to his room, turned on Smashing Pumpkins, and didn't come out until it was time to drive to his father's. When we arrived, he kissed me good-bye but wouldn't speak to Zack. He walked into the house and closed the door, then opened it again and waved. "See ya, Zack."

Zack waved back. "I'm glad he did that."

Home alone. The sun was setting, filling the house with shafts of apricot-colored light. Zack and I were lying on my bed, on the quilt of sinuous vines and purple roses. When I'd lived here with Jeff, the bedroom had been black, white, and gray, but when he'd moved out, I'd painted the walls a pale, araucana green and brought in leafy plants and overstuffed chairs and quilts and needlepoint pillows.

Zack lifted my arm and placed it above my head. "Leave it there." He undid my shirt, pulling apart the first mother-of-pearl snap.

"There's something we should talk about," I said.

"What's that?"

"Condoms."

He unfastened the second pearl snap.

"How would you feel," I said, "about having a test so we wouldn't have to use them?"

"Sweetheart, I'll take any test you want, but it's not necessary."

"Why?"

He pulled open the last snap and parted my shirt. "Because I haven't slept with a woman in five years." He ran his finger down the center of my chest.

"Are you saying I'm the first . . . since your wife?"

"Yes, ma'am."

He lifted my other arm and placed it above my head. I felt exposed, elongated, a bird with a trembling wingspan. "Five years?"

"I was mad. I didn't want nothin' to do with women and when I decided I did, I couldn't get one to hold still for me."

"I find that hard to believe."

He kissed my nipples, setting off beestings of pleasure. "I must've been giving off some kind of bad black smoke. One lady got turned off by my truck. When I asked her for a date, she said, 'Don't even think about it. I'm having nightmares about your truck.'"

"Luckily, I haven't seen it."

He laughed, raking his fingers across my chest.

"I've been craving this, just craving it," I whispered. I told him that for years, I'd never gotten a hug from Jeff that I didn't ask for. We almost never made love unless I initiated it, and often he'd turn me down.

"Now I find *that* hard to believe," Zack said. "How could you tolerate that?"

Because, I explained, the marriage had never been about sex. When I'd met Jeff, I was thirty-seven and desperate to have children. Jeff was eager to get married and start a family, and I thought he'd be a dedicated father and loyal husband, which he was. "I got pregnant right away, but then I had premature labor and was told to stay in bed for six months, during which we couldn't have sex. When Sophie was born, as soon as the doctor gave us the okay to make love, we got pregnant again and there was another entire year when we couldn't have sex. Gabriel was born eleven months after Sophie."

"Same thing happened to us," Zack said. "Two kids in the first two years."

"You know what it's like—you've got two babies in diapers, two creatures who need bottles and baths and constant attention, and you don't have private moments except when they're sleeping and you're exhausted."

So sex took a hike. We kept saying we were waiting: when the babies slept through the night; when Jeff got his new agency up and running; when we learned to get along better; when we finished building our house, moving in; and then there was a moment when I realized we'd be waiting the rest of our years. We were at a screening of *Lawrence of Arabia*, which had just been rereleased. We'd had a fabulous dinner at Chinois and the film was imparting a sense of awe and I kissed his cheek and said softly, "When we get home, let's make love?"

I felt his body stiffen.

"What's wrong?" I whispered.

He crossed his arms and stared at the screen.

"What?"

He shrugged. "There's no juice. I don't know what else to say, Sara. I can go through the motions but . . . the desire's not there anymore."

I suggested we see a counselor. "Couldn't we try to rekindle the desire?" But he said he didn't think that was possible.

I did not see the rest of *Lawrence of Arabia*. I was staring down a long, cold corridor: years and years, an indefinite future with no sex. And it wasn't just sex, there would be no touching, no hugging, no chance of being looked at or desired as a woman. I knew people who'd made their peace with this falling away of the physical. They'd replaced it with warm friendship or cozy collegiality, but I could not. There were many deep fissures in the marriage, but sex—the utter absence of it—came to stand for the entire unsound structure.

So I came hurtling out of divorce court into the dating market of 1990, ready to jump in bed with the first male body that had a pulse and I couldn't get laid. The world had changed. There was no more sex on the first date, as there had been the last time I was single. Quaint as it seems, during the sixties and seventies there *was* sex on the first date, sex because it felt good, sex because we had the Pill and no one was sick and we were invulnerable. By 1990, though, AIDS had put a skeleton's head on every bedpost. There was no sex until you got to know the person well, no sex until you were ready to say you wouldn't have sex with anyone else.

"Can't we just have fun?" I asked the first man who took me on a date, a divorced rabbi. After kissing and groping on the couch in his apartment, he said he didn't want to fuck because "I get emotionally attached too quickly and I'm not ready." Then he lay down on top of me and started dry-humping, grinding his hips through two layers of clothes. I looked at the ceiling and thought, I'm forty-six. What is this?

"That guy ought to be horse-whipped," Zack said.

"There was a train of guys like that. I went out with a doctor, a stockbroker—there was even a New Age yoga teacher who drove an electric car—and they all said something like, 'I want to get to know you better so we'll be making love, not fucking.' That was supposed to be *our* line."

"It's a damn good thing you found your way to Elko," Zack said.

"Damn good."

"So I'm the first . . . since your husband?"

"Well, no. After a while, I did find a willing partner. I cried the first time, I was so overwhelmed, but it didn't take long before I saw that it wasn't just sex I was hungry for."

I told him that on New Year's Eve, I'd flown to Las Vegas with a stand-up comic who was tireless in bed and wanted to buy me lingerie. I thought he meant beautiful lace teddies and silk briefs, but he showed up with a box of half bras that stopped below the nipples and panties that had no crotch. We rode in a limousine to Caesar's Palace, where he was performing in the lounge, but when we walked into his suite, I was hit with a wave of nausea. I didn't want to put on a trick bra and crotchless panties and get drilled in the heart-shaped bed. I wanted to go home.

"I've been thinking . . ." Zack said. He slipped the shirt off me and dropped it on the floor. "About the things you showed me last time."

"I didn't show you that much."

"All the time I was sitting at my table, braiding knots, my mind was roaming over the terrain." He ran his hands across my rib cage and down my stomach. "I'd think, What would happen if I did this . . ." He took one rib between his fingers and traced its curving path. "And at the same time, I did this . . ." I sighed and closed my eyes; it was like listening to music on a superb hi-fi system where you could hear each note, crystalline and distinct.

I had a sense memory of being ten, when I would sleep over at my best friend Linda's house. We'd wait for her mother to say good night and turn off the lights, then we'd push the twin beds together and lay on top of the covers.

"Do my arms?" Linda whispered. "Five minutes?"

We took turns running our fingers over each other's arms and legs, seeing how long we could stand it without wriggling or laughing out loud. It was a safe way to toy with the new sensations stirring in the body.

"My turn."

"It hasn't been five minutes."

"Yes, it has."

"What do you want?"

"The back of my legs, please?"

We stroked each other for hours, and many years later in a darkened theater, I felt an illicit thrill when I watched Mariel Hemingway in *Personal Best*, running her fingers up the arm of her female lover. "I used to get paid for this," Hemingway said. "A nickel an arm, a dime a leg, a quarter a back."

Zack's fingers were cunning, approaching but never crossing the threshold of tickling, making the nerves come alert, sector by sector, so that every plane and crook, every crease and fold, every fleshy mound and bony point of the body was lit and added to the fire. When I tried to touch him the same way, though, he twisted aside. He wanted to be rubbed and pinched and have his hair pulled and his back raked with fingernails that left red marks. The rougher I was with him, the softer he was with me. At times he wouldn't move at all, he'd just rest a finger in a strategic spot and my body would strain and point.

"I love your hands," I said.

"I take real good care of 'em. In the old days, I'd use 'em like hammers. At the feedlot, we had to open three or four hundred gates a day and if they were stuck, I'd just punch 'em." He whacked the side of the bed.

He said he was happiest when his hands had a job—braiding, cutting—and when they were idle, they'd start, almost without his willing it, to pet whatever creature was nearby—a cat, a horse, me. "Marianne said it annoyed her."

"Really?"

"You don't mind if I do this?"

I shook my head.

"You're the first woman who's let me. I don't want to hurt you. You'll tell me if it bothers you, all right?"

"I don't want you to stop."

Even when he was in me, his hands were in motion, turning up the heat as if adjusting a rheostat. He'd keep things bubbling along, then let them fall to simmer and take them back again to boil, full boil, violent boil with the water foaming and spattering and threatening to spill. Then he stopped and I was flopping like a beached sea animal.

"Let's take a break," he said.

"No."

"I'm going down to the kitchen."

"Please."

"Get some more tequila."

"Not now." I grabbed his arm but he pulled himself free.

"I'll be back in just a minute."

"Why are you doing this?"

"Because you want me to," he whispered.

He was an agitated sleeper. He thrashed and talked and just as I was falling asleep, he had a coughing fit. When I opened my eyes in the morning, he was standing at the window, sipping coffee. The sun was at his back and when he turned, I felt a shock, he looked so beautiful. He was lean, slimmer than I, but with sharply defined muscles in his arms and thighs. Although his face was tanned a permanent brown, the rest of him was astonishingly white.

"What do you feel like doing today?" I said.

He shrugged.

"We could go for a hike. Walk on the beach."

He didn't answer.

"Go riding." I waited. "Spend the day in bed."

He smiled. "Let's do that."

Isn't it obvious? We were two famished souls and we were having a feeding frenzy. We both had stores of bottled-up desire and all the locks, the latches, the safety clasps were being tripped. We could let ourselves go. I didn't have to pretend to be a dainty eater, I could be ravenous, I could gorge. The divorced rabbi had told me I was loaded for bear and it spooked him but Zack didn't care. He wanted bear.

We looked out the window and there was sunlight and then there were stars. We dashed to the airport for the last plane at midnight—Zack speeding, me pressing myself against him, kissing like fools and screeching to a stop. We jumped out and ran around to change places and Zack was tucking in his shirt, adjusting his Stetson. I was bowlegged and sore and didn't care.

"You be sweet," he called.

I waved as he ran inside the terminal. Then I drove away, steering around the cloverleaf and onto the exit ramp for Highway 1, which would take me back to Santa Monica.

Good, I thought, this was good. It's out of my system.

4

I drove into the underground parking garage as if I were approaching Checkpoint Charlie. I stopped, the kids got out of the station wagon and walked across the cement to where a dark green Mercedes was idling in the darkness. They opened the door, climbed in the back, and the driver pulled away, giving me a subliminal nod.

We did this every week but it seemed we were doing it continually: at houses, in doctors' offices, at schools. We once did it in Grand Teton National Park. I'd flown with the kids to Montana and Wyoming for a vacation and I'd met Jeff at a prearranged time in Jackson Hole, where he was taking them white-water rafting. We met by the general store in Moose, Wyoming. I pulled in, the kids got out of my rented car, jumped into the back of his rented van and off they drove and I was by myself. In Moose.

The transitions—the hours before and after we made the exchange—were still nerve-racking. We'd had a difficult one this afternoon. I'd spent the day with Sophie, taking her to the Santa Monica mall to buy a dress for a party—her first boy-girl dance party. She was straining like a puppy on a leash and I'm embarrassed at how happy and grateful I was to be with her. We walked into Contempo, where Mariah Carey was singing "Dreamlover" and the mannequins were fitted out with the hottest, wildest styles for teens.

Sophie started fishing through the racks. I watched her and smiled: she was all arms and legs, with her ashen hair swept up in a ponytail. She turned and looked at me. "Don't talk to the saleslady."

"I'll just ask where to find your size." She wore a size one and there were never very many.

"Mom, I know where to look. Please, it's embarrassing."

"Okay." I held up a pale blue dress with a lacy jacket. "How about this?"

"Disgusting." She made a face. "No offense, but you and I have, like, way different taste."

She believed I was not to be trusted in matters of fashion. I didn't wear makeup, I had "bad clothes," and, most unforgivably, I did not wear a bra. I'm one of that band of women who stopped wearing a bra in the sixties because it was fashionable and sexy and a political statement: you were casting off the male-chauvinist halter. It was also comfortable. I loved the freedom of not wearing straps across my chest, and even when it stopped being fashionable and there was a backlash against "bra burners," I never returned to wearing one. Zack said when he saw me in Elko, "I noticed your hair, your eyes, and that you weren't wearing a bra. And it wasn't just a comfort thing, you were saying: 'I won't wear the uniform.'"

When I was Sophie's age, though, I wore a training bra. I

remember going to a girls' assembly at school where a thin-lipped, gray-haired woman gave a lecture on how to fit your-self for a bra. Hook it in back first, she said, then bend over and let yourself fill the cups, then tighten the straps. I hunched down in my seat, my face burning. I didn't have enough yet to fill a cup, but I believed that if I wore the train-ing garment, I would grow more quickly and when they did arrive, my breasts would be "trained."

Sophie wanted to buy a different bra for every outfit. At Contempo, she picked out a dozen dresses and three bras in coordinating colors. As she headed into the dressing room, she asked me to wait outside. For months, she hadn't wanted me in the room with her. She didn't want me to see her bud-ding figure and of course I was dying to see it. I found a chair, sat down, and pulled a script from my briefcase and started working on revisions of the next episode we were shooting, "Cooper vs. Quinn." I'd learned, by necessity, to carry my work wherever I went. I'd written in the bleachers of Little League games and in the waiting room of the orthodontist.

In "Cooper vs. Quinn," the father of Dr. Quinn's adopted children—the man who abandoned them—comes back and says he's taking them off to San Francisco. Dr. Quinn goes to court to try to keep the children, but she's on shaky ground. In 1865, I'd learned, after doing research on family law in the nineteenth century, it didn't matter whether the father was a drunkard, a thief, or if he beat his kids, he had absolute cus-tody and the mother had no rights. The courts believed they should not intrude on the privacy of the family by attempting to determine who was fit to be the father of any child. "That's up to the Almighty," the judges wrote.

Sophie walked out of the dressing room wearing a sequined,

short, black Lycra dress that clung to her from the shoulder to the thigh. She looked proud, shy, thrilled, as she swiveled in front of the three-way mirror. "I *love* this!"

"It's awfully tight."

"So? That's the way it's supposed to be. That's the style."

"I don't think it's appropriate," I said, without conviction. I'd worn extreme miniskirts and form-fitting jeans myself, but in sixth grade? The dress seemed too suggestive, but I knew I was waging a losing battle. We lived in California, near Hollywood, and the girls in her school, all the models in teen magazines and on MTV dressed like hookers, wearing skimpy tops with their bra straps showing and tight short skirts that looked like slips and high-heeled platform shoes and decal tattoos.

"I feel beautiful. I feel cheerful," Sophie said. On the speakers, Boyz II Men were singing "I'll Make Love to You." She did a few dance moves. I had to concede that the dress looked good, but she was so slender and willowy that everything looked good on her. She turned and stared over her shoulder at her back. "I love my back. I don't like my nose, I'd look better with a different nose."

"Your nose is lovely," I said. "Classic and straight."

She turned to the side and put a hand on her hip. "I can't wait to have big breasts."

I told her, gently, that the women in our family don't tend to look like Dolly Parton. "But small breasts are beautiful."

"I'm not like you, Mom. I'm not gonna turn out like you. I'll get breasts from Dad's side."

"Okay." I smiled.

"So, can I get this?"

I hesitated.

"Please," she begged, "it's my dream dress. I feel like it was made for me. I'll never find anything I love as much."

"All right."

"Thanks, Mom!"

Jeff had asked me, as a favor, to bring the kids to his office on Sunset Boulevard instead of his house so they could make it to a Lakers game on time. As Gabriel and Sophie started gathering up their books and clothes and stuffing them into shopping bags, I felt myself growing anxious. In the car, Sophie said, "I don't want to go to the game. I hate the Lakers."

"I thought you liked the Laker Girls," Gabriel said.

"I don't like watching people play sports. I like doing them myself."

"I feel the same," I said.

"Can I stay with you tonight?"

"We have to follow the schedule."

"I'm sick of the schedule. Why do I have to go to Dad's house anyway? I don't like that house."

"I do," Gabriel said.

"It's empty and cold. I can't sleep."

"Why can't you sleep?" I said.

"I'm afraid. My room is too dark. You know how every room has a feeling? At Dad's house, my room says, 'I wouldn't sleep here if I were you!'"

"That's crazy," Gabriel said.

"No, it's not."

"Okay, what does my room say?" he asked.

"'Keep out!'"

He nodded, satisfied.

I bit my lip not to smile. "At my house," I asked, "what does your room say?"

"'I love you. Come in and get cozy.'"

"And what does my bedroom say?" I asked.

She thought a moment. "I don't do adults' rooms. Only kids'."

I laughed, then took a breath. Another. "Why don't you ask your dad to help you make your room more cozy? Get him to be part of your team. He's a great problem solver. If you ask him, he'll be flattered."

"Yeah, like . . . you could really make it cozy," Sophie said.

"You could paint it a nice warm color. Put more posters on the wall." I pulled into the underground garage. "Listen, Sophie, I'll be home most of the weekend and you can call me anytime. Anytime. All right?"

She slumped out of the car and followed Gabriel across the cement. I drove home, and when I walked inside, the house seemed painfully silent. Sounds were magnified. The water heater switching on. Gabriel's computer humming and blipping. I walked through the rooms, pulling brown leaves off the plants. Is Gabriel wearing his retainer? Did Sophie take her math book with her? I felt panic in my chest—despite all the times I'd done this, it never was easier—and I had to tell myself: Two days, they'll be back in two days.

I made a salad and sat down at the kitchen table. I leafed absently through the *L.A. Times* and the *New York Times*. I looked at the clock. Zack would be landing in two hours. If I got up from the table now, if I started moving, I could take a bath, wash my hair, shave my legs.

◆

Zack had been flying to California every few weeks and I'd been buying most of the tickets. Each time we said good-bye at the airport, we didn't speak about when he'd return. For the first few days afterward, I'd ache for him and then I'd get distracted and be riddled with doubts about what I was doing, but after two or three weeks, I wanted to see him again.

I made most of the phone calls and he sent letters, which he worked on with a dictionary but which still had nightmarish spelling. It did not concern me that I made the calls, as it would have with other men. I'd been insecure with the president of the network and would not have dreamed of calling him if he hadn't called me. But I was not insecure with Zack—a cowboy who'd sent me a leather key and urged me to use it.

Once, though, when he didn't answer the phone for five days, I grew rattled and apprehensive and when he finally called, explaining that he'd gone to visit his daughters in Casa Grande, I was angry. "You need to let me know. You need to stay in touch."

"I didn't think thataway," he said. "I guess I've been on my own too long."

For most of our visits, he arrived on Friday so we could spend time with Gabriel and Sophie before they went to their dad's. Then we closed the doors and saw no one but each other. On this weekend, though, we'd decided it was time to venture out among people: to a party for the cast and crew of *Dr. Quinn.*

"You like this shirt?" he said, coming out of the walk-in closet. I turned to face him. He was buttoning up a Western shirt whose turquoise color brought out the green of his eyes and the rosy brown of his skin. "Yes, I do." I put my arms around him but recoiled at the touch of the shirt. "It feels like cardboard."

"That's because I asked for extra starch."

"You're kidding." I'd never known a man who asked for starch. When I'd taken Jeff's shirts to the cleaners, I always had to tell them, "No starch, please!"

Zack started pulling on a pair of boots I hadn't seen: turquoise blue with black stitching in the shape of feathers. He pushed his jeans inside the boots. "Starch is part of the cowboy way. A true hand doesn't show up without a crease. I've got my own iron and ironing board and cans of spray starch. When I worked at Red River, I'd get up at three in the morning to starch and press my shirt and iron my jeans."

"Why?" I was slipping on a beige lace blouse and black silk pants.

"It's about looking good. Cowgirls iron their jeans until the creases are so sharp, they'll cut you."

I thought about the cowgirls I'd seen at Elko. Their jeans did look stiff and dark, nothing baggy or stonewashed. And their shirts were crisp and had long sleeves fastened at the wrist, not rolled up in cuffs as mine were. And of course they had cowboy hats tipped over their faces and wore pink lipstick.

"I like my pants pressed so hard that the two sides stick together and you gotta pry 'em apart," Zack said.

"I like comfort, softness."

"So do I, and if I want to get thataway, I throw off all my clothes and lie down, hopefully not alone." He took hold of my blouse, pulled me to him and kissed me. "Your clothes are very relaxed and that's right for you, because you choose to present yourself as loose and relaxed."

"Are you kidding? I'm tense and frazzled."

"Your hair's all free."

"I thought you liked the way I dress."

"I do. I'm not criticizing. This is just my roundabout way of saying that look is right for you but when it comes to me . . ." He tucked in the stiff shirt and buckled his belt. "This starch attitude is gonna stick."

When we pulled up to Beth Sullivan's house in Sherman Oaks, there was a line of Porsches and Lexuses and Jeep Cherokees. Jane Seymour was standing on the sidewalk, dressed not in the long frontier skirts and aprons of the show but in sleek black pants and a V-necked sweater that accented the extraordinary lines of her body: lush breasts, small waist, graceful legs. She waved toward my car. Zack tipped his Stetson.

"You know what the definition of a weed is?" he said.

"No."

He stepped out of the car, walked around, and opened the door for me. "I learned this when I took a class in agriculture. It's a plant that's out of place."

"You feel like a weed?"

"I'm out of place."

I kissed his cheek. "I love you."

No one seemed to notice at first. Then everyone was staring. Jeanne rushed over and Zack caught her in a hug, and Beth broke away from the group she was with and hurried over with her arms stretched out. "I'm so glad to meet you. Welcome!"

If I'd been nervous about her response, I needn't have worried. When you're in your twenties and thirties, I'd found, your friends will adopt a brutally appraising eye to any new man you bring around. They're concerned: Is this a potential mate? Is he right for her? Is she settling for too little? Would I want to be with this person? But when you're forty-nine, your close, true friends don't care if he's the elephant man as long as he's making you happy. They'll open their doors, "Hello, Mr. Elephant Man, good to meet you!" And then they'll take him aside and tell him, "Sara's been much more relaxed since you've been around."

"He's great," Beth said as Jeanne hooked her arm through Zack's and walked him across the room to the bar where they took glasses of champagne.

"We don't look like we go together."

"What do you care what it looks like or what people think?" Beth said. "He's a free spirit, right? And he's crazy about you . . . " Her attention was pulled away by a swarm of people, all wanting to ask a favor or inform her of a problem. I made my way through the crowd, greeting the camera operators and the actors who played the townsfolk of Colorado Springs. Unlike Beth and Jeanne, the rest of the crew eyed us with amusement and curiosity. In most circles, a man can appear with a woman who's younger or less distinguished and she's accepted, swept right along with him, but a woman is expected to appear with a man of at least equal stature. If she's not, it's regarded as suspect, telling. One of the most frequent observations made about Marcia Clark, which was supposed to be revealing about her character, was that she'd been married to a backgammon player and then to a Scientologist who was a low-level computer programmer.

I joined Zack at the bar. Pete O'Hara, a short young man

who was head of postproduction, walked up to us. "Nice boots," he said to Zack.

"Thank you, sir."

Pete was wearing a charcoal shirt and Armani slacks. "Where'd you get them?"

"Oh, a little ol' feed store in Casa Grande," Zack said.

"You ride in those?"

Zack smiled. "They're dress boots now, but as my riding boots fail, these'll work their way down."

"I bet my brother would like them. He's in Iowa."

"You gotta order 'em special. But any ol' feed store'll do that for you."

"Feed store, hmm? I'll keep my eye out for one," Pete said, enjoying this.

As the night wore on and Zack drank more champagne, he started talking more like a hick. "Little ol' this" and "big ol' that." Pete said, "If you're really such a cowboy, why don't you come out to the set and show us?"

"I might."

I took Zack's arm. "Let's get something to eat?"

Zack shook his head. "I'm gonna step outside a moment." He winked and reached in the pocket of his denim jacket for cigarettes.

"You having culture shock?" Pete said.

"Tad bit," Zack said. "This ain't Kansas anymore."

"Just relax." Pete stepped closer. "If you stand there and don't say anything, people will drive themselves crazy trying to figure out which country-western star you are. I'm serious. We've had Johnny Cash on the show. Willie Nelson. You look sort of like Dwight Yoakam. Yeah. Just keep your mouth closed."

Zack grabbed Pete by the shoulders and shoved him up against the wall. "I don't know who the fuck you think you are. I imagine if you was two or three inches taller you might be a halfway decent human being. But you ain't, and if you don't get outa my face, I'm gonna show you what culture shock can do."

I grabbed Zack's arm, trying to pull him away, saying, "It's all right, take it easy," and everyone was staring and Pete was sputtering, "Hey, I didn't mean anything. What's your problem?"

"I don't have to prove shit to you or nobody else," Zack said. "I know who I am, and where I come from, you wouldn't make a pimple on my ass!" He glared at Pete, gave him a final push toward the wall, turned, and walked out of the house as if it were fucking *High Noon*.

"I never said I was housebroke," Zack said. We were back in my bedroom and I was brushing and flossing my teeth. He pulled off the turquoise boots. "That jerk needed someone to let him know how it is."

I walked into the closet and Zack followed. "All right," he said, "maybe I overreacted."

I took off my shoes, my stockings, my silk pants. "I don't care about Pete. He's a no-count."

"I know," Zack said. "You're thinking, 'What the hell am I doing with this . . . individual? It's all a mistake. It can't go nowhere.' You don't think I've asked myself the same question? Why do I have to get on a fucking airplane and fly to a country I don't know?"

He leaned forward and started to unbutton my blouse. "Let

me help you with that." He slipped it off my shoulders. "You were the most beautiful woman at the party."

"Zack."

"You were. To me."

I pulled on a long cotton nightgown, walked to the over-stuffed chairs, and collapsed against the down-filled cushions. Zack slid into the chair beside me. He kissed my neck, ran his hand under the gown.

"I'm not in the mood."

"I'm not concerned," he said. "You will be."

I moved to the other chair. "I think we're two desperate souls who stumbled on to each other. And this is the only kind of relationship I can handle—where you live in a different state and fly here when it suits me and then go away."

He smiled. "Every time I leave here, I think, This could be the last. I don't want to get sidetracked. I worry about that."

"What do you mean?"

"Want some brandy?"

"Okay."

He took the bottle of Amaretto he'd brought from the kitchen and poured two glasses. He knew about beer and tequila and called everything else brandy. "I want to be the best rawhide braider in the world, and I don't care what it takes. I'm gonna do it." He downed the Amaretto in one shot. I asked how long he'd had this ambition, and he began to tell me how he'd learned about rawhide from Mexican vaqueros at the ranches where he worked.

The art of braiding rawhide into bridles for horses was a Western craft that had flourished in the nineteenth century and nearly died out. "There was this old guy, Joe Pintero, who was my foreman at Red River, and he was one of the last guys around who still knew how to make rawhide," Zack said. "I asked him lots of times to teach me and he said, 'Hell no, you pay me a hundred dollars and I'll show you.' He knew I didn't have a hundred dollars. But I wouldn't leave him alone. I said, 'Let me make you payments.'"

Zack stood up, walked into the bathroom, and came back with baby oil and two towels, which he spread on the floor. "Lie down, I'm gonna rub your back."

"You don't have to."

"Come on." He helped me down from the chair and as I stretched out, he placed his thumbs on the muscles in my shoulders and began to probe.

"So did . . . Joe show you how?"

Zack nodded and said they first had to find the right animal. "Every day there's cattle that die in the feedlot. But you don't want to skin any animal. If it was sick and got bloated up, the hide will be weak. You want a quick, clean kill. Say, if the animal got hung up on a fence and died right away—that's a good hide."

"Right there, yes," I said. "That's where it hurts."

Zack said that when Joe found a good animal, they hauled it away in his truck. "We skinned it with knives, starting at the back of the neck where the hide is thickest. Joe kept telling me, 'Pay attention, Zackary. Goddamn it, I'm only gonna show you this one time!'"

He lifted my arm and it snapped—like the snapping of a twig. "You're tight," he said.

"No kidding."

As he went on with the massage, he cracked the vertebrae in my back and neck.

"After we skinned the cow," he said, "we staked the hide to

the ground. While it was drying, we scraped away all the meat and muscle, and when it was clean, Joe cut the hide into one long string."

"Oh!"

"Too hard?"

"No, no. That feels good. How did he do that?"

"Sort of the way you peel an apple. He made one continuous circle, starting at the outside of the hide and working in toward the center, avoiding the brands. When he finished, the string was a hundred yards long. It took the two of us to lift it. We brought it to the feedlot and stretched it on a fence and let it dry a few more days."

Zack poured more baby oil into his palms and worked it into the muscles of my lower back. He said that during breaks at the feedlot, he and Joe would take their knives and shave the hair off the string. He demonstrated, making a shaving motion. "It was the old-fashioned way. It was the hardest, most god-awful way in the world, but I'd never seen it done and I thought it was fantastic!"

I started to raise myself. "Let me do your back—" But Zack pushed my shoulders to the floor. "I'm not done with you."

He went on: "Now that we had the rawhide in one long cord, we had to cut it into narrow strings we could use for braiding. And that's the coolest part."

He moved his hands down to my buttocks and I flinched. "Relax, baby." He said that Joe showed him how to make a *máquina* to cut strings. They chopped a four-foot branch off a mesquite tree, buried it in the ground, and carved a notch on top where Joe could set two knives. "I had to feed the rawhide through the notch while he cut it on both sides. Then we had our strings."

He was working on my thighs now, letting his fingers graze. He told me that many years later, he designed his own machine to cut strings—a metal cylinder with clamps and razor blades. "To be a good braider, you first have to be a master string cutter. The better your strings are, the greater your work is."

"Can't you buy the strings somewhere?"

"No, ma'am. I've had offers from people just to buy my strings and I've said no. Strings are a sacred part of it." He said he's learned to cut strings that are impossibly thin—one sixty-fourth of an inch. "And they're beveled on both sides. But you can only cut strings like that on certain days. Magic days, when you tingle all the way down to your fingertips and your hands are floating and the strings are whipping out."

He turned me over and he was not massaging anymore.

"When you braid rawhide, you're special." I looked up—his face had an air of exaltation. "Rawhide is the strongest thing there is. It speaks to me. Rawhide is what held the West together."

I pulled him down and kissed him. Everything felt good now. We rolled around the floor, arching our bodies against each other. "This is the best it's ever been," I said. Then we laughed, because I said this every time. I knew the body could not remember pain, but I was discovering the body can't remember physical pleasure either. Every time Zack flew back to Arizona, I could remember what we'd done in great detail—the moves, the progressions—but the actual sensations . . . I couldn't re-create them. So each time he returned and we reached that point of utter and inexpressible bliss, my mind would reel.

"You're like a young horse," Zack said. "They jump all over. They're unpredictable."

I laughed. "That's not a quality most people would find desirable."

"That's true. But I like riding a horse nobody else can ride."

"Pretty sure of yourself?"

"Yes, I am. I know that if I hunker down and ride through the bucks—"

I grabbed his hair and yanked his head back.

"God! You'll quit bucking and I'll have my way with you."

5

I later came to look at them as our salad days—the first few months of Zack flying in and out like some masked rider on a white plane. The children loved coming with me to the airport to pick him up. When he was around, we seemed to laugh more, there was a spirit of lightness and unpredictable adventure. We rode horses, climbed rocks, and searched for treasures at garage sales, slithered through the haunted house at the Pumpkin Festival and ate fried shrimp on picnic tables at Neptune's Net.

And then things turned. Not long after Thanksgiving, I went upstairs to help Gabriel clean out his room and heard him playing his drums to Metallica's "Enter Sandman."

I knocked. He couldn't hear me, even though he was using SoundOffs—rubber disks that fit over the top of each drum-head and reduce the volume. I walked in, carrying storage boxes and a black plastic garbage bag. He had Metallica on the radio and his best friend, Jason, was on the speaker phone, playing electric guitar.

I cleared a space on the floor for the boxes. The gray carpet could hardly be seen—it was covered with CDs, sheet music, skateboards, toys, books, baseball caps, a trumpet and music stand, and sticks of incense and transistor microchip boards.

Gabriel had started playing trumpet in kindergarten and two years later fell in love with drums. He could reproduce almost any song—tune, rhythm, words—after hearing it only once. When I started playing Beatles tapes in the car because I was sick of "The Wheels on the Bus," he went home and picked out the trumpet riff from "Penny Lane."

He'd always liked to keep his room orderly, but in recent months he'd let things fall to chaos. Veronica, the dark-haired, rotund, compulsively thorough housekeeper who'd lived with us for eleven years, was upset because she couldn't vacuum. When I'd ask Gabriel to straighten his room, he'd push things to the corners and under the bed and after a day it would be chaos again.

I told him we needed to clean out his shelves so there'd be room for the toys and papers that were now on the floor. "Yes! We killed it!" he cried as he finished "Enter Sandman" with an extended roll. He said good-bye to Jason, turned off the radio, and swiveled around to face me.

I picked up a dusty, three-level space station that we'd bought when he was five.

"I'm not throwing that out," Gabriel said.

"You don't play with it anymore."

"I don't care."

"Okay, we'll put it in a box and keep it in the garage and any time you want it, you can just open the box. All right?"

He nodded, reluctant. He walked to the bookshelf and took down a basket filled with action figures, tanks, and planes. He held each G.I. Joe in his palm, remembering the feel, the heft, then put it in the box.

"This guy stays here," he said, fingering an astronaut with an oxygen helmet.

"Why?"

"I want to set him on fire."

"Gabriel."

"I'm serious, Mom. I'm gonna burn him in the wastebasket and see if the helmet works."

"You're not burning anything here."

"Outside."

"Not outside either."

"I'll be careful."

"This is not negotiable."

"But Zack said if you fill a bucket with sand and burn it outside, it'll be safe."

I thought a moment. Was this some male tropism, the urge to set things on fire? Should it be tolerated, channeled in a constructive direction? "Zack's coming Friday. You can talk to him and if he wants to supervise this, you can do it."

Gabriel dropped the astronaut into the storage box. "No thanks."

"Why?"

He picked up a paratrooper. "I don't want to do it with Zack."

"I thought you liked him."

"I did. But . . . "

I told myself to speak calmly. "But what?"

"You're different when he's around."

"Different?"

"I don't like the change."

"How am I different?"

He picked up a plane whose tail had broken off, studied it, then dropped it into the box.

"I feel happier when he's here," I said. "Is that it?"

"No."

Gabriel had come to the bottom of the basket and started weeding through his books. "I remember this—*Cars and Trucks and Things That Go.*"

"I still have plenty of time for you. You'll get just as much attention—"

"But I don't."

"We have our special trip coming up next month."

He shrugged.

Once a year, I took each child on a trip, just the two of us, to a place like San Diego or Palm Springs. When Gabriel was six, we'd driven to Santa Barbara and I'd taught him how to ride a Boogie board in the ocean. Every time we caught a wave, he'd reach out his small hand and grab mine as we felt the rushing curl pick us up and shoot us out like missiles— two missiles scudding in unison over the water to the shore. The next year, I taught him to ski, holding him in front of me as we coasted down the bunny slope.

He was game for adventure and fearless—he wanted to ride the fastest horses and ski the black-diamond runs. When he was nine, we'd gone hiking in Colorado with my friend Jodie and her two sons, and at a waterfall near Durango, the boys wanted to scramble up the cliff instead of driving up the road to the top of the falls. Jodie and I watched them leap from rock to rock, grabbing for handholds. When they were halfway up, I saw them start to slip, stop, try a different route, stop again, and call to each other, pointing. I went up after them, thinking I could help, but after I'd climbed about twenty feet, rocks started sliding away from under me. I was wearing tennis shoes and the cliff was covered with loose scree. Gusts of wind blew sprays from the waterfall over the rocks. I kept probing for footholds and grabbed on to a shrub but it started to pull away from the mountain. I looked up— the three boys had made it to the top and Jodie had driven there and they were all staring down at me as I yelled, "Help!"

Jodie tried to hike down but she was wearing flip-flops and slipped and fell on her backside. I was stretched out flat now—a mistake, I learned later; you want to keep your body curved against the slope. Since I had no traction, I was slipping, slipping. The plant was tearing loose. My feet were shaking, my whole body was shaking. I looked down. I could die. No. I tried to dig my feet under the small wet rocks but that made me slip more and the plant was hanging by one last root and then Gabriel was there. He'd made it down the cliff and was standing above me, holding out his hand.

I don't dare grab it, I thought. I'll pull him down with me.

"Mom, look. There's some grass over there."

I turned my head and saw a small patch of grass to my left, about four feet away. If I could get to it, but those four feet seemed . . . a chasm. What if I fell before I could reach it?

He kept holding out his hand. "You can do it, Mom. Put your right foot on that big gray rock. Go ahead. It's not far, you can make it."

I looked at him: he was reaching, watching, and then I lunged. I was on the grass. I scrambled up after him to the road and collapsed, jerking and gagging from the adrenaline and the cold slap in the face, the reminder: the holds we have on the earth are tenuous.

◆

When we finished clearing out the bookshelves, I said, "Let's do the area around your bed." I looked under it and found his old stuffed dog, Joe Joe. The cloth puppy had been placed in his crib when he was born, but it did not resemble a dog now. Its fur, once brown, was dishwater beige, the tail and ears were missing, and it possessed a mildewy smell that I couldn't bear but which Gabriel found comforting.

"Do you still sleep with Joe Joe?"

"'Course not."

"Then maybe you don't need to keep him here."

He held the dog in his palms, hesitated, then placed him carefully in the box. I reached under the bed and pulled out a poster for Nine Inch Nails. Gabriel unrolled it and tacked it above his headboard. I felt a wave of tenderness. He'd just started his growth spurt, his chest was long and narrow, and his limbs had the unformed look of an ungainly young bird. He was still a child who liked to take his G.I. Joes into the bathtub and pretend there was a tidal wave, and he was a young man who wore a chain wallet and dark glasses and played his drums while tuned to KROQ, the alternative rock station.

He dragged a box of Lego toys out from under the bed. He studied each piece: an owl, a helicopter, a monster that had six legs and was motorized. Jeff and I had given him the monster for Chanukah the last year we were together and he'd assembled it entirely by himself. He flipped on the switch and it started to move, crablike, across the carpet, going *tat-a-tat-a-tat*. He looked at me with his large, luminous brown eyes and started to cry. He didn't close his eyes but kept them fixed on me as his face muscles quivered and the tears ran down his cheeks. I had the impulse to turn away, it was so intimate.

"Is it hard to let go of your toys?" I said softly.

He shook his head no. Then he went to his bed and threw himself on it facedown. I sat on the edge and rubbed his back.

"What, Gabriel? What's making you sad?" I waited. "I wish you'd tell me."

"I can't."

"You'll feel better . . . "

"No." He turned away from me, toward the wall.

"Is it something about your Dad? Sophie?"

He didn't answer.

"Me?"

"Yes."

"Something I did?"

"Yes."

I was surprised. "Are you angry with me?"

"No."

"Just sad?"

He nodded.

"I feel bad. Please, tell me, so I won't do it again."

His body jackknifed with a paroxysm of tears. "You can *never* do it again. Never!"

I wracked my brain. What could it be—what could I never do again?

"Please, Mom, I don't want to talk about it."

I sat quietly and rubbed his back.

On Friday afternoon, Sophie had a costume fitting and rehearsal for *Beauty and the Beast*. In the evening, Gabriel's class at school was having its project night, when they'd be displaying their art and science projects and giving a choral performance. We drove to the airport to pick up Zack between the dance rehearsal and project night. Sophie was pulling off her jazz shoes, then yanked out the rubber band so her ash blonde hair fell down her back. "I don't like Zack and neither does Gabriel," she said. "When are you gonna break up?"

"We just got together. Why don't you like him?"

"He's mean. I've tried being nice to him but it doesn't do any good."

Gabriel said, "He's bad at heart."

"What are you guys talking about?"

"He uses foul language," Sophie said.

"He does," Gabriel said.

"He's ugly, very ugly. I hate his hair. I hate his whole body. And you're always kissing. Can't you just be friends and not kiss? It's disgusting."

"Well, he likes both of you," I said.

"No, he doesn't," Gabriel said. "He wants to be with you so he has to be nice to us to get to you."

"You like him better than us," Sophie said.

"That's not true. You and Gabriel come first and always will."

"I'm gonna tell him that."

"Please do. He already knows."

We pulled up to Southwest Airlines, I stepped out of the car and told the kids to get in the backseat. The tan Stetson separated itself from the blur of people on the pedestrian island. When Zack grabbed me in a hug, I turned my face to avoid his lips.

He got in the car and gave the kids presents, as he always

did. He handed Gabriel one of his pocketknives and said he could keep it, "if it's all right with your mom."

"As long as he's responsible." I turned to Gabriel. "You're not to point it at anyone. Even in play."

" 'Course not," Gabriel said.

Zack gave Sophie a silver bracelet with a horse charm. "I don't wear bracelets," she said. "Mom, can we have dinner at California Pizza Kitchen?"

"Hey—what do you guys say to Zack?"

They both mumbled, "Thank you."

"You're very welcome," he said.

I looked at my watch. "We don't have time. Project night starts at seven."

"But I'm hungry."

I pulled into a McDonald's and headed for the drive-through lane. I asked the kids what they wanted and shouted into the voice box: "Two Happy Meals, one with chicken nuggets and a Coke, one with a hamburger and a Sprite."

Static erupted from the box.

"What?" I shouted.

"Seven dollar . . . window." I drove to the window.

Zack reached back and touched Sophie's arm. "You're happy to see me. I know you are. You just don't want to admit it."

She jerked back—as far from his reach as she could. "Can't you find a girlfriend in your own city?"

I laughed, nervous.

"A lot of people have asked me that question," Zack said. "And I tell them I've never met a woman like your mother. I'd go halfway around the world to be with her, if she'd have me."

Sophie and Gabriel pretended they were throwing up.

I paid the man with the microphone headset and drove to the second window. Zack turned so he was facing both kids. "Would things be better for you if I stopped showing up here?"

"Yes," they said.

"Well, here's the deal. I'm gonna keep coming back. So you can be a plus or a minus."

Sophie folded her thin arms; her eyes looked bruised. "I'm a minus."

Gabriel flicked the knife open and wagged it at Zack. I reached back to take it but Zack caught my arm and Gabriel snapped the blade shut.

The fifth-graders were lined up on risers at the front of the gym. Gabriel was standing in the center of the back row. Our family—our cobbled, dysfunctional group—was camped in a line on folding chairs. Sophie sat in the middle between Jeff and me, and Rose and Zack were on the edges.

The music teacher, Ann Huxtable, a Valkyrie-like woman with thick, brown curly hair, raised her baton and the class started singing "They Call the Wind Mariah."

Sophie put her hand to her mouth, struggling not to laugh.

"What?" I whispered.

"Look at Gabriel."

All around him, the students were moving their lips, trying to form round tones as they wailed the mournful falling notes, "Mar-iiiiiii-ah." Gabriel kept his mouth closed.

"Why isn't he singing?" Jeff asked.

I shrugged and shook my head.

"He thinks it's a dumb song," Sophie said.

"That's no excuse for not participating," Jeff said.

When the class finished "Mariah," we clapped dutifully as they filed off the risers for intermission.

"He can't stand Mrs. Huxtable," Sophie said. "I can't either. She makes you stretch your mouth like a dork, and she picks the worst songs." She laughed again.

"It's not funny," Jeff said. "If he doesn't want to sing, he should at least move his lips. This kind of behavior is not going to get him anywhere."

Sophie spotted a friend by the refreshment table and ran off to join her.

I turned to Jeff. "You're right. I'll speak with Gabriel about it."

Jeff and Rose exchanged a look. "It's his attitude," Jeff said. "You let him run the house and he thinks he can do whatever he likes. The whole world will cater to him."

"He does *not* run the house."

Rose, who was wearing blue-tinted glasses and a black suit, said, "He needs limits. They both do. They may kick and scream, but in the long run, they'll be grateful."

Zack looked down the row at her. "You have children, ma'am?"

"No," Rose said. She shot a glance at Sophie. "I thought I wanted kids . . ."

"I've got three," Zack said, "and I'll tell ya, there's no sure-fire way to do it right. If you're too lax, they'll run away on you, but if you ride 'em too hard—that's what I did—they go sour. I think Sara's doing a great job."

He kissed me on the cheek and stood. "I'm gonna step outside for a minute." He walked to the door, reaching in his pocket for cigarettes. When he paused in the courtyard, we could see him lighting one.

"Does he smoke around the kids?" Jeff asked.

I waved to Sophie, motioning her to come back.

"Sara?"

"That's not your business."

"This is a health issue—secondary smoke."

I stood up and started easing out of the row. "I'm going to go look at the science projects."

On Saturday, Zack and I took the kids to the Griffith Park Equestrian Center for a cutting-horse show. Zack had braided headstalls for some of the contestants from Arizona, and he was eager to see his customers compete. As we walked across the parking lot, Gabriel wedged himself between Zack and me, forcing our hands apart. Zack tried to take Sophie's hand but she yanked it away. "Come on, baby," he said, "can't we all just get along?"

"Don't call me 'baby.'"

"All right, darlin'. I mean, Sophie."

I shot Zack an apologetic look. He brushed his hand in the air as if to say, Let it go.

We walked into the arena and climbed the steps of the bleachers, which were spotless and painted a fresh white. When I sat down, both kids scrambled for the seats on either side of me. Zack sat down next to Gabriel. Below us, a gate was opened and thirty cattle trotted into the ring.

"Here's what's gonna happen," Zack explained. "The rider has to cut one of the cows, keep it out by itself, and stop it

from reentering the herd. He can't use his hands. You'll see—
he drops his reins on the horse's neck."

"Can we get popcorn?" Gabriel said.

Zack waved to the vendor and bought popcorn and Cokes.

"How does he communicate with the horse?" I asked.

"With his body weight and feet. There's mental telepathy,
but it's not spoken of. Bottom line is—you've spent two years
training this animal and now you just let him work."

Sophie opened the top of her Coke, spilling some.

"Be careful," I said.

"Watch," Zack said, "here comes the rider."

A woman with platinum hair, wearing a shocking-pink
Western shirt, rode into the arena on a palomino. Zack sat
forward. "That's Jacy Walker. See the headstall? It's mine." I
squinted. Zack had told me about Jacy as we'd driven to
Griffith Park. She'd won first place at the national cutting-
horse finals in Fort Worth the previous year, and she'd bought
what Zack considered his finest bridle.

Jacy walked the palomino among the cattle, seemingly at
random, but suddenly she had the herd divided in half and
then she had one cow stranded by itself. The cow started darting and running but the horse seemed to anticipate each
move, keeping the cow in front of him as it zigged and
zagged. The horse raced to one side, came to a skidding stop
and wheeled about so sharply that Jacy's body tipped far to the
side and her knee brushed the dirt. Then the horse raced in
the opposite direction, all the while Jacy sat limp and loose. It
was astonishing—she was utterly relaxed and fluid.

"Yee-haw!" people yelled. Gabriel and Sophie started
laughing and took up the cry, "Yee-haw!"

"You have no idea what a thrill it is to ride an animal who's that intelligent and that fast," Zack said. "There's a moment when you're on the horse and his eyes are on the steer and the steer is looking at him. And you feel that breath go back and forth. That's what I love—to feel the stillness and the breath, in that moment before they jump."

A bell rang. Jacy picked up her reins and trotted to the back of the arena. Five judges sitting on a podium composed their tallies. The crowd roared as the number 220 flashed on an overhead screen. "That's real good," Zack said. "A perfect score is 240."

We watched four more rounds and then the lights came on for intermission. Gabriel and Sophie went outside to look at booths where people were selling jewelry, toys, horse gear, and Western clothing. "There's Jacy," Zack said. "Come say hello." Jacy was standing by the horse pens, surrounded by men. She turned a cold eye on me when Zack introduced us. She kissed him on the mouth. "Where the hell've you been?"

"Tryin' to stay out of trouble," Zack said.

I heard a scream—Sophie. I wheeled around. There was a horseshoe court outside and she and Gabriel had started pitching them. She'd thrown one wild, lobbing it into the side of a trailer. Gabriel was laughing and she was yelling at him to shut up.

I hurried over just as the owner of the trailer, a gray-haired cowboy with wire-rimmed glasses, came up to inspect the jagged dent.

"I'm sorry. It was an accident," Sophie said to him.

"We'll pay for the repair," I said.

He looked at Sophie, then at me. "Don't worry about it. This trailer's seen a lot of miles of bad road. This ain't the first or last dent."

I hustled the kids back toward the horse pens. "You're lucky," I said to Sophie under my breath.

"When can we leave?" she asked.

"I'm hungry," Gabriel said.

"Zack has to talk with some people about business. Now you can stay with me and behave yourselves, or you can wait in the car."

They looked glum as we reached the railing where Zack was standing, talking to trainers. Jacy was on a sorrel horse, warming him up, but I noticed she kept glancing at Zack and me.

"How late do you think this will go?" I asked Zack. It was almost six.

"Nine," he said.

Sophie started complaining that she was tired and her stomach hurt. "Could we please go home?"

Zack nodded toward Jacy. "I'm hopin' to sell her another piece, but I can't really talk to her till this is done."

"I understand."

"It's boring here," Gabriel said, pulling my arm.

"Let go," I said, wresting free, but part of me sympathized. The contest was not that riveting unless, I imagined, you'd tried the sport and knew the fine points to watch for.

I turned to Zack. "I don't think the kids are gonna make it."

"Take 'em home if you want. I'll catch a cab later, or get a ride."

"You wouldn't mind?"

"Go ahead."

"You sure?"

He took my face in his hands and kissed me. "I'll be back right after the show."

◆

I drove home, fixed dinner, cleaned up the kitchen, and read to both kids as I did every night before putting them to sleep. When I turned off the lights in their rooms, it was ten-thirty. I figured Zack had made his sale by now and was on his way home. I walked into my bedroom, pulling the door shut behind me. I took my time in the shower, washing my hair, giving it a conditioning treatment. Then I slipped on a white terry cloth robe and walked into the sleeping area to see if Zack was there. He wasn't. It was eleven-thirty.

I walked down the hall of the second floor to my study, which had a balcony. I scanned the street: dark, silent. No cars were passing and only a few lights were on in the entire block of neat, two-story homes. I went to the shelf and picked up *Funny Sauce* by Delia Ephron, a diabolically humorous and edgy book about children of divorced parents and blended families. I'd read it years before and laughed aloud at the chapter, "Mom in Love," but when I got in bed and started rereading it, the story had pointed meaning. I was reassured. It was normal for kids to wish for their mother's new love object to be dead.

At midnight, I called the equestrian center. The phone rang six, seven times and then a male voice answered.

"Is anyone there from the cutting-horse show?" I asked.

"Naw, they cleared out over an hour ago. I'm just locking up." I calculated: it was a thirty-minute drive to my house, maybe less at this time of night. Had Zack gotten lost? He had a poor sense of direction, he was always making wrong turns and didn't know the city.

I turned off the lamp and tried to sleep. I'd given him a key and he would wake me. I dozed and when my eyes snapped open, the fluorescent numbers on the clock said one-thirty. Something was wrong. Maybe he'd been in an accident and the authorities had called his home in Arizona. My heart started pounding. I dialed his number. Zack had told me Nathan always stayed up late, painting and watching old movies, but no one answered. Then I remembered, Nathan was spending the weekend with his mother in Casa Grande. I called information but Marianne had an unpublished number. Now what? It struck me that I didn't know the names of any of Zack's friends, his parents, other family.

Jacy Walker. Maybe she'd given him a ride, they'd stopped for beers. He'd gotten drunk. I should have left the kids at home with Veronica and gone to the show with Zack alone. I should have insisted the kids stay to the end and we all go home together.

I walked to the bathroom and took a Valium. I felt as if I was coming down with flu. I kept twisting in the sheets and then it was three in the morning. He wasn't coming home. Goddammit, is this what I bought along with the cowboy? Staying out all night, chasing women, not calling? It was rude, it was cruel. Who the hell did he think he was! I was shaking inside. If this is how it is, if this is your code—always alone, riding off, can't be tamed—then give me my key and take your turquoise boots and rawhide flyswatter and get the fuck out of my life!

The phone machine. I hadn't checked it; he might have called when I was in the shower and I hadn't heard the ring. I walked downstairs and stopped. His Stetson was sitting on the counter by the machine. "Zack?" I called. No answer. I flipped on the light in the kitchen, then walked into the living room. He was on the couch, sleeping. "Zack!" He didn't move.

I shook him hard, and he jerked and raised his fists. "Huh! What are you doing?" he said.

"What the hell are *you* doing?"

"Trying to sleep."

"How long have you been here?"

"Oh, I got back about eleven."

"Why didn't you come up to my room?"

"I did. The door was locked."

"No it wasn't."

He was sitting up on the couch now. "It was. I know a locked door when I run into one."

I considered: I had pulled it shut when I took my shower. Had I pushed in the lock by reflex?

"I didn't mean to lock it."

"You did."

"I was going to take a shower, and I guess I could have locked it out of habit. I always feel vulnerable when the water's running . . . "

"I thought you were teaching me a lesson. For staying out so late. I got to talkin' to folks and before I knew it—"

"Didn't you hear me open the door? I must've walked back and forth between the bedroom and the study five times, checking the street."

"I heard you."

"Why didn't you say something?"

"I wasn't gonna beg."

I threw up my hands. "You know how worried I've been! I called your house. I even tried calling Marianne."

"What for?"

"I don't know anything about you. I don't have the names of your parents, your friends."

"That's right. I never told you because I didn't think it was any of your goddamn business. But I ain't gonna fight with you. When I found the door was locked, I asked myself: do I handle this the way I normally handle a locked door? Knock the motherfucker down? Or do I try a different way. Go downstairs and sleep on the couch."

"Did you consider . . . knocking?"

He put his chin in his palm. "Well, now that you mention it, that does seem to have its upside."

I forced myself not to smile.

"Sara, I love you."

"I thought you were with Jacy."

"Hell, no." He stood up, took hold of my shoulders, and kissed me but I didn't kiss back.

"I didn't mean to cause you concern," he said. "I know humility is the key here, but short of crawling on my knees . . . I'd like to walk through this."

I had to smile. He kissed me again and my mouth opened, by increments. "I was scared. With the kids acting up, I thought you were throwing in the towel."

"I'm tougher than that. I always said I wanted a woman with no kids or real young ones. If they're small, you can get 'em to mind you. Or if they're grown, that's all right too. But yours—they're right in the red zone."

I told him Gabriel had started crying several nights before and wouldn't tell me why. "It was the divorce. I know it was the divorce. He was crying because he thinks I made his father leave. I remember the night we told them—we sat them down on the living room couches and said, 'Mom and Dad are getting a divorce.' Gabriel shouted, 'No!' and water ran from his eyes. I wanted to cut off both my arms, fall to the floor and die rather than do this and I couldn't not do it. He wants us back together—they both do—and you're in the way."

"That's a fact."

"If it's any consolation, they hate Rose too."

"Well," he joked, "in her case, it's understandable."

We laughed softly and walked upstairs where we fell into bed, exhausted. I turned on my side and fitted my back against his chest. "We'll get through it, sweetheart," he said, "with patience. We'll wear 'em down."

I pulled his arms around me.

6

The week after Christmas, Jeff took the kids to Boston to visit his parents and I caught a Southwest Airlines flight to Phoenix. Zack and I would have five days—the longest time we'd spent together during our four months of intermittent weekends—and I was filled with trepidation. I would be meeting his son, seeing the house where, he'd warned me, he didn't have a bed, he slept on a couch—not a fold-out sleeper but a couch he'd found on the street and dragged inside. I'd told him to book us a room in a motel.

Before I left, I closed myself up in my study and pounded out an episode in which Dr. Quinn's sixteen-year-old son wants to get married and she tries to prevent it. I dropped the script at Beth's and had no idea whether she and the other writers would love it or run over it with a bulldozer. For a week, I didn't want to think about it.

Zack met me at the gate carrying a single pink rose. I could generally gauge his mood from the boots he was wearing and the ones he had on were confidence builders, red with gold arrows.

He kissed me. "Nervous?"

I nodded.

"I just had a beer. Let's sit down."

He led me to a row of gray, immovable chairs near the gate. He leaned forward in the seat. "Hey, baby."

"What is it?"

His green eyes looked straight into mine. "You know I've been working the last three weeks on that headstall?"

"Yes." I knew he'd been making a piece for a cowboy art show at the Arizona State Fairgrounds this weekend.

"It took a lot longer than I planned. I finished it at one this morning and ran it over to the show at eight. Just made it under the wire."

"Congratulations."

"I'm flat broke."

I looked at him.

He explained that he hadn't finished the work he'd planned to do for Dunnings Custom Tack, which would have given him cash. "I wanted to take you out and show you a good time, but I can't do that now. I don't even have money for gas. If you want to get up and leave, I'll understand."

I looked out the window at the orange-and-gold planes parked on the tarmac. I would have to pay for all our meals, the motel, whatever we did. I considered going to the ticket counter and booking a seat on the next flight home. The kids would be gone and I could catch up on errands and call friends I hadn't seen in months. "I'm here, and I'll do it this time, but I'm not going to be comfortable if I'm always the one who pays."

"Nor am I," he said. He picked up my two bags with one hand and slipped the other arm around my shoulders. "You gotta be tough to run with me." His truck, Willie—the '68 Chevy that had given women nightmares—sat at the edge of the parking lot, faded red, covered with dents and gun-metal patches where the paint had worn off. But when Zack turned the key, it started. "Willie's got heart, even though he's foul-headed. The door on your side's stuck. If you want to get out, you gotta bump it with your shoulder."

I tried a few times before it creaked open. "Now that I know how to do it, I'll wait for you to come around and open it."

"I expected no less," he said.

He wanted to drive me straight to his home in the Coronado section, an old neighborhood of small houses with overgrown front yards, populated mostly by Latinos. In the month before the trip, I'd hired a designer to redo my living room. When Jeff and I had built the house, we'd chosen a Japanese architect who created a living room with a twenty-foot ceiling and a wall of windows shaped like Mondrian squares. It was dramatic but felt cold; no one ever sat there. I'd asked the designer to make it cozy, which she'd accomplished by installing a huge, three-trunk Kentia palm and filling the room with rustic antiques, like a freestanding windmill from Woodbine, Iowa. She had charged me four hundred dollars for the rusty piece, plus her commission, and as Zack drove me to his house, I saw the exact same windmill lying on its side in someone's yard, ready to be carted to the dump.

When we pulled into the driveway, Nathan was sitting on the porch step. "Hey, dude," he called.

"Nathan, this is Sara."

As Nathan walked toward me, I had to fight the reflex to startle. He was no more than five feet tall, with thinning dark hair caught in a ponytail. His face was like a Cubist painting: the forehead was large and jutted out, the nose was small, and the cheeks were wider than the forehead. He wore thick, Coke-bottle glasses that made the light bounce back at you, and yet there was a joy, a radiance about him.

"Carry," Zack said, nodding to the truck. Nathan took out my bags and followed us into the house, moving with a web-footed glide.

It was hard to know what to do—stand, sit? The house was a single room, with chunks of plaster missing from the ceiling. A bare bulb was hanging from a cord and an exposed gas duct was stuffed with rags. There was a flea-bitten chair facing the sofa where Zack slept, and behind the sofa was Nathan's bed and drawing table. Along one wall was the kitchen area—a dingy sink, refrigerator, and hot plate—and across from it was a bathroom like the ones you find at the rear of auto-repair shops. In the back, Zack had his worktable set up with tools and rawhide strings dangling from hooks. There was no insulation; the wind seemed to blow right through, carrying the dank smell of decay. No one I knew had ever lived in such a place. Veronica's house in El Salvador was nicer—neat and painted bright blue—I'd seen photographs. And Zack told me he and Nathan had spent a day cleaning up the place.

"Want to look at my drawings?" Nathan said.

"He's determined to show 'em to you, so we might as well get through it," Zack said.

I walked around the sofa as Nathan pulled out a worn leather portfolio. "I've been riding the bus a lot. It takes hours to get to school and back, so I started sketching people." He showed me a drawing of a Latina woman with her hair in a loose bun. She was rendered with precise, almost photographic detail: the sad eyes, the beauty mark above her lip, the shoulders slumped in an attitude of resigned and uncomplaining patience.

Then there was a sketch of a black boy who looked about five, sitting beside the hulking shape of his mother, though you couldn't see her face. The boy was crying and the tears looked as if they might slide right off the paper.

"These are wonderful. The boy—"

"He was just sitting there, crying. Nobody paid any attention."

I'd expected Nathan to draw in an abstract style but his sketches were hyperrealistic. "Nobody can figure out how he sees what he does," Zack would tell me later. "But since he was three, he's been drawing the world."

Nathan put away the drawings and showed me a series of oil paintings, stacked in the closet, which were markedly different: fantastical, hallucinatory. "This one is called 'Indifference,'" he said. It showed a man's face rising from the ocean, his long hair tangled with the waves. "That's a self-portrait."

"I see that now." I hadn't caught it at first because he'd painted himself without glasses. I asked how he'd done that.

"I had to stand right against the mirror, because without my glasses, I can't see anything that's more than two inches away. I'd take off my glasses, look at my eyes, then put the glasses back on and draw."

I studied the painting. "Why 'Indifference'?"

He rubbed the bridge of his nose. "I was trying to get across an attitude. I'm not gonna change my direction, no matter what the world says." Nathan smiled. "I'm gonna paint and I don't care if anybody else thinks it's good. It's good for me. Mozart died penniless. So did van Gogh. But they did what they had to do."

I felt a muted sting; it was humbling to see the two of them holed up in this room, where they would draw and braid leather while they listened to Joseph Campbell tapes. When there was no money, they lived on coffee and cigarettes, and when cash came in, they went to the grocery store or a Mexican restaurant, La Cucaracha, to splurge on burritos and beer.

"Let's take her to The Cockroach," Nathan said.

"You hungry?" Zack said.

"I'm always hungry."

We walked out to the truck and squeezed into Willie's front seat.

The Cockroach was painted dark green, with Formica tables and unmatched wooden chairs. I'd always found it interesting to see how "Mexican" food is prepared in different regions of the United States. In California, every dish is loaded with guacamole and shredded cheese and sour cream, but at The Cockroach, the food was unadorned. A burrito came with chunks of beef inside and nothing else, and it swam in a sauce that looked like thin red gruel. Zack and Nathan ate with zest, Nathan holding the fork in his fist.

The waiter brought margaritas. Nathan told me about his classes at Phoenix College, where he was studying art and mythology. He was the first in his family to go to college, which he'd accomplished by winning grants and applying for federal aid to the disabled. "We're studying the Hindus now, and that stuff about reincarnation is so cool." He grinned as he spooned more sauce over his burrito. He was so buoyant it was infectious; I'd stopped seeing the asymmetry in his face. "I know I've been here before, and I must've done something reee-al bad."

"That's not necessarily the case," I said.

"I was given the power to create, but I was also given this." He touched his face.

"You might be here to see things in a deeper way."

"Really," Zack said, looking at me intently.

"As I understand it, the concept is that you keep taking different forms to experience all of creation, in all its facets—the horror and the beauty."

"I'd like to come back as a tree one time. Or a rain cloud," Nathan said.

"I don't wanna be a fucking rain cloud," Zack said.

"You already are, at times," I teased.

He laughed. "I got the right to be off center once in a while. You're not always on the money yourself, darlin'."

The room Zack had taken for us was in a complex called the Wooley Suites, located in the run-down heart of the city and frequented by civil servants. Every unit was a suite—bedroom, sitting room, and kitchenette—for $54 a night. It was clean and impersonal, and I was relieved.

"What'd you think of my son?" Zack said. We were lying on the bed, listening to Ian Tyson sing about a Navajo rug that had disappeared, the rug on which he'd made love to his first girlfriend.

"He's inspiring. So bright and devoted to what he's doing."

Zack exhaled. He was visibly relaxing. At any point on our

route today, from the confession at the airport to the ride in Willie's creaking cab to the dank house and The Cockroach with Nathan, I could have flapped like an alarmed bird and rustled for home. Why hadn't I? Why was I still here in the Wooley Suites? Zack said that when Nathan was born, he'd been afflicted with so many physical problems that the doctors had said he'd never walk or speak, let alone see. "They told us to put him in an institution, but we said no." He cut the air. "You stay with your family."

"He has such light in him."

"He's been in some real dark places."

"I don't see it."

"Adolescence was tough on him. The girls treated him like he was some kind of teddy bear. They'd have these soulful talks but when it came to sex, they wanted the big blond jocks."

"Didn't we all."

Zack said Nathan had tried to cut his veins with a razor and landed in the county mental health hospital. "They were ready to throw away the key. Once you get in those places, you don't come out. Nathan refused to talk to me, to anyone, but I kept showing up. And he finally realized, if he ever wanted to see the outside world, he'd have to get himself together."

I wrapped my arms around my chest.

"Tired?" Zack said.

"Is it cold in here?"

"Not especially."

I took a Kleenex from my purse and dabbed at my eyes. "I feel sad. I don't know why, I don't know where it's coming from."

"That's all right. You go ahead and feel whatever you want."

He put his arm around me and patted my back. The sadness was building, threatening, pushing up from deep reaches.
"Don't hold it in," he said. "The quicker you can get it out, the
quicker it'll move on." I cried helplessly against his stiff,
starched shirt. "You're my princess."

"No."

"Sara, you're the most independent woman I know, but it's
my job to take care of you."

He rubbed my neck, relaxing the muscles around each ver-
tebra, then he kissed my forehead and eyelids and temples and
gradually, softly, in the run-down heart of Phoenix, we made
our way to the closeness we so relished. The Wooley Suites,
the falling plaster in his house, the bare lightbulb—everything
faded and dissolved away.

"John Deere Green" was playing on the country station as
Zack drove Willie south toward Casa Grande. At first I'd
thought the song was about a town square called John Dear
Green, something happened in John Dear Green. But the
song had been playing every time we turned on the radio in
Phoenix and I'd learned it was about a boy who spray-painted
"Billy Bob Loves Charlene" in giant letters that were John
Deere green.

I shifted gears so Zack could keep his arm around me. An
ad came on: "You're a cowboy, a man alone. A dusty trail the
only life you've ever known. And you think, Maybe I wouldn't
be so lonely if my clothes weren't wrinkled." I shot a look at
Zack. "Wrangler," the announcer said, "the wrinkle-resistant
shirts and jeans."

"You were right," I said. "But you know what they're saying—if your clothes aren't wrinkled, you'll get laid."

Zack laughed. "A lotta hands are buyin' that too."

We pulled into the San Tan Cattle Company, the feedlot where Zack had worked for many years, where cattle were shipped from all parts of Arizona to be fattened until they were ready to be slaughtered. There were rows of beat-up metal pens in which thousands of cattle were kept in groups, determined by their sex, weight, and owner. A dozen cowboys on horses were working in the pens, and I noticed their jeans did look remarkably wrinkle-free.

"My reputation is fixin' to soar," Zack said.

"Why?"

"In twenty minutes, everyone in Casa Grande will know I was here with a woman from out of town."

"It's that obvious?"

"You're not from this country, and word travels fast. Folks know instantly who gets fired from what outfit, who gets in a fight, who gets caught with somebody else's wife. We used to call it, 'As the Feedlot Turns.'"

He held my hand as we walked to the saddle house. The cowboys in the pens stopped working to stare. I heard one yell, "Zack's here with his girlfriend from Hollywood!" They came nearer, craning their heads as if to catch sight of a movie star.

A tall man with a black mustache came up and slapped Zack on the back.

"Sara, this is Freddy."

"Pleased to meet you, ma'am." Freddy tipped his hat. "You got any rich girlfriends you could introduce me to?"

"I'll have to give it some thought."

"I want one who drives a Mercedes." He winked at Zack. "A convertible."

"Any particular color?" I said.

"Gotta be gold." Freddy grinned, and I could see two teeth were missing. The other hands had come closer and were standing with their legs apart, hips thrust forward and thumbs hooked into belts with large rodeo-prize buckles. But what I saw was not romantic; I saw poor teeth and threadbare shirts and prematurely wrinkled skin. Poverty covered by bravado— big hats and spurs.

Freddy motioned me over to the horses he'd saddled by the fence. "You ride this one. Name's Joker. Used to be a cuttin' horse but he's retired."

"I don't know if I'm good enough—"

"Ma'am, he's survived eleven years on the cuttin' circuit, he can survive a two-hour ride with you."

I felt their eyes on me as I climbed into the saddle. Zack rose onto his horse in that single fluid motion I admired, and we rode out past the cattle pens and across the rocky sand. He started to lope, zigging and zagging around mesquite bushes and paloverde trees. I stayed right behind him. I can do this, I thought. Then he started loping faster and turning more quickly and he cut to the right around a big red barrel cactus so abruptly I couldn't react and loped straight ahead. He burst out laughing. "I knew you weren't gonna make that turn. I could tell just by listening."

"I wasn't paying attention."

"If you'd made it, I wouldn't have quit. I'd have cut harder the next time."

He rode his horse alongside mine and I felt Joker shift between my legs, filling his chest and blowing out. I was in a state of arousal. I'd always known there was a sensual affinity between women and horses. All the riding classes I'd taken when I was young had been made up exclusively of girls. Jane Seymour loved to ride; she wanted to do her own stunts and we knew that on a day when she rode her horse in a scene, she would be in an ineffably good mood.

The obvious appeal is that you're controlling an animal that, by logic, you have no right to control. It weighs twelve hundred pounds, it could throw you and crush you, and for even the most proficient rider, there's always a frisson of watchfulness, if not fear. And yet, the horse responds to the touch of your calf, the pull of your finger on the bit in its mouth. And the saddle, well, it's perfectly contoured for the female body. It rises to a peak at the most sensitive region, and as the animal moves, there's a continuous gentle contact.

"Lucky saddle," Zack said.

We stopped the horses to kiss. When we opened our eyes, we saw a herd of a thousand cattle coming up a rise with sand swirling above them like a mushroom cloud.

"They're moving that herd in from the desert. Want to help out?"

"Can we?"

Zack trotted over and talked to the trail boss, who shielded his eyes to look at me. Then Zack rode back and spoke quietly. "Okay, we're not gonna go charging at the cattle or they'll get nervous and run. And running makes 'em lose weight, which is the worst sin around here. We're just gonna nudge 'em ahead, real easy."

We walked our horses along the flanks of the herd, watching for strays and circling around behind them. "Each cow has a comfort zone," Zack said. "When you cross the line and enter that zone, he'll move away." Sure enough, when we came within a few feet of the strays they turned and ambled back to the herd. But one black cow stood his ground, glaring at me and snorting. I looked for Zack but he'd ridden ahead. The black cow lumbered toward me, his eyes flat and hard. I told myself I shouldn't be nervous, I was elevated and the cow was below me. My heart started jumping. The black cow was running straight for me and I froze but Joker's old cutting instincts kicked in. He lunged at the cow, making him stop in his tracks. Joker halted, his feet splayed in front of him, his head down, all twelve hundred pounds fixed on that cow. The black steer darted to the side and Joker cut him off, stopped, and swerved 180 degrees to run back the other way. My limbs seemed to fly out in all directions but I kept hold of the horn and I wasn't falling. I was scooping with the horse, this way, that way—*whoosh, whoosh*—swift as a knife. It was as if I were riding on a sedan chair and there was commotion all around me but I was being borne along in a smooth, exalting rhythm. Zack came riding up at an angle and shouted, "Hee-ah! Get on back there!" The renegade black let out a bellow of protest, turned, and trotted back in the direction of the herd.

"Did you see that!"

"Yes, ma'am."

"It felt fucking wonderful."

"Some folks say it's better than sex. I don't agree, of course."

"How do you train a horse to do that?"

"There are steps, it's a progression, but they're born to do it. They don't like cattle. There's a natural animosity between horses and cows but the horse is smarter. Cattle are stupid—that's the reason we can pen 'em up and slaughter 'em. You couldn't do that to any other species, they'd mutiny."

He said that when cattle arrive at the feedlot, "they're

hooked up to a chute and in forty-five seconds, the steer gets his horns sheared off—so he won't gore another animal; he's given six shots, he's branded with the owner's number and castrated."

"Do they use an anesthetic?"

"No, ma'am. It hurts like hell. Those cows are in shock for days. But that's how people get treated in life, too."

"Come on."

"It's true, Sara."

It was hard to look at the cattle now. As they approached their new metal pen, they began to bunch up by the gate until they were a sea of roiling flesh. They seemed to be excreting continually—the ground was covered with steaming green dung—and copulating. The cows would come up behind one another, rise up on their hooves and hump, with their heads resting on the other animal's rump. If the herd moved, they would waddle along on their back legs, humping as they went. It was mesmerizing: bodies would arch up out of the sea—a brown one, a black one, a brown and white—and then they'd sink down and a dozen other bodies would rise like flying fish in their brief trajectory over the water.

"They're mating?"

"No, these are heifers," Zack said. "All females."

"Then why—"

He laughed. "It's the way of the barnyard. When they come into heat, they give off a scent that makes the ones who aren't in heat try to mount 'em. The steers do it too. But it ain't gonna do 'em no good."

As if they'd been cued, the animals began to moan and bray. "Let's go," Zack said. "See that bunch of trees? It's a pecan orchard. I'll race you."

I squinted at the orchard: it was a mile away, a straight shot across the open desert.

"Give me a head start."

"Much as you want."

I tightened the reins, squeezed my legs, and Joker took off like an accelerating jet. It was glorious, with the wind singing and the sand kicking up in swirls as the mountains turned purple in the late afternoon sun. I heard Zack's horse pounding up behind and it made Joker frantic to keep the lead. I stood up in the stirrups, balancing on the narrow rings, leaning forward over his neck and praying I wouldn't lose a stirrup and fall. My horse was blowing and panting and we were almost to the trees and then I reined him in but Zack went tearing past me into the orchard where he skidded to a stop. He jumped off his horse and came back to lift me off mine.

"I won," I said.

"The hell you did."

"I got to the trees first."

"I got to the center of the orchard and that's where the finish line was."

"Who says?"

He turned to tie the reins to a tree, and I tackled him from behind and we laughed and wrestled until he had me pinned to the ground.

On the ride back to Phoenix, I sat wedged next to Zack as he told me about his favorite job at the feedlot: loading cows onto trucks and receiving new calves.

"Why?"

"Because I worked alone. It was prestigious, and I got to

move at my own pace—slow and thorough. That was my nickname. 'Slow and Thorough.'"

"Works for me." I kissed his ear and was running my lips down his neck when the red light in front of us changed. Horns started blasting. He shifted into first and told me that with cattle, the amount of money earned was determined by number and weight. "So it's real important to count 'em accurately. Oh, baby . . . "

He reached over toward my lap. "Joe Pintero, he was my maestro . . . "

"I remember."

"He taught me to count a certain way. You position your horse at the gate, pick a spot, and fix your eyes on it. You don't look left or right." He worked the zipper loose on my jeans. "You don't move your arms or upper body. If you're quiet, the cattle will keep going past you in a nice, even flow." He demonstrated with his fingers.

"Yes."

"Every time you reach a hundred, you put one finger down and start counting the next hundred."

"Why don't you use those metal clickers?"

"They don't work. It's real easy to lose track of when you clicked on which cow. And the noise makes 'em nervous." He swerved into the parking lot of the Wooley Suites. "Besides, it's not the cowboy way."

By the time we made it into the motel room we were in a fevered state. We had acquired, by now, a rough map of the places we went when we made love, and there were landmarks. The first was when we both agreed it had never felt this good. Zack loved to think of new ways to crank up the torture. For someone who, when I'd met him, "didn't know what the clitoris was for," he'd acquired not just knowledge but command. He could make me aware that this tiny structure had a microstructure: ridges, slopes, and stem as well as the hooded peak. He took the stem between his fingers and squeezed it gently. I offered to give him anything. "You can have my kingdom. You own me." And this was landmark two—when I told him he owned my body.

"Yeah, I know," he said. "But when you've got your clothes on, I can't see my real estate." I started to laugh. "You're not this easy to get along with when you've got your clothes on."

The more we made love, the more sensitive our skin, muscles, nerves became. When we began, my mind was skittering about, worrying about the script I'd just turned in and the conference I'd had with Sophie's teacher, who'd told me she was not doing the required reading. Both my kids hated reading, even though I'd read to them every night, the concept of sitting alone with a book was alien and that was the unkindest cut. I was conscious of Zack's touch but it was like the scratching on a door, and then I'd sink deeper into the body and I wasn't thinking much, and then there was that moment when I wasn't thinking at all. The small chain was pulled and the light went out. I loved that moment. I told Zack we were lapping at the edge of it now. "That's a great description," he said, "lapping."

What was happening? How could I be so driven, obsessed, besotted by sex? I was almost fifty, starting on the path toward what the literary lionesses—Germaine Greer, Simone de Beauvoir, Colette, Isak Dinesen—extolled as the third stage of a woman's life—"triumphantly post-sexual." Colette had viewed carnal love as a virus she'd barely survived. Francine du Plessix Gray wrote, "the more fortunate among us serenely accept that we may never again be seen as objects of erotic desire ... that we must acquire instead a deepened inward gaze."

Not me. I was not going gentle down that path, and I was flummoxed. I'd thought the best sex was behind me. I'd been at Berkeley in the sixties, for God's sake—smack in the epicenter of the sexual revolution—when lust was in the air like perfume and you could breathe it in and everyone was game to try it with everybody else. Now, thirty years later, it all means more and there's a startled sense of gratitude when you encounter a good fit purely on the physical level—your fantasies are the same, your rhythms are the same, your tastes and body chemistry and levels of desire mesh and blend—because you know this is not to be found on any corner, just ahead.

"I want you so much," I said hoarsely.

"You're supposed to," Zack said.

Was I mad, or lucky? Was this craven? Depraved? Was it going to pull me down to the lower depths? I thought of stories I'd read as a teenager in magazines like *True Romance*, stories about women who possessed the secret affliction, nymphomania, and would do anything to be "touched." Was sex a substance you could abuse, like alcohol or heroin? Would I have to go to a meeting in some church with strangers sitting in folding chairs and say, "Hi, I'm Sara and I'm a sex addict"?

I looked in his eyes. "You've created a monster."

"I like riding monsters."

This was landmark three. We called it "Monsterville," when we couldn't bear to be apart from each other, we had to be touching. If Zack wanted to get up and walk outside to smoke, I'd grab his arm and throw myself on top of him so he couldn't leave the bed.

When, in the early hours of the morning, we allowed ourselves to come, I felt as if I were riding the prow of a ship, rising and crashing like one of those carved nude females arching out over the sea. I heard Zack murmur through breathless laughter, "That was . . . large." We curled up and drifted to sleep, but I was awake again at five. I couldn't lie still, it was too exciting just to brush against his flesh. I thought about waking him but he was sleeping so peacefully, I decided I'd wait until seven, that was decent. I lay on my stomach with one of his legs flung between mine and I was tingling just to lie like that. I ran my hand down his back, over the smooth, firm buttocks. It was six-thirty now. He turned over and I slid down and put my mouth around his cock. He was stirring but not conscious, floating toward the surface and then a smile broke out. He moaned and opened his eyes. "Oh, baby, I thought I was having a dream."

"You don't mind . . . ?"

"Mind?"

"I've been waiting an hour, trying to restrain myself."

"Don't."

Around nine, he put on one of the terry cloth robes that hung in the closet of every Wooley suite, walked barefoot to the rec room, and returned with a tray of orange juice, coffee, and powdered sugar doughnuts.

The next time we got out of bed it was six at night. We had to get dressed for the opening-night party at the cowboy art show. I pulled on jeans, a purple sweater, and my new boots from Powell's, the "little ol' feed store" Zack had told Pete O'Hara about and where he'd taken me after riding. Zack said Powell's was "the focal center of Casa Grande." The owner, Dick Powell, a gregarious and canny businessman, had bought numerous pieces of Zack's at a fraction of their worth when Zack was broke and needed cash. Dick refused to sell them now; he told Zack that one day they'd be worth something.

Zack had stood me in front of a wall of boots that came in the most exotic array of colors, decorated with flowers or longhorn steers or broncos rearing and pawing the air.

"Which ones do you like?"

"I'd never wear them."

"Let's just try some on for the fucking fun of it."

I pulled out a pair of low-heeled ropers, green with yellow roses twining up the sides. I tucked my jeans into the boots, walked up and down in front of the mirror, and Zack said, "I'd follow you anywhere in those."

The cowboy art show was held in an exhibit hall at the fairgrounds. All the traditional crafts were displayed: horsehair hitching; rawhide braiding; leather tooling; saddle and boot making and silver engraving. Zack took me to the case where his pieces were arranged. The bridle he'd spent the last month making was the most intricate design he'd attempted. He'd used twelve strings of rawhide instead of the customary eight, and wine-red leather braided in chevron patterns and fine horsehair tassels. He'd set the price at fifteen hundred dollars, but there was no red dot on the tag indicating a sale.

I took one of the knots between my fingers. "It's so intri-

cate, it's like something from nature—a seedpod or shell."
Other people came by to look and admire and when they
checked the tag, walked on.

We circled the hall, browsing and talking with other arti-
sans and I was struck by the eccentricity of the breed. Cheryl,
a weaver who wore her hair in braids, had taught herself to
raise sheep and shear them, spin the wool into yarn, and
weave the yarn into blankets for horses. She was giving a
demonstration to a group of children, sitting at her spinning
wheel surrounded by blow-up photos of her sheep. "That's
where the wool comes from—I gave my sheep a haircut."

Wayne, who'd driven down from Canada, hammered silver
into many-petaled roses to decorate spurs, belt buckles, and
bits. Martin braided black kangaroo—that was the only hide
he used. Chris forged and shaped iron into furniture using
tools that had been devised in the Stone Age. They were toil-
ing alone with few or no colleagues, and almost no one on the
outside understood why their products cost so much. That
was the sorrow—and as they saw it, the purity—of craft. The
joy was in the doing—the spinning of yarn, the cutting of
rawhide strings, the layering of wafer-thin silver. They could
never be compensated for their time. The market wouldn't
bear it, so they had to charge as little as they could manage
and live close to the bone. They drove old trucks thousands of
miles to sell their work at shows, because it cost too much to
fly. And these were the most successful craftsmen, the elite
who'd developed a following. The ones trying to arrive at that
level couldn't make any money at all.

Zack had earned his subsistence by doing piecework for
Dunnings Custom Tack. They would give him a dozen
machine-made bridles and ask him to braid simple knots on

them, but Zack couldn't do anything simple. He had to find ways to create variations in each knot. Mike Dunning didn't care if the knots looked alike, but Zack did.

"Come have dinner with us later," Wayne, the silversmith, kept saying and others asked too, but Zack made excuses. As we walked out, he shook his head. "I ain't in the mood for company."

It was New Year's Eve, and every place we tried to stop for dinner was completely booked. Zack looked straight ahead, he drove straight ahead unless I pointed out a restaurant we should try. We ended up at the Lone Star Steak House downtown, sitting in a vinyl-covered booth with sawdust on the floor. What's wrong, I kept asking. Zack cut up a few pieces of beef and stared at them. "So far I've got a perfect record. I've never sold anything at a show."

I put down my fork. "Your work is beautiful, it's just that you're creating for a very narrow market—people who are rich and own horses and are willing to spend fifteen hundred on a headstall."

He drank his beer.

"Have you thought about making pieces that would be more accessible? Something less elaborate that would sell for, say, two or three hundred?"

He sighed. "I thought for sure I was gonna sell this piece. I was countin' on it to pay my bills."

I took a bite of steak and chewed, savoring the forbidden red meat, the blood-rare juices. "What about trying some of the galleries and boutiques that specialize in Western stuff, like in Scottsdale . . . "

He pushed his plate away from him. "Let's not talk about this anymore."

I signaled the waitress for the check and gave her my Visa card. We drove in silence to the Wooley Suites, parked, and went to our room. As we started pulling off clothes, I noticed my watch and unfastened it, setting it on the night table.

"What are you doing?" Zack said.

"Hmm?"

He nodded toward my watch, a waterproof Shark Free Style with a black plastic strap. "You never take that off, unless I ask you to."

"I wasn't thinking about it."

He smiled, for the first time since we'd left the cowboy art show. "I fucked it off you."

"What?"

He pulled me down to the bed. "I wanted you to take it off but I wasn't gonna say anything."

"Is that so?"

"It took me three and a half days but I did it. Yes, ma'am, I was feeling poorly before but now I'm plumb proud."

I was in lust again, and I thought, He doesn't hold back. He holds nothing back. He's right here with me and I don't care how loudly the voices in my head may object. It doesn't matter why I picked him out of all the creatures in this wide world or what interpretations might be drawn. I love this man.

We moved slowly, enjoying the scenery, cruising with the top down and making rest stops. But there was a point at which we gave up meandering. Zack started pumping for the finish line and I wrapped myself around him as he barreled to the edge and leapt off.

"Happy New Year," he whispered. He nestled me against him. "Let's make a date. We're gonna celebrate next New Year's just like this."

I smiled and nodded, but I couldn't imagine there was a way we could keep this going another whole year.

7

On a windy day in February, we were shooting an episode I'd
written in which Dr. Quinn's ten-year-old son, Brian, builds a
primitive flying machine and crashes it into a haystack.
Because of the relentless wheel of series television—we had to
turn out a new script every seven days—I rarely went down to
the set unless there was an emergency or I wanted to watch
the shooting of a critical scene. But this morning, one of the
ADs had paged me and said a war was erupting over the flying machine. I drove down to Malibu Creek in a golf cart.
Burt Campbell, one of the stunt coordinators, walked out to
meet me on the dirt road. Burt was a bodybuilder whose arms
stood out from his chest and who walked like a pumped-up
peacock.

"What's the problem?" I said, getting out of the golf cart.

Burt pointed at me. "You wrote it. *I'm* trying to solve the
problem." He said the flying machine was too big. "We've got
to cut it down four feet and lose twenty pounds."

"Beth wants it big."

Burt crossed his arms. "It's not safe. It weighs sixty pounds. The boy has to run with it, holding it over his head. We've got winds blowing and we're gonna have a wreck. People say, 'Don't listen to the stunt men,' but we *are* the movie. We make the exciting stuff happen and we know how to do it."

"Let's go look at it," I said.

The cast and crew—about three hundred people—were camped at the bottom of a sheer rock face that jutted out over the creek. Below the rock they'd constructed a fake hayloft and beside it, the flying machine, which looked like a cross between Icarus's wings and a homemade hang glider. The plane had ten-foot wings made of yellow gingham stretched over balsa wood and a harness in the center for Brian to step into.

Gordon Blue, the prop master, stood guard in front of the plane. He was furious because the day before, the director had told him to cut the machine, then Beth and I had objected because it was too small, so Gordon had worked all night rebuilding it and now here was fucking Burt Campbell telling him to cut it again. Big, small, big, small.

The director, Chip Landau, came over and hugged me. Chip was tall and rangy, with a mane of white hair; he'd shot hundreds of hours of television and possessed the survivor's talent for getting along with everyone. "I don't know what your thoughts are," Chip said, "but if safety's at stake, I can live with the smaller machine."

"I just don't want it to look rinky-dink," I said.

Burt showed me where he wanted to shorten the wings. "If you explain it to Beth, I'm sure she'll approve."

But Beth had left the ranch, her assistant was out sick, and we couldn't reach Beth in the car or at home.

"Cut the wings," I said.

Gordon said, "If Beth blows up . . . "

"She won't."

"If she does?"

"I'll take the hit."

He started sawing off the wings. Burt walked over to check the hayloft, a rickety structure with stacks of empty cardboard boxes inside, hidden under the hay. Burt insisted that empty boxes piled on top of each other were the best thing to break a fall.

"How do you know the stack is big enough?" I asked.

"We base it on body weight and distance. This is a thirty-foot drop, so we've got eight stacks of boxes."

"But are you sure?"

"There's nothing sure, Sara."

We could not rehearse the jump because the plane was designed to break apart on landing. We would have only one chance to shoot it, so Chip was lining up three cameras to film simultaneously from different angles.

"Quiet, please," the first AD called.

The sawed-off flying machine was hoisted up to the top of the rock face, where a twelve-year-old boy dressed to look like Brian stood waiting. He was slim, wiry, the son of a stunt man. He stepped into the harness.

"Marker."

The assistant cameraman clapped the sticks. "Scene forty-three, take one."

"Rolling."

"Speed."

Chip called, "Action!"

The stunt boy hoisted the forty-pound plane over his head

and ran toward the edge of the cliff, but the wings started wavering and tipping perilously. Before he could jump, he lost his balance and the plane thudded to the ground.

"Cut!" Chip said.

"Wind's come up strong," Burt said.

"Everybody stay put!" Chip said. "Let's see if it dies down."

We stood, hushed, feeling the gusts of wind hitting our faces. After ten minutes, Chip walked over and told me we had to do this soon or drop the shot and move on. This was the last day of shooting on this episode and in an hour, the sun would be setting.

"We can't lose the jump," I said.

"We may not have a choice."

"But it's the climax of the story."

Well, Chip said, running a hand through his white hair, maybe the jump could take place off screen. "Write some dialogue where Brian tells his mom about it later. How scared he was. How humiliated."

"That's weak," I said.

He smiled and shrugged. "This is television, not brain surgery."

The phrase "It's not brain surgery" was repeated so frequently at all levels of the industry that it had become a code. When lines were dropped, when guns didn't fire, when good scenes were replaced by trite, mediocre ones and you'd fought for the good and slammed into a brick wall, you'd look at your colleagues and say, "All right. All right. It's not brain surgery."

My walkie-talkie buzzed. It was the receptionist at the trailer. "Your friend's calling from Arizona. Want me to patch him through?"

"Sure." I opened my flip phone and walked to the edge of the creek.

"Hello there," Zack said.

"Where are you?"

"My favorite pay phone, on the road going outa town."

I smiled. I was standing beside a trick hayloft on a fake Western set and he was standing in the Arizona desert surrounded by cattle and tumbleweed.

"Just fixin' to make my reservation for the weekend. What time would suit you?"

It was my birthday and we were planning to drive to Santa Barbara for the weekend. "Whenever you'd like. The kids go to Jeff's on Saturday morning."

"How 'bout I sneak in after that?"

"That would certainly make things easier."

"Then again, maybe those kids need to see my face. How 'bout Friday?"

"Wind's died down!" Chip yelled. "Let's shoot this."

"Sure. Gotta run. Come Friday." I put the phone in my purse and hurried toward Chip. Burt shouted to the stunt boy, "Ready to do it?"

"Ready," he called in a reedy voice.

"Action," Chip said.

The boy lifted the yellow gingham wings up, ran straight for the edge, and jumped. He hovered in the air for a fraction of a breath, then dropped. I grabbed Chip's arm. What if he missed the hayloft, he would crash on the rocks and die and I would be responsible. He fell straight down, straight into the loft, and we heard a sickening *shoof shoof shoof* as the cardboard boxes imploded. The wings cracked off and the boy disappeared under a flurry of hay. All was silent.

"Oh, God . . . "

"Hold on," Chip said.

After what was perhaps three seconds but seemed an eternity, a small arm poked up out of the hay. Burt reached in and pulled the boy free.

I nearly crumpled with relief, falling against Chip as the entire crew broke into applause.

Zack flew in late Friday night. I put the kids to bed, left them with Veronica, and drove to the airport, but I didn't pick him up at the curb because he'd said he was checking luggage. I parked and walked down the causeway toward the gate, scanning the crowd streaming toward me. I couldn't spot the Stetson, but I did see a flurry of excitement—a crowd buzzing and lunging around some person who was advancing. When I'd worked as a reporter, this was what it had looked like when Bobby Kennedy or Muhammad Ali arrived at an airport.

It was Zack, in full regalia: baby-blue boots with the jeans tucked in, a belt fastened with an enormous silver buckle, and the Stetson tilted down at a mischievous angle. Over his shoulder he was carrying a pouch made of golden elk skin, and sticking out of the pouch were about a hundred peacock feathers, their turquoise eyes and iridescent green strands fluttering out behind him.

I laughed to myself. I was turning fifty and this was what was coming for me. He looked like a fucking cowboy cupid.

I kissed him. "What's that?"

"Your birthday present."

The crowd continued to swarm around us. A heavyset woman asked Zack, "Are those peacock feathers?"

"Yes, ma'am."

She turned to her companion. "They sure are pretty. Have you ever seen a peacock?"

Zack was tense, though, tenser than I'd seen him. "I've had a crowd trailing after me since I got to the airport in Phoenix. I spent all day cutting up cardboard, making boxes, because they've got to be a certain size or the airline won't let you bring 'em." He collected the oversize boxes from the carousel and lugged them to the exit, where the guard fumbled with the luggage tags. "You're not too goddamn handy, are you," Zack said under his breath.

By the time we drove home, though, he'd calmed down. He took from his duffel bag a bottle of Dom Perignon. I was touched and appalled: he didn't have a bed, he didn't have air-conditioning when it was 105 degrees, but he'd spent eighty dollars on champagne? "Your birthday only comes once a year," he said.

He'd also brought a rare, antique army saddle made in 1910, which he'd traded for one of his pieces and which he said I could "hold on to," and a stand he'd made of weathered oak so we could display the saddle in the living room. My house was taking on a decidedly Western character. In addition to the braided flyswatter and the saddle, we had a set of steer horns mounted on wood that we used as a coatrack, and several lamps Zack had created out of his old boots.

We went up to the bedroom and Zack undid the elk skin, unveiling my major present. It was a fan, which he'd made of saguaro cactus ribs that opened out to a six-foot span, with the peacock feathers ruffling between the ribs, laced together with wine-red leather. It was exotic, voluptuous. Zack attached it to the wall above the bed so the feathers waved out like a canopy that was alive.

"It's gorgeous! I love it. Thank you."

"You remember Chris? That high school teacher who builds things out of iron? He drove me to the airport, and he said, 'You got a lot of nerve walking around with that thing.'" Zack held out his foot. "That's why I put on these boots. If you're gonna pack peacock feathers, you gotta strut."

"What did Chris say to that?"

"He thinks I'm a nut. He calls me 'the frequent flyer,' who's gotta fly all the way to Los Angeles to get laid. Chris says, most nights, he wouldn't walk across the living room to get laid."

He put on a cassette he'd brought, George Strait singing "All My Ex's Live in Texas." He took hold of me and we did the two-step, twirling around the bedroom. Some time later—minutes? hours?—we'd finished the Dom Perignon and were making love under the winking eyes of the peacock feathers when I heard a noise, rattling.

"What's that?"

"Nothing." Zack was in the flight pattern.

There were two doors between the hall and my bedroom and both had push-in locks built into the handles.

"Did you lock the doors?" I said.

"Yeah."

"You sure?"

"Mmm." He was coming in for the approach. I heard a clicking at the outside door. "Oh, sweetheart . . ." I could feel his body rippling, humming, seconds away, and then the inside door burst open. We jerked our heads to the side—it was Gabriel.

Shock, fascination, then triumph passed across my son's face. Shock, horror, and mortification passed through me.

There was an endless moment when he looked at us, we looked at him. "Git," Zack yelled, "out of here!"

Gabriel slammed the door and ran down the hall. I grabbed a robe, pulled it on, and went after him, marching over the carpet. Gabriel ducked into his room and tried to close the door but I pushed it open.

"What did you want?"

"I was sick, Mom."

"Sick?"

"I threw up."

He nodded toward the bathroom. He didn't look sick, but what if he was?

"You have a fever?" I reached out to touch his forehead but he jerked back from me.

"You should have knocked," I said.

"I did, but you didn't hear. You were making so much noise. You were moaning and screaming. I thought you were hurt. I'm serious!" He was trying to look self-righteous but his eyes were full of smug glee.

"My bedroom is private. So is yours. You know that. If the door is closed and I don't answer, you *do not come in*."

"God, Mom, I was sick! Don't you care? No, you don't. I could have passed out and you wouldn't care. Never mind, good night!" He went to the bed, threw himself on it, and turned on his side, yanking the comforter over his head.

The next morning when I woke up, Zack had dressed and left the bedroom. I went to the window and saw him in the yard, putting together the saddle stand with Sophie. He'd charmed her into the project by letting her use his electric drill. She was kneeling on the grass, totally absorbed in tightening screws with the drill while Zack held the wooden pieces in place. The sight cheered me, but an hour later, when I called them in for scrambled eggs and bagels, Sophie deliberately moved her chair away from Zack's. When I turned to the stove, she pretended to vomit on his plate. Gabriel clomped down the stairs but instead of sitting at the table, he went to the freezer and opened it.

"How're you feeling?" I asked.

He shrugged and took out a Snickers ice cream bar.

"Not in the morning, Gabriel."

"Come on, Mom, it's Saturday."

"Not in the morning."

"You have all these stupid rules."

"You were sick, right? Have some toast. I'll make you tea."

"Can I go to Dad's now?"

"After breakfast."

"I hate it here. I hate you!" He threw the bar back in the freezer and slammed the door.

Zack said, "Son, that's not right. One day, you're gonna appreciate how lucky you are—"

"I'm not your son."

"It's a damn good thing you're not. If you were, I'd whip you good for talking like that."

"Shut up, you hick."

"Gabriel!" I said.

But he'd grabbed his skateboard and was heading out the door. Sophie now sat angelically, taking ladylike bites of her eggs. When I asked her to clear the table, which she never did without grumbling, she said, "I'd be happy to, Mother."

As soon as we'd cleaned up, I drove them to Jeff's, parked in the driveway, and opened the hatchback to help them unload their bags. Butterball leaped out of the car and ran straight for Jeff's door. He was a joint-custody cat, he knew the drill. Gabriel came around the side of the car and stopped. "Sorry, Mom, for . . . you know." He leaned over and kissed me on the cheek. "Happy birthday."

"Thank you."

Sophie said, "We stayed at Dad's last weekend."

"Your dad and I switched, remember?"

"So you can go away with Zack?"

"You'll be with me next weekend and the weekend after."

"But I want to stay with you this weekend, on your birthday. You didn't even ask me. You and Dad just make your plans and it's not fair to me."

"You're right, it's not fair. But this is something the adults decide."

"I hate going back and forth." She dropped her duffel bag and kicked it. "Like, I don't know where my black shoes are right now. I can't find Butterball when it's time to go. My friends call one house when I'm at the other, so I miss out on lots of things. You never had to do this, Mom. You don't know what it's like."

I knelt down so I was at her eye level. "Sophie, I know how hard it is. It's hard for me too. I miss you terribly when you're away. I miss hearing you laugh, and watching you dance around the yard with Butterball chasing you. I wish I could be with you all the time. I wish you didn't have to move back and forth. But it didn't work out that way and we've got to make the best of it."

Jeff walked out of the house. She put her arms around me and hugged me tightly.

"Sophie," I said gently, "it's time to go."

She shook her head, clinging.

Jeff started taking her hands off me. "Let's go, Sophie."

"No, Mom!"

He led her toward the house and she started to cry. "Just get in the car and drive away," he called. "She'll be all right."

"Those kids work you over real good," Zack said. We were driving north on the Pacific Coast Highway and I'd just used the car phone to call Jeff, who'd told me Sophie had stopped crying as soon as I'd left.

"Have you thought about going to court?" Zack said. "The child's unhappy."

"Going to court is brutal for everyone." I sighed. "And as much as I'd love to have her, I know it's in her interest . . . she needs to work things out with Jeff, or she'll be working them out with men the rest of her life."

He put his hand on my leg and patted it. "You're a great mom."

"I'm sinking into a pit here."

"I mean it. You encourage your kids, you give them lots of attention, you expose them to all kinds of opportunities."

"I created this . . . schizoid life. On the holidays, they light two sets of candles for Chanukah and spend two separate days carving pumpkins for Halloween. And birthdays! Sophie goes to Benihana's two nights in a row with two different parents and gets two Polaroids taken by waitresses singing "Happy Birthday" in Japanese. Gabriel wants us all together, so we have a tense dinner at Madame Wu's, where Gabriel eats Wu's beef and hardly looks up from his plate while Jeff and Rose and I smile and talk about business."

"Let's just leave all that on the highway behind us, okay? Let's not be such a grim Gus. Let's take a vacation. All those problems will be right there when we get back and we can fret about 'em then, if we want to."

I slid over next to him.

We checked into the Miramar Hotel, one of my favorite places on the California coast. The Miramar sits on an incomparable stretch of floury, white sand beach in Montecito, lush, privileged. But the hotel hasn't been upgraded in so many years that it has the feel of an aging beauty going to seed. There are blue and white bungalows connected by trails that wind around palm trees and red hibiscus and pools surrounded by AstroTurf. Inside the rooms, the sheets are threadbare and the bathrooms have tiny sinks that stand on four metal legs. Railroad tracks run through the center of the grounds, and at scheduled times, the Amtrak Coast Starlight goes clickety-clacking right past the bungalows. But on the beach, there's a string of rooms that jut out over the ocean as if you're on a ship, and I'd reserved one that had a private sundeck.

Zack was elated. We took off our clothes and stood at the railing of the deck, watching the waves and feeling the salt air on our skin. He turned to me with the wind blowing the dark curls back from his face. "Usually I'm cold, but this isn't cold, this is alive!"

For the next two days, we drifted between the sundeck and the bed, keeping the sliding doors open so we could hear the gathering, rising, cresting—*foom!*—of the surf. We ordered hamburgers from room service and bought candy at the gift shop. Zack liked peanut M&M's and I liked Snickers and Reese's Pieces. We dozed and woke and it was sunset or was it sunrise? The room had become a bubble of heightened feeling and the people outside on the sand—drinking a soda, throwing a Frisbee, tuning a radio—seemed to exist on a different plane that was shallow and dull.

How was this possible, I thought. How could two adults build a relationship on sex? One of my women friends in New York had told me, "I can only do sex for so long and then I want to get on with things." What things? There are few times in life I'm aware of that we feel this good. For me, it's skiing down a bowl of packed powder when you're in the zone, or sitting at your desk when the words are rushing out and you want to drop to your knees and look skyward and say, Thank you. Or that rare moment with your children when all is in harmony and you stare at their perfect hands and cheeks and unique personalities and feel such awe.

"But what do you talk about?" my friend from New York asked. We did not talk about books, history, politics. We talked about people, children, animal and human nature. Zack told me about his past: he hadn't been raised to be a cowboy. His father was a structural engineer who moved his family to each new job site around the South: Spartanburg, South Carolina; Mobile, Alabama; De Queen, Arkansas. When Zack was nine, his father bought him an erector set and Zack spent weeks building elaborate motorized Ferris wheels. "My dad thought I was a prodigy and gonna be the greatest engineer in the world," Zack said. But at seventeen, he joined the navy, got married and moved with his wife to southern Arizona where, after making a pest of himself at every ranch in Pinal County, he was hired and trained as a hand. "My parents stopped speaking to me," Zack said. He had committed what, in many circles, is unpardonable—moving downclass. "My dad never forgave me."

We watched the sun turn crimson as it sank below the ocean and the air turned chilly. I got out of bed and put on one of Zack's shirts. I fished in my bag for some grapes and Zack's peanut M&M's. Zack went out to the deck to smoke and when he came back, he had a red silk scarf around his neck.

"What's that?"

He slipped off the scarf. "I found this at a swap meet. I love silk."

He sat down on the bed. "You know how to tie a double bow knot?"

"Can't say that I do."

"It's a forehand knot. You start with a loop in the center, you thread both ends through the loop and it makes a double bow." I watched him fold and tie the silk and I thought of my father, an accountant, who'd seen the world in terms of numbers. Until his last days, my father could remember every number he'd ever looked at or heard. All of life, he'd told me, could be explained in terms of numerical relationships—sets and chains and intervals that spiraled to infinity. Zack, I thought, sees the world in terms of knots.

"The beauty of the double bow is, you can make it large or small . . ." He fashioned what looked like one large bow with two floppy loops. "Put your hands through the loops." I did, and with a jerk, he pulled the silk. The loops snapped tight around my wrists, binding them together. I was shocked.

"You see, with one pull, the double bow becomes a handcuff knot. You've been handcuffed, baby."

He raised my arms up over my head and tied the other end of the silk to an opening in the wooden headboard. He must have thought about this, prepared for it, and I hadn't seen it. "Traditionally, they use rawhide for the handcuffs instead of this nice silk cloth. They wet the rawhide and when it dries, there's no way your hands can slip out."

I looked in his eyes. I knew he wouldn't hurt me but being bound and immobilized was terrifying. I was surprised at how primal the fear was—I was trussed, helpless. He moved closer, bringing his face next to mine. "I'm your man. The one who loves you. Now let's see, how much do you trust me?"

"I don't want to do this!"

He ran his hand down my torso and I felt hot, edgy. He went to his bag and pulled out a black scarf with small red roses. "There's a funny thing about the senses," he said. "If one's impaired, the others take up the slack. They get magnified." He tied the silk over my eyes.

I was scared, excited, this was too much, no, all right. I couldn't see his face, I couldn't see what he was doing.

"You're always quick to help out," he said. "But tonight, you're gonna get nibbled and not have a chance to nibble back. Can you go through a night and not help out?"

No, I couldn't do that. Zack always wanted me to lie still while he kissed and stroked me and I loved it, but it made me uneasy. "This isn't even," I would protest, "give me a chance to return the pleasure."

"You are," he said, "by letting me do this to you. It makes my dick hard."

"I feel I'm getting the better deal."

"That's the way I want you to feel."

At some point, I would insist on reversing positions and taking the lead, but tonight, with my hands tied to the headboard, I couldn't reciprocate. I had to be passive, which was a challenge—nearly impossible. I always have an opinion, a preference, a wish. Hardly ever do I just go along with the group. And yet I yearned to be passive. I'd read that people who are aroused by sadomasochism find it important to be completely immobilized. They say this leads more quickly to surrender, or to trauma, and I could feel the two like alternating currents: submission and panic. He would arouse me, then fear would slam through my body and then I gave up. I'd caught the wave. It was lifting me, carrying me. I had no power of my own and no more wish for it. I felt him resting a finger inside me and gradually, the skin began to grow warm. The whole area began to throb. Nerves started firing that had not fired before.

"What are you doing?" I asked.

"There's this little hollow, right here . . . "

I nearly rose off the bed. He had his other hand on top of me and sensation was coming from all directions. It was four-part harmony, quadraphonic, omnidirectional, Dolby Surround Sound and I thought I would pass out.

The bed began to shake. Was it me, my state? No. The whole room was trembling. I could hear objects jiggling on the desk. There was a loud, screeching whistle.

"What the hell!" Zack said. I felt him jump off the bed, springing to his feet.

The room was vibrating now. "It's the train," I said.

"What train?"

"We saw the tracks, remember?"

There was a high clang-clanging along with the whistles

and rumbling. I started to laugh. He yanked the blindfold off my eyes. He looked tense, buck naked.

"How often does this occur?" he said.

"Two or three times a day. Whenever I come here with the kids, we go out and put pennies on the tracks before the train comes. It's a ritual—all the guests do it. Then, after it's gone, we search for the pennies, which are all flattened out—"

"I got a better idea." Zack slid inside me while my hands were still tied with silk to the headboard and the room still shook from the surf on one side and the train rushing past us on the other. It was funny and ludicrous and "goddamned exciting," Zack said. I began to make foghorn moans. We came with the bed vibrating and the ocean roaring and the train clang-clanging on its way north to San Francisco.

He untied me and flopped on his back. "Did you arrange that?"

"No."

"Yes, you did. You timed it perfect."

"How could I—"

"If you keep doing this, I'm gonna love you all my life."

"Wait a minute. Are you swearing undying love? Yes! It took eight months but I got you to do it."

He pulled me to him and we curled up together facing the ocean. "All I know is, I want to figure out how we can spend more time with each other," he said. "I want to move forward. It's time to take a deep seat, nod for the gate. You up for that?"

I thought about the children. I kept seeing Gabriel's face when he'd burst into the room and stood facing the bed, his eyes stung with amazement. "The kids—"

"If I'm around more, they're gonna have to figure out how to get along with me."

I was quiet.

"What are you thinking?" he said.

"You've seen me at my best. You have no idea . . . how thorny I can be."

"I'm aware of that. You've seen me with my best foot forward too." He smoothed the hair back behind my ears. "I'll take you on your worst day."

He was smiling, looking in my eyes, but the words didn't land. I couldn't hear what he was saying. I thought he meant he'd put me through the worst day I'd had. And then, as if by delayed reaction, I understood.

The next day, it rained and the sea turned gray and gloomy. I paid our bill, reviewing the charges and signing for it while Zack stood behind me, looking away. "It blows my mind how much you're spending," he said. I'd thought the Miramar was reasonable—$150 a night for an oceanfront room.

Traffic was miserable; the rain beat ceaselessly and the cars crept along. We fidgeted in our seats. Zack hunted through the tapes. "Dwight Yoakam?"

"If you want."

He steered the car into a different lane and as soon as he did, the new lane came to a stop. "So, you had a good birthday?"

"It's a relief that it's over. I've been dreading it the past few years. I kept practicing saying the number."

He put his hand on my thigh. "You look good, sweetheart."

I turned my face toward the sea. It didn't matter how good I looked, how fit I was, or how few wrinkles I had around my eyes. I was fifty. I was not, in any conceivable light, "young," and there was no dodging the backward glance, the weighing and stocktaking, the sighting ahead—to what? "I feel loved and appreciated, except possibly by my children."

"They'll come around."

"We had some sweet moments, actually. Before you arrived, they gave me a lemon cake they'd baked with chocolate frosting. It's my favorite, but they insisted on putting fifty candles on top. It made quite a blaze."

"I bet your son lit the match."

"Many." I took a drink of cranberry juice. "Sophie put on a special concert for me. She made up a dance to 'Good Vibrations.'"

"Sounds entertaining."

"It was. Gabriel gave me a sculpture—he must have worked on it for weeks at school, in his art class."

"What kind of sculpture?"

I looked at him and considered whether to continue. "It's two black swans made of papier-mâché. They're swimming in tandem, tucked together." I took another sip of juice. "I thought at first it was me and you, but Gabriel said no, it was me and him."

Zack hit the brakes and muttered under his breath. When I asked what he'd said, he shook his head. "Let's pull over a minute." He swerved to the right and stopped the car in a turnout by Point Mugu, a huge bald rock that perches precariously on the cliffside. The rain had let up and he leaned against the hood of the station wagon and lit a Kool. I walked back and forth, kicking idly at the sand.

"Did you ever try to stop?" I asked.

"Lots of times. I ain't trying now because I don't like to fail."

I nodded. I understood—this was something that would not respond to my prodding or trying to be helpful. I had my own addiction, overeating. I could not leave food on a plate and was perpetually on a fast-glut cycle. I'd eat skinless chicken breasts and steamed vegetables and salad with low-fat dressing until I couldn't stand it, and I'd eat guacamole and chips and cake and then I'd go back to the skinless chicken. When Zack would say, "You've got such a beautiful body," I'd cringe. "Do you realize," I said, "I've gained six pounds since we met?"

"Do you realize," he said, "I don't give a shit?"

Zack stubbed out the Kool with his boot. "I don't expect to live long. If I'm sixty, I'm gonna be in sorry shape."

We got back in the car and nosed into the snail-like procession down the highway. "So, you gonna celebrate your birthday at work tomorrow?"

"We did that Friday. The writers all took me out to lunch. Beth gave me a really beautiful skirt and sweater from my favorite store on Montana. Josef gave me a new edition of Anne Frank's diary."

"Who?"

"Anne Frank." I paused. "You know who she is?"

"What did she do?"

I looked out the window at the fog, which was advancing over the water, blotting out everything. How could he not have heard of Anne Frank? Her diary had been translated into twenty-seven languages, made into a play that won the Pulitzer prize, a movie. My kids had read it in school.

"Have you heard of the Holocaust?"

He switched on the turn signal and looked in his rearview mirror. "If you want a peer, a colleague, I suggest you shop elsewhere."

He moved into the left lane and I turned on the radio, trying to find a station that would come in without static. I leaned back and closed my eyes.

I must have dozed because when I opened my eyes, we were in Malibu. We stopped for dinner at Carlos 'n Pepe's, where the bar was packed and salsa music was blasting. I asked the waitress if we could move to a quieter table away from the speakers, but she said they didn't have another table. I asked if the volume could be turned down. She shrugged. "I'll see."

Zack was smiling at me.

"What?"

"I like watching you."

"I don't like being watched."

He opened a packet of sugar and stirred it into his coffee. Why was I doing this? He was tiptoeing around me and the more he tiptoed, the meaner I was getting. We ate our burritos in silence and I paid the bill while he went to the men's room. It would always be like this. As long as we stayed in my house, the issue didn't come up, but when we ventured out, I'd pick up all the checks and feel awkward or Zack would offer to pay and I'd feel bad because he had so little.

We got back in the car and water poured down in sheets, bringing traffic to a standstill.

"I think I outclassed myself here," Zack said.

"I should have known about the traffic. Sunday night."

"I've been thinking about getting a job." He took the red bandanna from his pocket and wiped the steam off the front window. "I need to go back to work with horses, so I'll have something to teach you, something to bring. Other than sex."

By the time we pulled into my garage, we'd been fighting the rain and fog and mulish lines of cars for almost five hours.

I took a shower and when I got in bed, Zack was asleep. He had a troubled night. "Let's go now! *Andale!*" he yelled, waking me up. "Hand me that thing!"

"What thing?"

He didn't answer. I leaned over to look at his face but he was out cold.

When the alarm woke me at eight, he was gone. I'd put twenty dollars in the pocket of his shirt the night before and he'd left for the airport in a cab.

8

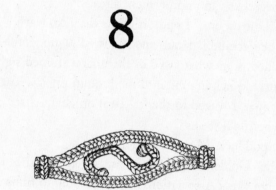

On the night of the Golden Globe awards, Josef Anderson, my fellow coexecutive producer, came to pick me up in a limousine. We stood outside the black coach with tinted windows while Gabriel and Sophie climbed inside, drank Cokes from the bar, ate Hershey's kisses from a dish, and turned on the TV. "There's champagne in the refrigerator," Josef said. "We can drink it on the way. Better yet, let's open it now."

He reached inside for the bottle. Josef's ancestors had come from Scotland by way of Arkansas, and he was tall, bearded, manly, with a flicker of whimsy in his eye.

Sophie rolled down her window and watched Josef uncork the champagne. "Are you gonna break up with Zack and date him?" she asked.

"Josef is married," I said. "And how do you know you'd like him any better than Zack?"

Sophie turned to him. "Do you smoke?"

"No."

"See, that's an improvement already."

"Come on out," I said, "it's time for us to leave."

They scrambled out and I kissed them good-bye. They watched, somewhat awed at the unaccustomed sight: Josef in his tuxedo helping me into the limo in my low-cut black velvet gown. I waved to them. "Turn on channel six in an hour. Maybe you'll see us."

"Good luck, Mom," Gabriel called.

The Golden Globe awards, given by the Hollywood Foreign Press Association, were presented to films and television shows on the same night. They were not the Oscars, but in recent years, they'd become important and commercially beneficial, so almost all the stars who were nominated appeared. When we pulled up to the Beverly Hilton, a long red carpet had been laid from the street up the walkway to the hotel. On either side of the red carpet, swarms of reporters, photographers, and TV cameramen were straining and pushing against golden ropes. There was a chorus of clicks and pops and staccato flashes of white light as the camera strobes fired: *wocketa wocketa wocketa.*

I took Josef's arm as we started up the gauntlet. We tried to appear stately, entitled. The people behind the ropes were staring and not reacting. I wondered if I should make eye contact or look straight ahead? I tried to keep facing forward but curiosity made me turn and I caught the eye of a young photographer with three large cameras hanging from his neck. "Who's that?" he asked the veterans around him.

"Nobody."

Then, from a dead rest, the swarm went into full buzz, snapping and shoving and yelling: "Julia! Over here! Julia—

you're gorgeous! Julia, smile!" Josef and I turned to glance at Julia Roberts before ducking gratefully into the lobby.

We made a slow tour of the ballroom, checking to see who was already there. Only a few souls were sitting at their tables. The most important players stood in the cocktail area and did not move. All the others came to them, forming conversational clusters that circled and shifted like gears turning around a few central pins. It was an art: knowing when to cut into a cluster, when to speak to the linchpin and when to drift away, not to overstay.

I was not a linchpin but I knew tricks. Josef and I established a position near the door, so that everyone coming in would have to walk past us. We chatted with producers and executives and writers and smiled at those we didn't know and then my ex-husband walked in with Rose.

"Good evening," Jeff said with a genuinely warm smile, and touched my arm. "Best of luck."

"Thanks, but we're not going to win. Hi, Rose, you look fantastic." She was wearing a midnight-blue kimono slit up to the top of her thighs. She had the legs for it. I didn't; I had spider veins that had blossomed after my pregnancies.

"Thank you," Rose said and nudged Jeff ahead. "There's Bruce. I need to say hello. Maybe I can close my deal."

"Is that Sara? I don't believe it!" Jeff and Rose walked into the ballroom as a birdlike woman gripped my arm. I stared at the freckled face, the smartly cut black hair.

"How are you?" she said, with an accent that was dimly familiar.

"Fine, great, how're you?" Who the hell was this? I struggled to come up with a name, a setting . . .

"It's Nava," she said.

"Nava!"

"It's gotta be, what? Fifteen years."

Nava was a movie producer, an Israeli who spoke with charming bluntness and with whom I'd often played tennis and gone to parties when I was single.

She turned to Josef. "Sara used to be a hot girl on the town."

"This is Josef Anderson—Nava Bernstein. What are you talking about?"

"When your book came out, remember? You were a hot new talent and a hot girl and everyone wanted to know you. Then you got married and disappeared." She raised her hands in a shrug. "Nobody knows— What happened to you?"

I forced a smile. "Did you ever have kids, Nava? I remember how much you wanted that."

Her eyes went glassy; her head swiveled like a searchlight on a pole until she spotted someone else she knew and rustled off, handing me her card. I gave it to Josef, who slipped it into his pocket.

"This is hard," I said.

"Shine her on."

"There's a lot of people here I haven't seen since we all started out."

"Good. You can get reconnected."

"But I'm not here on my own, for something I created."

"Josef!" cried a man with a bald head and a wandering right eye.

"Sara, this is Stan Fuchs."

We shook hands.

"Did your show get nominated?" Stan said.

"Yep."

"Congratulations. Good meeting you."

"Look at it this way," Josef said. "It's like the Olympics. What matters is that you're here. You're in the elite. You're one of the few who's made the team."

I nodded but I couldn't help it, I wanted to be captain of my own team.

The lights in the ballroom began to blink—a signal to move to the tables as the program was about to begin. We threaded our way toward table 125, which was not on the main floor but on the first tier around it. A distinguished-looking man brushed past me, his eyes fixed on the carpet, but as his shoulder touched mine, he looked up. It was Bill Tannenbaum, whom I'd dated in the seventies when I'd first moved to California from New York. His hair was gray, but he hadn't gone slack and flabby as I'd feared. He'd been a rising young producer when we'd met and his friends said he'd be running a studio one day, which he was. I'd liked him a great deal and wished I could will myself to fall in love with him. He owned a delicious wit, he made zinging observations, and he was a kind, generous, good-hearted man who never acted with anything short of integrity—a rare quality in the business. But I hadn't been aroused; the chemistry, the smells, weren't right. A few months after we'd stopped dating, he'd gotten married and gone on to have three children.

"You look exactly the same," he said.

"Liar."

He gave the laugh I remembered—a cackle of delight. We asked about each other's children and he said, "How's your love life?"

"I've been having a wonderful affair . . . with a cowboy artisan who lives in Phoenix."

He shook his head, satisfied. "It figures."

"What figures?"

"It's one of those things Sara would do. You're a pioneer. You travel out to the territories."

"It works."

"Of course it works. He's there and you're here."

"You'd have the same deal if you could get away with it."

He gave another delighted cackle.

I asked how the transition had been from producing movies to being chairman of a studio. "Has it been fun?"

"It's fun when things are going well and painful when they're not. And since there's always some of both, you swing between pain and pleasure and you can't rise above it or you don't care. I have a theory about this . . ."

The lights started blinking furiously. "I'd love to talk to you more, but . . ." He squeezed my hand and went off to his table in the center of the ballroom, where he and his wife were sitting with Tom Hanks and Bruce Springsteen.

I was the last to sit down at our table, where Beth and her husband, the actor Jim Knobeloch, sat between our stars—Joe Lando on one side and Jane Seymour on the other. Joe Lando's rugged features and long hair contrasted with the refined elegance of the tux and made his beauty more startling. Jane looked equally dramatic, wearing a brilliant crimson satin gown from an episode in which Dr. Quinn had gone to Boston and attended the opera.

Josef whispered, "You know how long it took to get her ready?"

I knew the costume designer had driven out to Jane's house that morning to adjust the gown so that it fit perfectly and to show her diamonds borrowed from a jeweler in Beverly Hills.

The hair stylist had started at noon, creating gold highlights and sweeping her hair up in a cascade of individually ironed curls, while the makeup artist was working on her skin to make it look opalescent. The effort had all paid off: she had the sheen of an exotic plumed bird. I was proud to be sitting with her and I felt like a supermarket mushroom.

Salads were placed in front of us on chilled plates but no one ate, I knew no one would pick up a fork until the awards were announced. I'd gone with Beth to the Emmys, the Writers Guild awards, and the Humanitas awards and *Dr. Quinn* never won for best drama. We were an eight o'clock family show and the award was always given to a ten o'clock show, a hip urban drama that the reviewers loved even if it received poor ratings. But as the moment drew near, Beth said we might be a long shot. Jane had legions of fans in Europe. That's true, I thought, this is the foreign press and they tend to have more popular taste. Maybe it's not out of the question.

They were announcing the award for best comedy series: *Seinfeld*. No surprise. We were next. Camera operators were dispatched to each of the tables where the stars of the nominated shows were sitting. Blinding white lights came on and the cameraman focused his lens on Jane, ready to go live. Jane smiled and tipped up her chin. No actress over forty wanted to be photographed with her chin down.

We watched the TV monitors while they ran clips from the five dramatic series. Jane had selected our clip, which was from an episode I'd written. Maybe, by some fluke, if the four other shows split the hip vote and we got all the other votes . . . please, a fluke . . .

N.Y.P.D. Blue.

The white lights went off. At the table next to ours, Steven Bochco and his producers and stars were yahooing and slapping hands as the cameraman skulked away from our table and we sat in darkness.

The sea was gray and churning with whitecaps as I drove to work the next day. When I walked into the writers' trailer, Brian said I had a call. I picked up the phone in my office.

"Hello there."

"Zack."

"How're *you*?" He always put the emphasis on "you."

It had been almost a week since he'd left my house in a taxi. "You didn't say good-bye."

There was silence, as if a line was being played out. "You were sleeping."

"Please . . . deposit . . . thirty-five . . . cents," a recorded voice cut in.

"I tried putting you out of my mind . . . " *Ding ding ding.* "It didn't work," Zack said.

"I'm sorry."

"You don't need to apologize."

I looked out the window and saw that the hillside, after the rains, was ablaze with orange poppies.

"You doing well?" he said.

"Not really."

"Maybe I should come back and see you."

"I wouldn't be much fun."

"Let me be the judge of that."

"I'm not in a good place, Zack. I'm not in a good place."

"Sweetheart, that's the time I need to come see you the most."

A monarch butterfly alighted on a poppy, which bent gently under the gossamer weight. "How's your work going?" I asked.

"Pretty fair. I'm braiding a hackamore for a show in Albuquerque. I'm trying something new—using horsehair rope for the reins instead of leather."

"Mmm."

He said he'd be finished in a week or two and we talked about getting together when he'd mailed off the piece. That night, after I'd read a chapter of *Treasure Island* to the children and tucked Sophie into her canopy bed and was ushering Gabriel into his room, the doorbell rang. I walked downstairs, alarmed at the intrusion. It was late, too late for messengers from the set to be delivering a script. I looked through the peephole and opened the door.

Zack gathered me in his arms, and what I remember specifically is the feel of the cowboy hat against my hair. "You didn't have to do this," I said. We kissed under the brim, as if under a sheltering tree.

"Let's just be together. All right?" he said.

I took him upstairs to the bedroom and made a point of locking both doors. We sat down in the overstuffed chairs that swiveled and faced one another. "I've been full of black thoughts. Just full of them."

"I heard that on the phone."

I told him about the Golden Globe awards and how they'd made me acutely aware of all the boats I'd missed. Other boats were leaving and I was missing those too. My career was a shambles. "I haven't created anything in years that's worked."

"I've always been kinda curious how you got into this business. You don't watch much television. I've seen a whole lot more than you."

I told him it had happened almost by accident. After I'd finished my first book, I'd written a screenplay for a film that was never produced, but I found it was restorative—going back and forth between the two mediums, like planting alternate crops on a piece of earth. "It takes me two or three years to write a book and then I'm drained, just wrung out. Doing a script is a good way to keep writing but you're using different faculties: you're telling a story through visual images and dialogue rather than with pure language, the music of words. You also get wonderful health insurance from the Writers' Guild."

When I'd become pregnant with Gabriel, I told him, my insurance was about to lapse so I'd needed to find a script job quickly. I was having lunch with a friend, Carla Singer, who happened to be head of drama development at CBS, and she asked, "Have you thought about writing a pilot?"

I'd never seen a pilot. She sent me five scripts, including *The Scarecrow and Mrs. King*, and after reading them I thought, I can do this. The first pilot I wrote wasn't produced, but the second was made into a series for ABC and then I wrote *Heart Beat*.

Zack hadn't heard of the show.

"It was about a group of women doctors who specialized in all areas of women's health. Some were married, some single, one was lesbian—the first gay character on network television. Their personal lives were intertwined with their cases."

"Sounds fascinating."

"It was ahead of its time. We got decent ratings, we were building a following, but the network didn't renew us."

"Why not?"

I shrugged. "What goes on the air and stays on is determined entirely by men. It's a fluke we were on the air at all.

But we'd gotten so far, we'd beaten the odds . . . I don't think I slept that entire year. I was like an octopus, trying to keep a hand on the scripts, the music, the costumes, the actors. I kept a pad by my bed so when I was twitching all night I could at least be productive."

Zack took one of my hands and began, absently, to massage the fingers.

"People congratulate me on my success with *Dr. Quinn*, and I don't know what to say. I mean, I like writing the show and it has important messages, especially for young women. But—"

"I understand," Zack said. "It's like me braiding for Dunnings Tack."

"I feel like I've stepped off the beam. Joseph Campbell talks about the pollen path—when you have the sense you're exactly where you ought to be? Pollen to the right, pollen to the left, pollen above me, pollen below."

Zack picked up the other hand.

"I'm not on the path."

"But this is not gonna last forever."

I told him this was the longest stretch I'd been away from prose. I hadn't completed a book in years. "I'm afraid I won't be able to. I've lost my confidence. My mind starts running along this track and it leads to blood and wreckage. And I'm ashamed—I've had more than my share of life's rewards . . . "

He moved into the chair with me and made consoling sounds. "You're having a creative crisis and that's all right. When you get through it, your work will be stronger."

How the hell am I going to get through it? "I'm sorry. I didn't want to inflict this on you."

His eyes were calm. "It's gonna be all right. I know how to take care of you. When you cried, I held you. When you got mad, I tolerated it. When you picked on me, well . . ." He looked at the ceiling a moment. "I went away."

I laughed softly. I actually laughed.

"You're perfect for me, Sara. I'll take you with all your luggage."

Tears came to my eyes. "I know satisfaction doesn't come from out there, from the hit book or the hit show, because I've had that. It's like a drug. You get high and then you need another fix and you can never get enough unless you love yourself and I don't have a clue how to do that!"

"I'm giving you an example," he said quietly.

I stared at him. The room, which had felt like an airless cell, suddenly was shot through with brightness. It was as if a cannon had been fired, the ball had rolled right through, and the enemy bodies were on the floor.

He would take me with all my luggage, even the torn, foul-smelling pieces. *I'll take you on your worst day*, he'd said in Santa Barbara. I'd never been able to do this for myself, but I could accept it from him. That was a start, but why was it so difficult? Why is self-love so elusive, so maddeningly elusive, despite massive doses of psychotherapy and inspirational books and spiritual courses and the common wisdom that what's needed, from cradle to grave, is self-esteem? What would that mean? To accept and embrace all aspects—your virtues as well as your pain, your sadness, your sense of worthlessness and shame? To be at ease with and actually take delight in the society of yourself? Which of us can do that? Even the teachers, the pathfinders, have acknowledged how little intimacy they've achieved with self-love. Abraham Maslow, who created the term "peak experience," told students at Harvard that he'd never had one. William James said he'd constructed his ideas about the varieties of religious experience as one constructs a house, but he'd never walked through the door. He was beset by depression and doubt.

Self-love would mean not merely accepting all facets—bright and dark—but accepting what you've done and not done and the limits of what you're able to control at all. Self-love is what Paul McCartney demonstrated when asked, in a TV interview, if the White Album should have been released as a single record. George Martin, who produced it, said it should have been edited down to one disk, and Ringo Starr said it should have been released as two separate albums. McCartney said, "I'm not for going on about, we should have done this or we didn't do that. It's the bloody Beatles White Album. Shut up."

"Thank you," I said to Zack, "for coming tonight."

He lifted my legs up onto his lap and slipped off my shoes. "It wasn't easy. I could've been real embarrassed showing up at your door, after last time."

I sighed and met his eyes, which looked like a cat's, flat green with amber diamonds. "I'm sorry. I was irritable and tired. But the thing about Anne Frank . . ."

"I know." He ran his hands up my calf, kneading the muscles.

"It filled me with despair, that you'd never heard of her. I don't mind teaching a few things, but right then, it felt like all of Western civilization."

"You're not telling me anything I don't know." He ran his hands up the other calf. "It's sorta similar to training horses. I like to start 'em when they're green, when nobody's ridden 'em and they've got nothing to unlearn. But you like 'em already schooled, so you can just add the finishing touches."

I smiled.

"Are you breaking up with me?" Zack said.

"No. I feel really close to you." I put my hand on his fore-arm and ran my fingernails down it. "Why can't I stay in this place?"

"Because," he said, teasing, "when you get your clothes on, you forget. You rationalize. It's just sex. I remember it was good but it can't be that damn good. There's more to life than that."

I laughed and burrowed deeper in my chair.

"This is gonna be the best visit ever." He lifted my bare foot and kissed the arch. "Right now, you've got lots of thoughts running across your mind and what I'm doing to your foot is just one of them. But that's gonna change."

He put his lips to my toe, kissing it, while he caressed the sole with his fingers, sending jolts of extreme sensation through me. I jerked my foot back but he held on. "You gonna make me stop?"

"No."

We sank onto the carpet. "I got you back where I want you." His fingers were walking right through my skin, right on the nerves, right up the long meridians that led through the body to the hot core. "You've got so many different moods and colorings, but this is the one I'm most interested in."

I moaned.

"Long as I keep doin' this, all is forgiven?"

"Yes," I whispered.

"It makes up for Anne Frank?"

The phone rang.

"I love you," I croaked.

"What was that? I couldn't quite hear . . . "

"I love you!" In my office down the hall, the answering machine was recording someone's voice.

Zack lifted his head.

"You look pleased."

"I am. When the phone rings and you don't jump for it, I know I've got your attention."

Zack stayed for the weekend and on Sunday, we drove out to the ranch to ride. The wrangler boss, Mike Riggins, was at the remuda, backing the water truck up to the horses' troughs so he could fill them. Mike was tall, flinty, sandy-haired, with small eyes that always seemed to be enjoying some joke at your expense. He told Zack which horses we could ride and watched carefully as Zack saddled them and tied on a bag.

"Take off those spurs," Mike said. "These horses aren't used to it." Zack unbuckled the spurs and put them in my car. I could tell he wasn't happy but he nodded respectfully at Mike.

"Aren't you the guy who gave Pete O'Hara what for?" Mike said.

"Yes, sir, I lost my temper but I don't plan on doin' that again."

Mike smiled. "I'm shorthanded tomorrow. You want to work?"

Zack and I looked at each other. It had never occurred to me that this was a possibility. "Doesn't he have to be in the union?"

"Not if everybody in the union's working," Mike said. "There's only thirty-four wranglers in the union, and right now we got a lot of Westerns shooting. Two features, a pilot, and this show. I could use you the next three days."

Zack and I spoke quietly. He could postpone his flight home, but what about the piece he was braiding, and Nathan? "Nathan can manage, and I've still got a week to finish that hackamore." He turned to Mike. "What time do you want me here?"

"Six-eighteen."

"I'll be here at six."

I gave Mike a grateful nod as we walked the horses out the gate. I was riding a large sorrel named Solomon and Zack was on a chestnut named Scout. Zack scooped his arm forward in a "Let's go" gesture and we galloped off toward the state park.

Because of the heavy rains, the hills were aswarm with poppies and a profusion of wild herbs—sage, mint, thyme. The air was so fragrant that just breathing was intoxicating. We loped across a field and through a cluster of live-oak trees. "Watch the branches," Zack called. I ducked under a low branch but then felt something catch behind the saddle. Solomon lurched and strained. There was a snapping sound and the saddlebag suddenly flew around to the left. Solomon put his head down and started bucking. I lost my stirrups. It was happening so fast I couldn't make a sound but Zack heard the commotion and rode back toward us, grabbing Solomon's reins just as I went flying into the dirt. I crawled away on all fours, scooting faster than I thought possible, terrified of flailing hoofs and the twelve-hundred-pound body landing on me.

"You all right?" Zack called.

I felt my legs, put my hands to my head. "I think so."

Solomon was bucking, darting in circles. Zack held on to Solomon's reins and stayed with him. Solomon stopped for a second, hyperventilating. The bag was hanging askew, to the left. "Whoa," Zack said in a low voice. "It's all right, son." He got off his horse and took a small step toward Solomon but the horse bowed his back and jumped straight up.

"Let him go!" I said. "He's crazy."

"Settle down, son," Zack said, reaching out his hand with the palm down. "Here, come and see." Solomon stamped the ground, then arched his neck forward. "That's right, I'm not gonna hurt you." The horse stepped closer to sniff. "That's it."

To my surprise, Solomon kept inching closer, still blowing hard, his chest muscles twitching. When he was near enough, Zack stroked his nose and face. Slowly, deliberately, he reached around to tie the saddlebag down with another strap. Once the bag was secure, Zack hitched Solomon to a tree. Solomon stiffened and jerked as if he might bolt in the air. "Easy, son." Zack patted his neck. "Good."

He came over to me. "You sure you're all right, baby?"

"What happened?"

"It was one of those freak little accidents. A branch must've caught in the loop of the saddle strap and broke it. Then, when the bag came loose, it gave old Solomon quite a scare. He thought that bag was gonna eat him alive."

"That's ridiculous."

"Not to him. That bag was some kind of demon. He wanted it off his back and he didn't care how he got it off."

"I would have let him go."

"You don't *ever* let him go, or he'll try that every time. He's got to learn his safety and salvation are with you." He kissed me and the kiss had the coppery tang of adrenaline. "If he was my horse, I'd take him back to the corral and tie that bag on and off him twenty times. But we're just gonna go on now and have a nice ride."

"I'm not getting on him."

"He'll be all right now."

"I want to walk back."

"I'll show you what to do if something like that ever happens again. It's real easy—"

"Not today." My heart was still knocking in my chest.

"Sweetheart, I can't let you walk out of here."

"I'm too shaken."

"Then I'll switch horses with you. Scout's calm, nothing bothers him."

I hesitated.

"You're not a quitter, I know that." He led me over to Scout and helped me on. Then he swung onto Solomon. "We'll just take it nice and easy."

I followed him across the meadow, which, because of the rains, was crisscrossed with rivulets and brooks. We rode the horses through them, splashing and jingling, and my confidence began to return.

Zack must have sensed it because he put his horse into a gentle, rolling canter. Slow and steady, as if on rocking horses, we followed a path that curved around the meadow and toward a waterfall. "I don't want to!" I shouted, but he waved me forward. We rode right through the space between the tumbling water and the rock wall and beads of icy moisture sprayed us. I cried out but the sound was muffled and then we burst into sunlight, coming to a halt by a stand of sycamore trees.

Zack spread a blanket on the grass. He undid the saddlebag—the demon bag—and took out the bottle of red wine I'd packed, cheese, sourdough bread, and his peanut M&M's. He propped his back against a fallen log and pulled me into his lap. Tucked together, we drank the wine and listened to the river rushing and tumbling and the *click click clicking* of hummingbirds as they sipped from wildflowers. His arms were around me and the sun was warm and sweet as melting butter, penetrating our skin.

We lay down on the blanket. "Now, aren't you glad we did this?"

"I'm still not riding Solomon."

"Just say, 'Yes, Zack.'"

"Yes, Zack."

9

He called me from a pay phone in Phoenix just before midnight. He'd packed up Willie with his clothes and tools and rawhide and was about to hit Interstate 10, which would take him out past the Big Horn Mountains and across the Mojave Desert to the high-rise office buildings of downtown Los Angeles and finally the off-ramp for Santa Monica.

"Drive carefully."

"Sweetheart, I will."

I lay in bed, reading magazines that had been gathering in an unruly heap on the nightstand. I kept trying to fall asleep, turning off the lamp and putting my head on the pillow and after ten minutes I'd turn on the lamp again.

I read a profile of Marvin Hamlisch and an interview with Steve Martin about his play, *Picasso at the Lapin Agile*, and I thought, I should be with a playwright, a composer. I read a review of a new restaurant with a hot new chef from San Francisco who was blending Pacific Rim flavors with California cuisine and I thought, I won't be going to those places anymore. Zack's favorite restaurant is Polly's, a coffee shop frequented by senior citizens, whom Zack calls the "gray badgers," where, for $5.95, you can get a hamburger, fries, and a slice of homemade pie: apple, banana cream, lemon meringue.

I must have dozed because at five in the morning I was awakened by familiar boot thuds. "I'm whipped," Zack said, coming in the door. "I've been running on coffee. Just let me lie down and hold you." He pulled off his boots and flopped on the bed, clutching me, his heart racing and his breath coming twice as fast as mine. His skin was sticky and carried the pungent odor of sweat and cigarettes. What have I done?

It had seemed so clear; I'd been so calm. Zack had worked with the wranglers for three days and then Mike Riggins had offered him a full-time job. This had given Zack the impetus to move and a way to earn his livelihood. He thought it would be good for his braiding career as well. There were significant numbers of people with horses and money in California, and Zack braided in what, during the golden age of the craft, had been known as the "California style."

On Friday night, I'd told the children at dinner, "Zack's coming here to work on the show."

They jerked their heads up.

"You said you weren't gonna get married," Sophie cried.

"We're not getting married, but we want to spend more time together, and he wants to see more of you guys too."

"Where's he gonna stay?" Gabriel said.

"With us."

Gabriel folded his arms. "No."

Sophie was shaking her head.

"Listen, I know this is a change and change can be upsetting, but I want you to give it a chance. Just wait and see how it goes—"

Sophie ran upstairs to her room and slammed the door.

"This is our house too," Gabriel said, "and we don't want him. That's two against one."

"You're right, it *is* your house. But it's not a democracy. I'm the parent and he's coming because I want him to."

"I'm not gonna talk to him."

"Yes, you are. You don't have to love him, you don't even have to like him, but you do have to be courteous."

Gabriel shook his head. "This sucks."

"Come on, I'll get Sophie and we'll go out for a treat. We'll get yogurt." I went up to her room and knocked. "Sophie?"

No answer.

I knocked again, then opened the door. She was lying on her canopy bed with the sheer white gauze curtains pulled shut and her cat draped over her stomach. She ran a red comb through his fur.

"You've ruined my life."

I parted the curtain and sat down on the bed. "He wants to be your friend."

"That's impossible."

"Why?"

"It just is. He smokes, he walks around with no shirt on. I hate that."

"I'll ask him not to."

"He yells at me. He does it when you're not around, and I'm afraid to tell you because you'll get mad."

"I won't get mad."

She shot me a glance, then continued combing Buttercup's fur. "Can I tell you what he said, without getting in trouble?"

I nodded.

"He said 'fuck.' He said that I fuck up everything."

"That's hard to believe."

"See! You take his side."

"Sophie, I know how you feel—"

"No you don't." She turned a pinched, pale face to me. "Do you know what it's like to be my age and have your mother have a boyfriend who's . . . who's weird, who's a creep, who's a stupid jerk that you hate!"

"No."

She burst into tears.

Zack slept until noon. I drove the kids to Jeff's and when I returned, he was unloading Willie, carrying in cardboard boxes and metal tubs filled with stiff, uncured animal hides. The beat-up red truck looked less exotic and charming than it had in Arizona. Parked on my street of two-story homes and manicured green lawns, it looked as if the gardener was moving in.

We made strawberry margaritas with lots of tequila and took them out to the Jacuzzi. "Ahhhh," Zack sighed as he lowered himself into the steaming water. "My knees and shoulders just instantly relaxed."

We got out of the tub and dried ourselves, refilled the margarita glasses, and carried them up to the bedroom. We sat down in our ritual spots—the overstuffed chairs by the Kentia palm. "I'm scared."

"That's good," Zack said, "so I'm not the only one going through it."

"It's no accident that I haven't lived with a man for four years."

"I could get in my truck and drive home right now."

I put my feet up in his lap.

"It was hard leaving Nathan. I mean, it's way overdue. He's twenty and he seems plumb tickled at the idea of being on his own. But when it came time to drive away . . ."

I lifted his hand and kissed it. "You feel guilty?"

He nodded. "What are you scared of?"

"The responsibility. You're here because of me."

"Com-mit-ment." He pretended to choke, and we laughed. He led me to the bed and I sank into his arms. He ran his fingers down my chest, over the silk robe, touching me so lightly it seemed he was touching just the silk above my skin. Relax, I told myself, all you have to do is relax. Breathe in, breathe out. I rubbed his back, squeezing the lean, hard muscles while I gnawed gently on his shoulder but things felt different. This was not a poignant short visit where we had to get the most out of every second and fuel up hungrily for the coming dry spell. Time stretched ahead indefinitely.

Sunday night, when the kids came back from Jeff's, I fixed their favorite foods for our first joint dinner, even though the foods clashed: spaghetti with pesto for Sophie, macaroni and cheese for Gabriel, corn on the cob, and coleslaw from my mother's recipe.

"Can I eat in the den?" Sophie said.

"No, I'd like you to sit in your regular place, please."

She stood with her back to the wall. "He smells."

"That's rude. You apologize or you'll go to your room and skip dinner."

"I just mean, I can smell the cigarettes and I'm very sensitive to that."

"I appreciate that," Zack said. "I'm not gonna smoke in the house."

"But it stays on your clothes. And, like, I don't want it in my room."

"Me neither," Gabriel said, nodding with satisfaction.

"I'm not gonna go in anybody's room unless I'm invited. But I am gonna stay here, so the best thing we can do is try to get along."

"Yeah, right!" Sophie said.

"Go to your room," I said.

"Mom, I'm sorry. All I said was—" And she changed her tone, making it neutral, "Yeah, right." She took her seat.

We passed the spaghetti and coleslaw. No one spoke. I felt as if I was chewing inert matter. I took Zack's hand under the table. He winked at me.

"Good corn, doncha think?" he said.

Silence.

"Back home, we used to grow sweet corn and eat it right off the stalk. You didn't even have to cook it."

Sophie rolled her eyes. "Whatever."

He looked at each of them. "I don't want to be your father. You've already got a father and I've got my own kids—"

Gabriel dropped his fork and it clattered on the tile floor. "Can I go watch TV?"

The next morning, Beth called me from the ranch before I was out of bed. "Did you read Kevin's script?"

"Yes, it's not good."

"It's a disaster. I'm letting him go."

"Already?"

"If he can't do it in two drafts, he can't do it in a hundred. How soon can you get here?"

"I'm on my way."

I hung up the phone and steeled myself. For three weeks we'd been on hiatus—that maddeningly short break between wrapping up one season and starting work on the next. Kevin Schwartz had been hired as a supervising producer for the third season. He'd arrived with a list of impressive credits but on day one, he was washing out.

I pulled on my jeans and a T-shirt, left a note for Zack, who was still sleeping, hustled the kids to school, and headed out to Agoura. As I drove along the ocean, I ran the affair with Zack back through my mind, back to Elko, and everything was recast in a tawdry light. I was bringing an uneducated cowboy from the feedlots of Southern Arizona to live in my house and work on my show. He didn't know the city, he didn't know how to call 411 for information. He was one more person I would have to take care of.

I walked into Beth's office right behind Josef.

"Did you read the script?" she asked him.

"Yeah, it needs work, but the story's good."

Beth looked at him as if he'd lost his faculties. "It's flat, it's dead. There's not one moment, one moment that's authentic."

Josef shrugged.

"I agree," I said, "the story doesn't go anywhere, there's no climax, and he doesn't have the characters' voices."

"He doesn't get the show."

"Give him time," Josef said.

"We don't have time," Beth said. She'd spent entire seasons training young writers, but she'd hired Kevin to go right to bat and score. We'd all worked on the outline with Kevin. He'd done a first draft, we'd given him extensive notes, but he'd written a second draft that was no closer than the first. "Better to cut our losses," Beth said.

Unfortunately, this left Josef and me as the sole staff writers. Toni G. and Toni P. had left the show the previous season. We needed a minimum of four writers to maintain a well-oiled series, because every seven days, we had a new show going into "prep," when all the departments were getting ready—sewing costumes, scouting locations, and casting; a second show being shot and a third in "post"—being edited and scored. Josef and I would have to rewrite Kevin's script from scratch, then we'd have to jump on the next episodes and we'd be chasing a train all year.

We stayed at the ranch until seven or eight at night, revising the story and turning out pages. We divided up the acts and sat in our separate offices, buzzing each other when we wanted to coordinate details. I'd set something in motion, he'd give it a good kick forward, and I'd put it away. On Thursday, when we assembled the pages and read them through, we were surprised at how decent they were.

We ordered comfort food for lunch—meat loaf and mashed potatoes from the Cheesecake Factory. "You still with the cowboy?" Josef asked.

"He's here."

"In California?"

"He's going to work on the show. He starts Monday."

Josef smiled and cuffed my arm. "Good for you."

"I don't think he's very happy. The kids are being awful. And I'm coming home late, exhausted, and the kids want help with their homework and when I finally get them to sleep, I've got one more person staring at me balefully, waiting his turn."

Josef winced. "I can relate to that."

"I don't feel sexy. Making love all day and night now seems like a senseless and absurd activity."

It was dark when I pulled into the garage. I could hear the kids screaming and when I opened the door, Veronica was waiting for me in tears. "What's wrong?" I asked. "*Los niños estan peleando.*" The children are fighting. There's nothing I can do. Nothing. She said they were "*malcriados.*" I wasn't sure what that meant but I knew it was bad. *Mal.* A bad creation.

"Mom!" Sophie yelled from upstairs. "I can't get on the computer. Gabriel fixed it so I can't and he erased my homework!"

I hurried up to the den where they were standing by the new pentium computer I'd bought them.

"I did not," Gabriel said. "She was threatening to destroy my files so I suspended her privileges."

"Hold it. You have no right to suspend her privileges. That's my job."

"But you don't do it. You let her get away with anything, anything, because she's a girl."

"Shut up!" Sophie shouted. "You're such a dork."

"You favor the girl," Gabriel said.

"Look," I said, "if you two can't work this out and share the computer, then no one will use it. I'll remove it from the house."

"Thanks, Mom! I'll flunk school because of you," Gabriel said.

"It's Gabriel's fault and I get punished," Sophie said. "That's stupid. You're the worst mom."

"Don't speak to me like that."

"Just go away. Go to your bedroom. Get lost!" she yelled, and then I was yelling and I yanked the plug from the wall and sent them to their rooms.

I walked into the kitchen and put my head in my hands. "Why do they act like this?"

Veronica wiped her eyes. "I don't understand, Mrs. Sara. You do everything for them. They want for nothing. And they have no respect. In my country, children don't talk to the mother like this. If they do . . ." She made a slapping motion with her hand. "But here, you can't do that. It's different." She shook her head. "*Muy diferente.*"

Veronica had come to work for us just before Sophie was born. She'd held Sophie in her arms the day I brought her home from the hospital, and when Gabriel arrived, she carried one baby in each arm. Veronica had had four children herself, but when her husband had died, she'd left the children—who ranged from eight to thirteen—with her mother in El Salvador. At first I'd been at a loss to understand how she could bear to leave her children. Once a year, she'd go back for a visit and when she returned, she was weepy and downcast until she resigned herself: she was earning money to send back for their schooling and food. "I sacrifice myself," she said.

During the twelve years she'd lived with us, she'd gone to night school to learn English, we'd taught her how to drive, helped her obtain a green card and become a citizen. Finally, the previous summer, she'd been able to send for her three sons, who were now eighteen to twenty-three. Her daughter couldn't come because she'd already married and had two babies. The sons stayed in our house for a time and they were polite, courteous, deferential. They treated Veronica like a queen.

Zack was lying on the bed, watching Clint Eastwood in *Fistful of Dollars* on the Movie Channel. He switched off the set when I came in. "Have a good day?"

I nodded down the hall toward the children's rooms. "Have they been driving you crazy?"

He yawned. "I sat in Sophie's chair at the table. I didn't know it was her chair but she made a big point of switching them."

I lay down on the bed, propping myself against the headboard.

"She said she was gonna tell you. I told her, 'Go ahead, your mom likes me.' Sophie said, 'She likes me better.' And I said, 'That may be, but she likes me pretty well. If you try to get me in trouble, you're gonna get it back yourself.'"

I folded my arms.

"So, what's going on at work?"

"Same."

"What are you writing?"

"I don't really want to talk about it."

He watched me. "You're on the peck."

"Excuse me?"

"You've got your arms crossed, your eyes narrowed. You're gonna peck just about anything that crosses your trail."

I laughed, and turned to look at him. "I'm sorry. This hasn't been a very nice welcome for you."

He put his arms around me. "I got an ideal."

I winced. He meant "idea." He fractured words and used them incorrectly and sometimes it was amusing. He once said "blondane" and I asked what he meant. Bland? Mundane? "Both of 'em." I could tolerate "blondane," but "ideal" was like fingernails on a blackboard.

"It's 'idea,'" I said.

"It's just a word. You know what I'm talking about."

"Words are my life. And the whole point of language is consensus—we assign a certain meaning to a specific sound and if everyone uses a different sound, there's no language."

"All right, baby, I'll try to remember." But five minutes later, he said, "What do you think of this ideal?"

"Zack."

"I need to get a place of my own."

Yes. I tried to conceal my joy. "You said we should be patient, give the kids more time."

"I want to set up my shop and start braiding and there's no place here I can do that."

"We talked about this—you can work in the den. We'll move out the Ping-Pong table and you can put your workbench there."

"But it doesn't have a door. Everybody else has a door."

"That's true."

"It's gonna be better for all of us."

We agreed we would try to find a small place for Zack nearby, but there was the matter of finances. He had arrived with literally no money and it would be weeks before he received his first paycheck. He still had to help Nathan with the rent in Phoenix, which was two hundred a month. I made calculations, and told him I could put in five hundred a month for a place here. If he could pay a few hundred, we could look for something in the six- to seven-hundred range.

We started that weekend. Our first choice was a studio or guest house somewhere between Agoura and West Los Angeles, where he could keep horses or preferably help care for them in exchange for rent. We put up notices on bulletin boards, at riding stables and supermarkets, checked the papers and real estate offices but at the end of the weekend, we hadn't found a single possibility.

Zack had to work only two days the following week—he worked only when the scenes we were shooting required horses. While I holed up in my office, he kept driving around the city, getting lost. We discovered there weren't a great many choices in our price range, so we expanded the search to include apartments. If necessary, we'd give up the idea of keeping horses.

He called to tell me he'd found a cottage he liked in Las Flores Canyon, but when I drove there to meet him, it had been rented. "If you like a place, rent it on the spot," I told him.

By mid-week, he'd seen dozens of apartments and couldn't remember one from the other. He was dragging his heels. "I saw a place by the freeway. It was fairly large, but . . . "

"Noisy?" I said.

"I could keep the radio on, I guess."

At home, he stopped speaking unless someone spoke to him first. He retreated into a silence that was black and spread through the house like something inflatable. He picked at his meals, drank continuous cups of coffee, and walked outside to smoke.

On Saturday, he took me to see the two best places he'd found. One was a trailer on a breathtaking piece of land in Latigo Canyon, surrounded by willow trees and a stream lined with rare silver succulent plants. It was next to a state prison for women and every ten minutes you could hear announcements being boomed to the prisoners over loudspeakers. That wouldn't have bothered me, but the trailer had one grimy window, no cooking facilities, and a bathroom so dirty and smelly it would never come clean.

The second was an apartment in the barrio around Slauson Avenue, which was a good value for the money—two bedrooms and an attached garage, freshly painted. Most of the apartments he'd seen for higher rents came with no garage. But there were steel bars on the windows and mariachi music blasting from every window of every apartment on the block. In the yard was a mound of broken glass—people threw their bottles out the windows—and a stripped-down car with graffiti on it. "I've lived in bad neighborhoods before," Zack said. "If you treat people with respect, they'll leave you alone."

I tossed and thrashed that night. Zack poked me in the eye with his elbow and had a coughing fit. How could I send him to live in a place where I wouldn't let anyone in my family live? Where I wouldn't feel safe driving at night? Maybe I should contribute more and get him something better, but how much more would it take?

In the morning, Zack said he wanted to start braiding and he could make do with the place in the barrio. "It's a start. It's got enough room and you don't have to come there, I'll visit you here. All right?"

I nodded. "The new listings come out today. Why don't you just check the paper one last time?"

He had no stomach for it, but he sat down with the ads and the phone and a cup of coffee while I went to my study to do rewrites for a script we were shooting Monday. After a while, he knocked on my door. "I think I found something. It's a guest house in To . . . Topago . . . "

"Topanga Canyon?"

"That's it. The lady says she's got some horses that need looking after."

"Better go right up. It's a beautiful area. And if you want it—"

"I know."

It was almost three hours before he came back, and he was smiling. "This could be it," he said. "It's six hundred bucks and it's small, but what it lacks in size it makes up for in atmosphere. You gotta drive down a private dirt road to get to it—"

"Did you rent it?"

"I filled out an application. The lady had a few others. She's gonna check us all out Monday."

"Let's go back," I said. We stopped at a florist and bought a dozen red roses. Zack told me the owner's name was Alice. When she opened the door, she was wearing a lime green jogging outfit and had her long white hair in a bun. Zack handed her the roses.

"What's this for?"

"This is a beautiful place you built," Zack said, "and I want you to know I'd be honored to live here."

She stood in the doorway, clutching the roses. I told her I'd known Zack a year, I knew his family in Arizona, and he was an honest, responsible person she could trust with her property and her animals. "I used to have a guest house myself, so I know how important it is to have the right person there." I said we'd already put a deposit on another place, but Zack would much prefer this one. If he couldn't have it, he shouldn't let the other place slip away. When did she think she might let us know?

She stared at me in silence, then at Zack. "Come on in, let me see if I have a vase around here somewhere." While she fussed with the roses, I wrote her a check for the first and last months' rent—I've never been so happy to write a check—and she gave Zack the key.

I'd campaigned for the cabin sight unseen, and when we walked inside, I was stunned. It was one large room with a natural wood floor, stained-glass windows, a Franklin stove, and a charming antique claw-foot bathtub. We'd been on the verge of renting an apartment in the barrio with a view of a stripped-down car and broken glass. This place even came with furniture. We opened the doors to the deck, which looked out on Topanga State Park, so that before us was an unbroken vista of eucalyptus and pine trees, hawks, deer, and green hills rolling to the sea.

We looked at each other, feeling dazed, humble. There are moments in life when you make a plan and everything thwarts you: the flight is delayed, a storm comes up, you get a flat tire and curse whatever prompted you to start on this venture. And then there are moments when you step into the current and it takes you. Locks click open, lamps come on.

"Let's check around back," Zack said. The one thing he'd wanted that this place didn't have was a garage, where he could keep his power tools and do messy work and leave skins hanging. There was a storage shed behind the cabin with a sliding bar across it. "I wonder if it comes with the place," he said, struggling with the rusty bolt. "It's probably packed full of stuff that lady's collected over a lifetime." He pushed open the door and sucked in his breath. "It's empty."

◆

He moved in the next day. I luxuriated, basked in having my privacy and solitude back—at least in the hours after the kids had gone to sleep. At the end of the week, I drove up to Topanga and found a wood fire going and Sawyer Brown singing "Some Girls Do."

"Hello there," Zack said, standing in the doorway, wearing jeans and a navy flannel shirt that made his eyes look brilliant turquoise. He'd hung a cow skull over the bed, put a bearskin rug on the floor and Nathan's paintings on the walls along with bridles, ropes, and spurs, creating what he called "the bunkhouse effect." Even the toilet-paper holder in the bathroom was made of braided rawhide.

I'd brought a bottle of Dom Perignon to christen the cabin. He opened it on the deck as he sang with Sawyer Brown that he wasn't high class but he wasn't white trash either. He let the cork shoot into the trees. He brought out a plate of Ritz crackers and Velveeta cheese—to him, this was living, but to me, Velveeta? At Berkeley, my roommates and I, newly awakened to bouts of passionate cooking, had recoiled, rebelled, cast out Velveeta. It was an artificial food with artificial orange color and it stood for everything processed and bland in American society but after several glasses of champagne, it tasted all right.

"I had a good string day today," he said.

"Great."

"Damn right it's great. You don't want to see me at the end of a bad string day."

"What's that?"

"You're just tearing and sawing at the hide. You can't get a flow going." He made a face.

I understood. There were days, sometimes weeks, when I'd

be slogging along, hacking at words and then putting them back the way they'd been. I couldn't find my voice, my rhythm, and I despaired that I ever would and wanted to hurl myself off the balcony. "Ernest Hemingway put a gun to his head."

"I'm sure there are braiders who've hung themselves on a bad string day," Zack said. "They probably even tied the knot on the noose."

We laughed and he poured more champagne. "But today— God, it was like playing an instrument." He took hold of a phantom guitar and plucked the strings. "It didn't come a minute too soon, either. I been . . . sorta upset the last few days."

"Was I the cause of this?"

He added a log to the fire.

"I've been mean, I know it. I couldn't stop myself."

He turned away, facing the window. "I took a walk this morning. There's a huge old windmill on top of that hill."

I tried to draw his attention back. "I haven't been making much effort. I stopped doing things like . . . shaving my legs."

He nodded toward the hill. "I'd love to get that windmill working. It makes such a cool sound."

"Zack, I think we should talk about this."

"Did you bring your boots?"

"Yes."

He took hold of my shirt and pulled me to him. "I'm gonna take you riding. Then I'm gonna fix you dinner. Then I'm gonna make love to you and drive you fucking crazy and let you drive me fucking crazy and then, if you still want to talk about anything, we can."

◆

The sun was setting when we started up the canyon. Zack said it was one of his favorite times to ride, especially with a full moon. He'd picked out two of Alice's horses which he said were "well mannered," but I found them dull, plodding with their necks down. "Come on, Susie, wake up!" Zack rolled his spurs over the horse's flanks and we started moving at a more sprightly pace.

"These horses aren't gonna do anything crazy," he said, "so it's a good time to practice what to do if you find yourself in trouble." He said I should keep an eye on the horse's head and ears. "If he starts to drop his head, take one rein and jerk it straight up. He can't buck if his head's up in the air. Try it." I yanked on the rein. "We're gonna do this as we go along, like a fire drill. So the minute you sense trouble, you don't wait for the first buck. You go on autopilot—pop his head up."

He scooped his arm forward and we shifted into a lope. It was dark now and I couldn't see what we were riding through. The trees were vague gray shapes and the air was full of noises—hooting, snapping, distant howling. When we reached the top of the ridge, we turned our horses in the direction of the ocean. Across the blackened canyon, we could see the entire curve of the coast outlined with winking lights.

"They call that the queen's necklace," I said.

He leaned over and traced, with his lips, the path of a necklace across my chest. A large band of cicadas were making their rapid sawing noise and it rose to a crescendo. He motioned me to ride down the hill ahead of him. I couldn't see, but the horse moved through the blackness in a confident rhythm and with every step, I was aware of Zack behind me.

He cooked steaks on the wood fire. After we'd eaten, he drew water in the claw-foot tub. While it was filling, he lit the oil lamps he'd scavenged from around the property and put on the Grateful Dead, *American Beauty*. I peeled off my jeans and eased into the water. He walked over carrying a bowl, a razor, and shaving cream. "I've had this for twenty years," he said, hefting the razor with his fingers. "I like it heavy. I don't like disposable."

He climbed onto the rim of the tub and sat facing me with his legs in the water.

"What're you doing?"

"Shaving your legs."

"No."

"Yes, ma'am." He lifted my right leg and set it on his lap, then lathered it with cream.

"I can't believe you want to do this." It was the grooming task I found most tedious and went to lengths to avoid. "I once thought of going to a barber so I could pay for it."

"Such business would be a thrill for the barber."

"That would depend on the woman, wouldn't it?"

"Right now, this is such a rare occurrence, you don't want to start cutting at the gate."

I laughed, and lay back in the tub as the oil lamps flickered and Jerry Garcia was telling us to come hear Uncle John's band. Zack started sliding the razor over my skin, bringing to the task that same concentration with which he did all things—slow and thorough. He used small strokes, over and over until there was a slim cut of skin that was perfectly clear. Then he moved on, clearing the next cut. "Could you turn your leg thataway?" I shifted in the tub. "There's a spot I missed."

"I never worry about those spots."

He finished the right leg and assessed it, turning it from side to side.

"It's beautiful. Thank you." I slid forward and kissed him. "That was fun tonight, riding in the dark."

He motioned me back and picked up the left leg, lathering it with cream.

"Don't you miss that life?" I asked.

"Sometimes." The tape had ended and he flipped it over. "I miss saddling up at four in the morning when there's no one around but the hands. You get on a horse that nobody wants to ride. They're all yelling—'He's gonna throw you!'—and then you don't fall off, or you do. Either way, you're in the game." He looked up at the dark windows facing the canyon. "And roping. God, chasing a five-hundred-pound steer, throwing a rope around him and tying it to your saddle and feeling the jerk. You get jerked good!"

He dipped the razor in the bowl. "Have you ever seen eighty-five thousand head?"

"Can't say that I have."

"When they made me assistant manager, I had to plot how to move thousands of cattle through the feedlot. It's like a chess game and I played it brilliantly. I was number two in the operation and I was set to be number one, but when number one quit I wasn't moved up. They gave the job to my best friend, and he fired me."

"Why?"

He bent his head down, making careful strokes around the curving bones in the knee. "He ran off with my wife."

"You never told me."

He wiped the knee clean with a washcloth. "They packed up my new Ford truck and drove away. Marianne took the girls and to this day, neither one of 'em wants to see me. I keep showin' up, though, and if I'm lucky, they fit me into their schedule."

"After all these years?"

"I was destroyed. But in a way, I had it coming."

"Why do you say that?"

"I was arrogant. I fucked just about anyone I wanted and expected Marianne to be there when I got home. At my high point, I was in charge of sixty people. If I wanted to hurt somebody, I knew how to hurt 'em and I did."

"I've never seen that side of you."

He checked the leg for errant hairs. "Part of it comes from moving so much, growing up. Every time I walked onto a new playground, there'd be one kid I'd have to beat the shit out of or the others wouldn't leave me alone. Once I whipped that kid, it was pretty much over."

I stepped out of the tub and reached for a towel to dry my legs, which were pink and so tender the towel hurt. "I've never had a shave this close," I said. He threw off the towel and held me against him while we both had a sheen of moisture on our skin. "Wild Nights!" I heard the poem by Emily Dickinson in my mind. I pushed him down on the bed and rubbed his back with baby oil. "Wild Nights—Wild Nights! . . . Rowing in Eden—Ah, the Sea!" I turned him over, rubbed his chest, and lifted the bottle over his cock, letting the oil fall: drop, drop, drop. He jerked and moaned as I worked in the oil and then he reached for my hips and eased me on top of him. We glistened, we slid, our bodies were conduits for heat that was almost unbearable. And I thought, He's fed and groomed me, laughed and played with me, taken me riding and to states of ecstasy and I'm complaining that he uses wrong words?

◆

We lay still, letting the room come back into focus. The fire crackling in the Franklin stove. Jerry Garcia singing "Truckin'." Up on the ridge, a party of coyotes were yip-yipping and ruff-ruffing and ah-oo-ing. I reached for the champagne glass but it was empty. "I'll get you some—" Zack started to rise but I grabbed his arm. "I'm back."

He fell on top of me. "I was afraid we were never gonna make it here."

"Me too."

"You know how many times I wanted to get in my truck and drive home? I got tired of trying to be nice."

"I didn't even try."

We stared at each other, drinking in the unexpectedness, the sheer outlandishness of the turn we'd taken. "What's going on?" I whispered.

He looked around the cabin. "Some days I believe I've died and gone to heaven in a limousine. And some days, well . . ." He turned his head. "Where's the back door at?"

I pinched his ribs but he grabbed my hands and pinned them down. "I know I'm gonna do great work here, Sara. You've inspired me. You make me want to work harder than I've ever worked." I tried to wrestle free but he held me. "I like to think I'm taking you to some new territory also."

"Maybe."

"You know I am." He started tickling me.

"You are!" He released my arms and I wanted him again. "This is our path," I said.

"It's a hellacious path."

"Without this, we've got shit."

"Without this," he said, "we've got what everybody else has."

We fell back on the pillows and the heat was there again and the phone rang. Zack answered it and passed it to me.

"Mom," Sophie said.

I sat up. "What's wrong?"

"I'm sick. My throat hurts really bad. I can't swallow. Could you please come pick me up so you can take care of me?"

"Your dad will do that."

"He took my temperature and it's . . . a hundred and three."

"A hundred and three? Are you sure?"

Her voice broke. "I'm scared."

I hung up and looked at Zack.

"You're leaving."

"I'm sorry." I started fishing for my clothes. "You could come with me?"

He shook his head no.

10

When I rang the bell, it was almost midnight and Jeff opened the door wearing a long black terry cloth robe. Rose was standing on the second-floor landing, squinting down at us.

"You shouldn't have come. I don't know why she called you," Jeff said.

"She's scared. She's running a high fever."

"I'm taking care of it."

"Mom!" Sophie threw open the door of her room and came hurrying down the stairs, flushed and glassy-eyed. I felt her forehead, the back of her neck. "I want to go to your house, please. I can't sleep." She put her arms around my neck.

"You see, this is what happens," Jeff said.

"Could I speak to you in private?" I told Sophie to go back to her room and wait. Jeff and I walked into the study and he shut the door.

"This is an unusual situation," I said.

"We stick to the schedule, that's our agreement."

"I know, and I've always respected that—"

"It cuts both ways. Gabriel wants to stay here all the time and I tell him no."

"She's burning up. Did you give her anything?"

"Tylenol."

"What time?"

He looked at his watch. "Eight."

"She could use two more. Jeff, please, let's just get her well. Let me take her to my place—"

"You want to drag her out in the middle of the night when she's running a fever? That's not smart."

"You can have extra days when she's better."

"You have no right to come here like this!"

"I'm her mother and if she's sick and crying, I'm not going to refuse to come and be with her."

"She's just doing it as a ploy. She knows what will happen. If she cries long enough, you'll break down and come get her."

"So what's your solution? Let her . . . cry it out?"

"Just tell her no, you're not coming. She'll get over it fast. I guarantee that."

"Are you going to take her to the doctor tomorrow?"

"What?"

"Cancel your appointments, stay home from work?"

"Come on, Sara." He opened the door of the study and headed for the stairs.

"Because I am. First thing in the morning, I'll take her to the doctor and get her medicine or X rays or whatever she needs, then I'll go by the school and pick up her assignments and books. So what's the difference if I take her with me now?"

He swiveled toward me with an expression that made me apprehensive.

Rose called from the balcony, "Jeff."

He poised on his toes, like a prizefighter. Then he turned, walked up the stairs, and followed Rose into the bedroom, slamming the door shut.

I slept not at all. I lay beside Sophie on her canopy bed, telling her stories—she loved to hear stories about when she was a baby and learning to walk and talk—until her eyelids fluttered shut.

I was not proud of my behavior at Jeff's. For weeks, sometimes months, we were able to go along maintaining a surface cordiality. We could keep up the illusion that we were partners collaborating on a long-term project. There were even moments when I felt gratitude—he'd married me and together we'd created these children. But the cordiality was thin and when I'd walked into his house tonight, I'd crunched right through it and wished for his disappearance in a pillar of smoke. There was no escape—that's what kept me awake and thrashing. When you have children, you can never separate, you merely encamp to different houses.

I showed up at the pediatrician's office when they opened at nine, although we had no appointment. Our doctor, Vicky Paterno, had a daughter Sophie's age and understood working mothers. She hustled us through in less than thirty minutes. She took a throat swab, looked at it under the microscope, and told us Sophie had strep throat. The nurse called ahead to the pharmacy so the antibiotic would be ready when I drove up. I gave Sophie her first dose, wrote out detailed instructions in Spanish for Veronica, and sped out to the ranch, arriving shortly after eleven.

As I drove past the remuda, I saw Zack's rusty red truck slouched against the fence. I parked in my designated spot in front of the writers' trailer, between Beth's gray Jaguar and Josef's classic '66 Mustang convertible.

The cars were a reminder: I was fucking down, but in the world of the set—a rigidly stratified world—I was fucking in the cellar. Since Zack was not a member of the wranglers' union, he was hired and paid as a "riding extra." He could only be employed as a "wrangler" if no union members were available, and he had to work twenty-two days in a given year as a wrangler to be eligible to join. The only way to qualify, Mike Riggins had said, was to go off on a feature for several months at a location so undesirable that none of the union members wanted to go. In Southern California, Zack would never get twenty-two days.

So he joined the Screen Actors Guild, which had simpler rules: if you worked as an extra, you became a member. Zack drove to the ranch every morning at six, helped the wranglers saddle horses, then walked to the wardrobe trailer where he was given a pair of wool pants with buttons (jeans and zippers hadn't been invented in 1865), a shirt, vest, hat (not a cowboy hat—they hadn't been created then either), and lace-up boots. Then he went to the makeup trailer where they glued a mustache above his lip. He hated the mustache but was paid eighteen dollars for wearing it. In the hair trailer, they combed and sprayed his hair so it looked authentic for the period. Then he stepped onto his horse in that graceful single motion and was ready to ride back and forth in shots.

He became part of the nameless, faceless mass who made up the lowest caste, although in Casa Grande he was now considered a movie star. The very word "extra" suggested their status:

expendable, non-people. They were referred to on the set as "background." When the director wanted to speak to them, he called, "Background!" Nobody bothered to learn their names. Before Zack had come to work, I'd scarcely looked at the extras and was irritated if one of them tried to make conversation as I dashed between the set and the writers' trailer.

The person in charge of background was the second assistant director. He placed them in scenes and choreographed their actions to create a moving tableau: two men on horses would come riding up to the saloon and dismount, while three women stopped outside the general store to look at potatoes and four children played with hoops in the street—all in silence. Our second AD, Marv Jabloner, was a balding young man with glasses who wore safari shorts and a cheap straw cowboy hat and carried a walkie-talkie. I liked Marv because he was so zealous but others found him irritating. He spoke to the extras with that wacky concentration of someone who's always been a nerd.

"I need a rider by the barbershop!" Marv called.

Zack looked around. He was the closest to the barbershop so he nudged his horse in that direction.

"I want you to get off the horse and look at his feet, like he's been limping and you want to see what's wrong."

Zack nodded. After several weeks on the set, he'd learned the unspoken rules. The first was not to be too eager. In the beginning, Zack had jumped up every time Marv called for a rider, but Earl McCoy, one of the senior wranglers—the one who'd sent me to the cowboy poetry festival in Elko—had come to him and said, "Zack, you've been in every damn shot. Sit down. You don't get paid any more for riding through the shot than for sitting it out." The goal of the wranglers was to sit out as much as possible, but Zack preferred to "stay busy."

The second rule was not to get noticed, but that was complicated. Every extra wanted to be discovered. If Marv picked an extra to walk up to Jane Seymour and hand her a letter, that was a big deal—a "silent bit," for which they'd get a thirty-dollar bump in pay. They'd talk about it for weeks and wait impatiently for the air date because the extra, standing next to the star, was sure to be seen on screen. But after that moment of glory, he'd be told by Marv to stay home because "we've seen too much of you." As Zack put it, "You want to get noticed but if you do, it costs you."

When I arrived at the ranch, one of the PAs beeped me and said the director needed me on the set. I grabbed my script and rode in a golf cart to the meadow by the church. As I walked through the clusters of crew members and equipment, stepping over cables and wires, people tapped me and called out questions. Chip Landau came over and hugged me. Zack had observed that *Dr. Quinn* was the "huggingest place." Beth had set the tone, hugging people when she greeted them, and everyone else had followed suit. Chip said, "I'm running late. I need some help if I'm gonna make my day. Can we cut these lines?"

I scanned the dialogue. "No."

"It'd save me an hour and a half. I won't have to do coverage."

"But we need to hear Dr. Quinn say this—she's changed her mind." I looked at the call sheet, which listed all the scenes being shot that day. "We could lose scene ten, if we have to."

"Thank you," Chip said.

I turned and looked around the meadow, squinting. There was a line of riders by the oak tree and one separated himself and rode forward. Zack would tell me later, "When I see you craning your head around, that's my cue." I walked to meet him and we stopped by the small wooden bridge that arches over Malibu Creek. He leaned down from the horse, I stood on tiptoes, and we kissed.

"Cut . . . that . . . out."

I turned and saw Marv, his eyeglasses glinting in the sun, speaking over his bullhorn.

"Leave . . . the girl . . . alone."

The crew members laughed and shook their heads. Jane Seymour's husband directed episodes, Beth's husband played the town barber, but I was the only woman from the group designated as "above-the-line" who was consorting with an extra. I didn't much care what the crew thought but Zack was subjected to nonstop hazing. The wranglers called him a gigolo and "Sara's boy." He kept protesting, "I take care of myself," and sometimes he disarmed them by saying, "I fucked my way here, all right? But I'm gonna make a good hand." One morning he stuck a wildflower in his lapel and Mike Riggins stopped him on the road. "What the hell is that?"

"Flower," Zack said.

"I know that. What's it doin' there?"

Zack shrugged. "I'm a sensitive guy."

"You're a whore."

The wranglers bunched up around Mike and laughed.

Zack stiffened. "You think it's easy to get a woman to pay you to do it? You show me one man here—I don't believe there's a man on the entire set, from the oldest to the youngest, from Joe Lando down to the lowliest extra—who's getting *paid* to do it."

They muttered under their breath and moved away.

The rage of the wranglers had taken me by surprise. I'd expected them to welcome Zack. He spoke their language, he'd worked at Red River Land and Cattle Company, the outfit owned by John Wayne, but they saw him as a threat.

When Zack dismounted and started tying his horse to the fence, McCoy, a big, beefy man with wattles, rushed over and grabbed the reins out of Zack's hand. He turned and called to the wranglers on the bench, "If there's one thing I hate, it's a goddamned extra who acts like a wrangler!"

McCoy told Zack that only wranglers were allowed to handle the horses and tack. The extras were supposed to get on, ride, and get off. That's it. Every time Zack showed up at six to saddle horses, he was making it possible for Mike Riggins to hire one less wrangler that day. McCoy told Zack, "You're keeping a good man home."

Zack went to Mike Riggins and asked if he should quit saddling horses but Mike said, "Nah, don't worry about it. Our guys are just lazy and they've got to have something to bitch about."

So Zack kept showing up at six, and McCoy kept grabbing the reins out of his hand. One of the old-timers warned Zack to be careful, to check his saddle and tack before he got on.

When the weekend arrived, on Saturday night, Zack and I took Gabriel and three friends who were members of his band to their first live rock concert—Nine Inch Nails. Gabriel had turned eleven the month before and the tickets were one of his presents. He'd been so keyed up all day that he'd gotten a stomachache and I'd had to settle him on the couch with a heating pad and a glass of ginger ale.

He made a spontaneous recovery when his friends arrived, followed by Zack.

"Good evening," Zack said.

"Why does he have to come!" Gabriel said.

I shot him a look. "You be polite . . . "

"I'm just asking why."

". . . or we'll call this off."

Zack held up his hands and waved them forward. "Let's all just move along now and have us a good time."

Behind his back, Gabriel mimicked Zack, waving his hands and wagging his head. His friends doubled up laughing.

"Let's get in the car now," I said. They crowded into the back of the station wagon. Zack helped me in, buckled my safety belt, walked around to the driver's seat, and we set off.

"I wanna go in the mosh pit," Gabriel said.

"You lie!"

"Nnnhhhhaaah."

"I'm serious!" Gabriel said. "I want to try crowd-surfing."

"Brrrraahhhh!"

The boys yelled and cackled and the air grew musky with testosterone. I swiveled around and told them I'd brought earplugs for everyone.

"Earplugs!" Jason, who was the leader, cried. Gabriel made a circling motion with his finger and pointed it at me.

"You'll see—even the ushers wear earplugs," I said. "When I worked for the *Boston Globe*, I did an interview with Pete Townshend. You know who that is? The Who? *Tommy*?"

No one spoke, then Jason said, "Yeah."

"Just before the interview, there were reports in the press about a scientific study which showed that listening to loud rock 'n' roll could damage your hearing."

The boys grunted.

"The Who were the loudest band around, so I asked Pete Townshend what he thought." I leaned toward Zack. "We want the next off-ramp."

"What'd he say?" Gabriel asked.

"He said, 'Rubbish! I'm around loud rock all the time. I fall asleep most nights with stereo headphones on my ears, and my hearing is perfect.'"

I turned forward in my seat. "Today, he's deaf."

Zack glanced at me sideways. I heard the boys whispering and Gabriel called, "Thanks, Mom, but . . . never mind."

We pulled into the parking tower of Universal City, which was crowded, confusing. To reach the amphitheater, we had to walk through the newly constructed mall—the Universal City Walk—whose designer had won awards but whose work was a garish vision of hell, "Ulysses in Night Town" expressed through the idiom of Las Vegas. There were neon palm trees, neon hot dogs, neon storefronts, all flashing and pulsing like slot machines. And the mall was inhabited by a race that dressed in black and colored its hair purple and green and had body parts—navels, eyebrows—pierced with rings. Zack was the only soul wearing a cowboy hat.

Our seats, which I'd obtained from a friend in the music business, were in the orchestra section so there was a chance we could actually see the performers. I handed Zack a pair of foam earplugs. The warm-up act was the Jim Rose Circus, which wasn't a band, I decided, but a group who did S&M performance art. While heavy metal played from speakers, Jim Rose put a glass to his mouth and ate it. Then he took off his shirt and flexed while the band members threw darts in his back. I looked at Gabriel and his friends, who were sitting forward in their seats, mouths open. Zack turned my face to him and kissed me.

On stage, the performers were hanging electric saws and toasters from rings in their noses, but the climax came when Jim Rose took two cement blocks attached to metal chains and clipped them onto rings in his pierced nipples. He let them dangle from his nipples, then gave them a push and set them twirling. I jammed my face into Zack's shoulder.

During intermission, the boys rushed to the concession stands to buy T-shirts, CDs, and chains. They'd just returned to their seats when Nine Inch Nails started playing. Even with earplugs, the volume was painful. The boys turned to me in panic and stretched out their hands. I tried to show no expression as I dropped a pair of earplugs in each palm. Zack and I hunched down in our seats. Tucked among the rows of bouncing fans, we could not distinguish when one song ended and a different one began. I stared at Gabriel. He was singing along and punching his fist in the air. Zack ran his hand up my jeans, trying to distract me. "I want to fuck you like an animal," my son was singing.

Fans started holding up cigarette lighters. Gabriel craned his head around, watching the small yellow flames flicker and multiply until the theater was a dome of fiery points. Zack took out his Zippo lighter and handed it to Gabriel. He looked at Zack, startled. He flicked it on and his friends buzzed about it. Then Gabriel held it up in the air.

Zack pulled me to my feet. "Let's go for a walk." He led me up the aisle and out of the theater. "It's embarrasing to be at a rock concert with your mom."

◆

The next morning, Zack asked Gabriel to help him unload skins and horsehair rope from his truck. He wanted to store them in our toolshed, since his own was already full. I unlocked the door of the shed and held it open as they carried in boxes from the truck. An old Champion lighter clattered to the ground. Gabriel picked it up. "What's this?"

Zack glanced at it. "Piece of garbage."

Gabriel had returned the Zippo the night before, after the concert. He tried flicking on the Champion but it made hollow clicks. "It's broken."

"It needs butane," Zack said.

"If you got some butane, would it work?"

"Yeah."

"Where do you get it?"

Zack shrugged. "Drugstore." They carried the last boxes over and stacked them in the shed. "That's it," Zack said.

"If I bought some butane, could I have it? I mean, if you're not using it?"

Zack squatted so his eyes were level with Gabriel's. "Fire's sort of a serious thing. You have to ask your mom first, but if you promise me you'll be responsible with it, I'll speak up for you."

"I promise."

"I'm gonna trust you to be smart about it. You can't light it in the car. You can't light it at school. And if you mess up just one time—it's gone."

"I won't mess up."

Zack turned to me. I gave a subliminal nod and he handed the lighter to Gabriel.

"Thanks, Zack!"

◆

Zack had given Gabriel many things—a bear claw, a pocket-knife—but nothing had the impact of that five-dollar Champion lighter. All weekend, Gabriel worked with it, lighting and relighting it, seeing how fast he could draw it from his pocket and flick it on. He refilled it with butane twice and Zack showed him how to pop it open with one hand and light it by snapping the fingers of the other.

In the days that followed, Gabriel wanted to be with Zack whenever he could. They drove to hardware stores and junk-yards, riding in the truck that Gabriel had ridiculed before. They built a ramp for his skateboard, and converted the storage room by the garage into a rehearsal space for Gabriel's band. They stapled insulation to the walls and installed lights. They also dreamed up pranks. Zack showed Gabriel how he could tie a string around a G.I. Joe and, holding the string, flush the soldier down the toilet. "That's so cool!" Gabriel said, pulling the soldier back out. Zack told him he could cuss around him, get it off his chest, "but never do it around other people and especially not around your mom or I'll take you out like a bad attitude."

The three of us made an excursion to Home Depot, which, to me, was an excursion to hell. I sat on a bench in a corner of the noisy warehouse crammed with things I didn't want or need, reading Frank Conroy's *Body and Soul*. Zack and Gabriel walked up and down the aisles, looking at drills that could blast through concrete and circular saws and tanks of propane.

After an hour, they came walking toward me carrying a metal contraption with pulleys and chains. They were an odd pair: Gabriel in his torn jeans and black Nine Inch Nails cap and Zack in his boots and Stetson.

"Can we get this, Mom?" Gabriel said.

"What is it?"

"A come-along."

"A what?"

"It's for stretching chain-link fence," Zack said.

"We don't have any chain-link fence."

"I've used it to pull a calf out of its mother."

"Only twenty-five bucks," Gabriel said.

"But what will you do with it?"

"Stuff."

Zack nodded at Gabriel. "He thinks it looks cool."

Right. I was sure he saw it as a means of torture and destruction.

Zack leaned over and said quietly, "I don't think he can do much damage with it." He told Gabriel he'd buy him the come-along as a late birthday present, if he still wanted it in two weeks.

Gabriel made a fist and yanked it down, as if pulling a lever. "Yes!"

I was mystified by the shift in Gabriel. It made me hopeful and I was reluctant to count on it because I knew he could turn like the wind. At the ranch, I told Josef I couldn't understand how the Champion lighter had had such a profound effect.

Josef smiled. "I understand. It's like an initiation. Fire is a symbol of sexuality, right? You've got a strong male who gives your son a lighted cock and tells him he trusts him to use it wisely."

The Santa Ana winds were blowing, turning the air hot and dry when I drove the kids to Zack's cabin for the first time. Gabriel walked inside and headed straight for the cow skull.

There was one horn free but he made a point of hanging his black Nine Inch Nails cap on top of Zack's Stetson.

"Come on out back," Zack called. "You gotta see this!"

We walked out the door and there, hanging down from the eucalyptus tree whose branches reached out over the canyon, was a long hemp rope. The kids made a wordless sound and ran to the rope as if to the Grail.

They toyed with it, unsure. "Let me show you," Zack said. He took hold of the rope, braced his foot against the knot he'd tied, and pushed off. He swung far out, twirling over the ravine to where the ground fell away, then swung back to where we were waiting.

Gabriel tried next but got rope burns on his hands, so Zack tied a loop in the bottom so he could put his foot in the loop and stand on that. Sophie wanted him to make a swing she could sit on.

"Try it this way," Zack said. "Put your foot right here. I'll hold you."

She shimmied away from him. "No."

"You won't fall."

"Can't we tie a board on it?"

"A board's not gonna work unless you've got two ropes, and I ain't climbing up there again." He nodded toward the branch, twenty feet above the ground.

"I was wondering how you got it up there," I said.

"I tried throwing the rope over it but that didn't work. So I climbed up on top of that shed and from there into the Y of the tree and then out onto the branch on my stomach."

"You're nuts."

"Of course. And I had to get it done before Gabriel got here or he'd have wanted to climb up too."

"Yeah, let's climb up now," Gabriel said.

Zack made a bigger loop at the bottom of the rope and told Sophie she could put her legs through it and sit on the loop like a swing.

Tentatively, she slipped one leg in, then the other. Zack moved forward.

"Don't touch me!"

He stepped back and held up his hands.

She looked at me, then pushed off gingerly and screamed. She stopped herself. "This is fun." She turned to Zack. "Could you give me a small push? Like, really small?"

He pushed her gently, respectfully, and each time she asked to be sent a little farther. "I might start to like you," she said. Two more pushes and she was swinging far out over the ravine with her head thrown back. Zack pulled me around the side of the shed and kissed me.

The children looked like sylphs that day, swinging and taking turns pushing each other on the rope and shooting water balloons from a slingshot into the trees. And they were calling, "Zack, Zack, look, Zack, push me, Zack, watch."

He helped Sophie launch a red water balloon that sailed clear across the canyon, exploding against a pine tree. She did a series of celebratory leaps across the grass. "That went the farthest yet."

"Yes, ma'am."

"Remember when I first met you?" she said. "I thought you were an alien from another world and I didn't know what you were gonna do to us."

"Still feel that way?"

"I still think you're from a different planet, but . . ." She placed another balloon in the curve of the slingshot. "Okay, fire!"

Later, we scrambled up the hill behind the cabin to collect firewood and halfway up, the brush became thick and blocked the trail. "We need a machete," Zack said.

"We can buy one at Home Depot," Gabriel said. "I saw one for nine dollars."

"But then we'd have to use it. Buying it's the easy part."

We carried the wood down and Zack and Gabriel built a fire of twigs and logs in the big steel barbecue drum. They held out their lighters at the same time and set the kindling ablaze. Zack said, "We're gonna let it burn a few hours, and then we'll have nice co . . . coal—" He began coughing, trying to stifle it with his fist, but each cough set off deeper spasms and more choking until he was crimson.

"Are you okay!" Gabriel said.

Zack nodded, waving us away. He leaned over and put his hands on his knees.

"It's because he smokes," Sophie said.

"I'm all right now." He took a few breaths. He straightened himself and asked the kids if they wanted to learn to drive the truck. "This is a private road so you don't need a license."

"I'm not driving that thing," Sophie said.

"It's a stick shift," Gabriel said.

"So? If you can drive a stick, you can drive anything."

"But I won't ever have a shift car," Gabriel said.

"I thought you wanted one of those racing jobs."

"I do."

"You gotta shift 'em."

"No, I went with my dad to test-drive a Porsche and they make them automatic."

Zack yanked open the door to the cab. "Climb in, cowboy."

He put Gabriel in front of him so he could steer and work the clutch. They went down the dirt road, turned the bend, and disappeared.

Sophie and I took a basket into the weedy garden that had been planted by previous tenants and picked tomatoes that were big as grapefruits. "I'm gonna make salad, and you can be my assistant," she said.

"All right."

As I rinsed the tomatoes, she sliced them into odd-shaped wedges and arranged them on a platter so they looked like the petals of a rose. Then she used wild mint we'd found to create leaves for the rose, and set the platter on the table. "Did you bring the camera?" she said.

"No. I'm sorry."

"Never mind. I'm gonna make place mats for everyone." She took out her watercolors and paper, settled herself on the deck, and started mixing colors to paint the Topanga hills.

I was struck by how spontaneous and unfettered Sophie was with her creative projects. Artwork seemed to pour out of her. She was constantly drawing, painting, working with clay, dancing, singing, baking, knitting.

Gabriel and Zack came driving up the road, Gabriel still wedged in front of Zack.

"How's it going?" I called.

Zack leaned out the window. "He's catchin' on real fast."

Gabriel yanked the wheel to turn the truck around and they headed back down the road, raising dust.

"Mom?"

"Yes."

"When you were my age, were you popular?"

I looked at Sophie, seemingly absorbed in spreading watery streaks of green on the paper. Her pale hair fell over the side of her face.

"No, I was always on the outside and I couldn't understand. Why were some girls popular and I wasn't? I didn't think they were any prettier or smarter than me. What was it?"

She started mixing shades of blue to paint the sky. "No one likes me at school. I don't fit in. Everyone's in groups and I don't belong in any group. I'm a nothing."

"That's a terrible feeling, but it's not true," I said.

"I don't really have any friends."

"What about Erin?"

"She's not a friend."

"She slept over last weekend."

Sophie put down her brush. "She's not inviting me to her birthday."

"Really?"

"She's going to Disneyland but she can only take three friends, so she's taking Megan, Chris, and Kate. They don't even talk to her that much, but she wants to be in their clique so she's inviting them and not me. And, like, I've invited her to everything! Every party I've had, every trip. At lunchtime, they were talking about it and I just had to sit there while they said, 'Oh, Sophie, too bad you can't come too.'"

Her narrow face puckered as she struggled to hold back tears. I put my arm around her; how I suffered with her. I knew girls were cruel at this age, gossiping, pecking, grouping and regrouping, trying to shore up a fragile sense of who they were by knocking down others. Their awakening feeling for boys was nothing—absolutely nothing—compared to the intensity of their relationships with other girls.

A few weeks earlier, Sophie had invited three friends to a

slumber party and all evening, when I walked past her room or brought them pizza, I'd hear them going at it:

"Did you see Annie dancing with Paul? She's so short, she barely comes to his waist."

"She wears those ugly shoes . . . "

"She was, like, throwing herself on him."

"Eeeoooh! She's such a slut." They burst out laughing.

"That's what she said about you."

"She said I'm a slut?"

"She said you dress like a slut. But don't tell her I said that!"

I cringed; I remembered nights in junior high when I would cry myself to sleep because A had told B something I'd said about her and B had turned against me. A had promised, sworn, she wouldn't tell anyone and then she'd told B, the very person she should never have told. So I'd called up B and insisted I'd never said those things, but she wouldn't believe me and she and A became best friends, cutting me.

"Listen, Sophie," I said as we sat on the deck in Topanga. "This is a phase. It happens to everyone at this age. It will pass."

She shook her head. "I'll never be popular. I know that now."

"Let me tell you something. People who aren't popular in school tend to be the ones who're most creative, who have special gifts. They're outsiders and later in life, their talents bloom. They make great contributions and have wonderful friends, while the kids who were popular often end up leading very dull, boring lives."

"Yeah? Like, who? Give me an example."

I thought of Mike Nichols, Kurt Vonnegut, Mary McCarthy, other luminaries who'd talked about being outcasts when young but their names wouldn't mean anything to Sophie. "Abraham

Lincoln. He was a loner when he was growing up—"

"They shot him!" Sophie said. "That's great, Mom."

I began to rub her back. "Yes, but people are still talking about him more than a hundred years later."

She wiped her eyes with her fists and I could see I was getting through. We heard the old truck rattling and chugging, drawing closer, and when it appeared, Gabriel was sitting by himself at the wheel and Zack was on the passenger side.

"Hi, Mom! Sophie!" His face was flushed.

"Gabriel!"

He put the truck in reverse and backed it up to turn around. It lurched and stalled. I could see Zack speaking to him quietly. Gabriel started it again and headed off, working the clutch, shifting and steering on the bumpy road.

It had happened so fast: he was driving a car. Sophie tore a new sheet from her pad and asked me to brush her hair while she painted. I sat behind her, running a brush through the strands of soft blonde hair as we watched the hills turn violet and magenta in the quiet hour before sunset.

"I feel so free," Sophie said. "I wish we could live here."

"So do I." The boys were driving and the cooking fire was burning and there was the comforting, cheering smell of wood smoke and I remember thinking, This is as good as life gets.

On Monday, I went down to the set to write some extra dialogue needed for a scene. Zack was riding by the saloon and when I waved, he beckoned me over. I walked toward him as Marv called through the bullhorn: "Lunch, for thirty minutes!" The cast and crew stopped what they were doing and hurried to the food pavilion. Zack stepped off his horse, looked straight at McCoy, and dropped his reins in the dirt.

"Valet!" he called.

Then he took my arm and marched me toward the lunch line, while McCoy scrambled to pick up the reins from the dirt before the horse trotted off or got tied up in electrical cables.

"You want him to kill you?" I said to Zack.

"No, ma'am. I'm showing him I'm crazier than he is."

At the food wagon, we picked up trays and utensils. A chalkboard listed the choices of the day: baked pork chops; orange roughy; chicken Kiev. Alfredo, the head cook, retrieved a plain chicken breast and steamed vegetables he'd put aside for me. Zack asked for pork chops and potatoes.

We carried our trays to the first long picnic table. There was an unspoken seating code in the pavilion. The "above-the-line" people—actors, writers, producers, and directors—had the table closest to the food. Behind them, at the second table, were the camera and sound crews, and behind them were the makeup, hair, and wardrobe people. Across the aisle were the editors, the art department, the construction and transportation crews. The wranglers took a table near the grass, and at the far back of the pavilion were the extras.

Zack slid in between me and Josef and across from Beth, who greeted him, as she always did, with an exuberant hug. All the crew members had to walk past us to get to their tables. McCoy gave Zack a black look, then forced a smile and tipped his Stetson to me.

"What time you going home?" Zack asked.

"Early, I hope. Why?"

"I could use a lift."

"What happened to Willie?"

He took a pack of Kools from his pocket and held it out. "I went to the remuda about an hour ago to get these, and found the two back tires dead flat."

"You don't think—"

He silenced me with a stare. "Somebody stuck a knife right through the sides of the tires, so they can't be repaired. I'm gonna have to find me two new ones." He glanced up and down the pavilion. " 'Course, no one knows anything about it."

"I'm sorry."

"It ain't the first set of tires I've lost."

"They're jealous. This is their whole world and it's not yours."

"They won't let me forget it."

"And you sit with us."

He took a bite of pork and put his fork down. "I've crossed the line. I don't belong here and I don't belong there."

"I'll get you tires . . . "

"I don't want to cause you trouble, Sara."

"I can handle this, if you want to stick it out." But I was sick with concern. Would the harassment stop eventually, or would it escalate? If necessary, I could enlist Beth's help but I was reluctant to do that because it would make the wranglers more resentful. Zack was out in the trenches on his own.

11

I saw the smoke and heard the siren, but I was preoccupied and didn't really take notice until I turned onto my street. A fire engine was parked in front of my driveway. Black smoke was billowing up from the side of the house. The kids! Sophie was at dance class but Gabriel had brought his friend Jason home. Were they in the rehearsal shed? Had there been some electrical short? Firemen in black slickers were feeding hose up the driveway into the yard. I jumped out of my car and went running toward them. "Is anyone hurt? What's happened?"

"This your house, ma'am?"

"Yes."

"No one's hurt, it's under control. It's just the fence between your yard and your neighbor's—it caught fire."

"The fence? But . . . how?"

"We're not sure. Might've been your neighbor's pool heater, or a leak in the gas line. We checked his house but no one's home."

"He works downtown. So does his wife."

I hurried up the driveway to the yard, where two firemen were blasting water on the fence and in seconds, the flames were gone, leaving nothing but steam and blackened wood. Ashes and cinders covered the driveway and lawn.

Veronica was standing by the side of the yard, her shoulders shaking. "Mrs. Sara," she said, "is terrible."

"It's all right now, it's over." I put my arm around her and comforted her. "Where's Gabriel?"

"In his room. *Arriba*."

I looked up and saw Gabriel and Jason standing at the window. I took a deep breath and exhaled. Thank God.

"Gabriel . . ." Veronica started speaking rapidly in a choked voice in Spanish, but I couldn't understand her. I was exhausted, impatient. This had come at the end of a day in which Zack's tires had been slashed, I'd had an hour-long battle with a network executive who wanted to kill a script, and I'd been stalled in traffic on the Pacific Coast Highway because of a three-car accident. "What? What about Gabriel?"

"You no believe me."

"I don't understand you."

She covered her face with her hands.

Gabriel and Jason came trooping out the back door into the yard. "Is it out now, completely?" Gabriel said.

"Yes. Did you see how it started?"

Jason gave me a wide-eyed look and shook his head.

"We were out front," Gabriel said.

"You tell your mommy," Veronica blurted.

I looked at Gabriel. "Tell me what?"

"I have no clue."

Veronica hurried inside and went to her room. I knew from

experience that it was pointless to follow—I'd have to wait until she calmed down.

"Did anyone get hurt?" Gabriel said.

"No."

"Did the house . . . did anything else catch fire?"

"Apparently not. Just the fence."

"That's good."

"Were you guys really scared?"

They answered as if to say, Are you joking? "Yeah."

"I'm sorry I wasn't here. But I promise, we're going to find out how this started and make sure it doesn't happen again. All right?"

They nodded.

I walked upstairs to my study and called my neighbor, who said he'd drive home right away and help investigate. I called my insurance agent and left a message. I started to call the handyman about repairing the fence when Gabriel walked in, holding a shoe box out in front of him. "Here!" he said. I took the box, looked inside, and saw his incendiary collection: the Champion lighter, cylinders of butane, matches, incense, and a barbecue fire starter he'd bought at the supermarket. "Throw them away. I don't want them."

My stomach lurched. "Gabriel . . . "

He shook his head and put his hands to his chest.

"Tell me what happened."

"I can't."

"Just tell me the truth. If you keep it inside, it'll hurt more. If you let me know, I can help you."

He said, with much hesitation, that he and Jason had been fooling around and wanted to see if they could build a volcano that spouted real flames.

"A volcano? But why?"

"I don't know. We just got the idea. We thought, maybe for the science fair or something." He said they'd taken an old toy tepee that was about a foot high, covered it with clay, and set a dish in the bottom of the tepee which they'd filled with butane. They fashioned a wick out of string and set it in the dish. They thought that if they lit the wick, the fire would rise up through the top of the tepee and sputter out quickly. But they'd poured on too much butane. The fire shot up into the air, raining sparks onto the driveway where a slick of oil that had leaked from my car caught fire. Before they could run for water, the redwood fence went up in flames.

"We tried to get the hose and put it out, but we couldn't find it," Gabriel said. The gardeners had moved the hose around to the front patio. They yelled, "Help!" Veronica, seeing the flames, called 911—a drill we'd rehearsed numerous times. The boys ran out to the street, where they cowered behind a hedge until the fire truck arrived.

"Why didn't you tell the firemen what happened?" I asked.

"We were scared. It was an accident. I swear. Please, you've got to believe me."

"I do believe you, but you should have had water ready nearby. You should have asked an adult to supervise this. Fire's not something you fool around with. Zack told you that."

"I know. I'm sorry. I'm really really sorry. Please don't tell Dad."

"I can't agree to that."

"All right. Just don't tell him now. Please, can you wait till next week? He was gonna buy me a bow and arrow this weekend—you know how long I've wanted one—and I'm afraid he won't."

"That may be a consequence."

He started to cry.

"Gabriel, I want you to tell your father yourself. And we have to go talk to the firemen."

He looked stricken, and shook his head.

"I'll go with you."

"But . . . will they put me in jail? Me and Jason?"

I took hold of his shoulders. "That's not going to happen. You're very lucky—no one was hurt. The damage can be repaired. But you're going to have to face up to what you did and pay the price. So will Jason."

"I'll pay! I'll give up my allowance for the rest of my life if I have to, but I'm not going down there."

That night Zack and I went to Jeff's for an interaction we'd come to dread—the summit meeting. We called these meetings when we had to discuss a problem with the children. At first it had been just Jeff and me, but then he'd started bringing Rose because she was living with him and involved with the kids. Zack had said he didn't want me going alone, he'd better come also.

We met at Jeff's, a high-tech house built of glass and steel with minimalist furniture that did not invite you to lounge. Jeff and Rose sat on one side of a six-foot-long glass table and Zack and I sat on the other side, in chairs made of black leather and chrome.

"What I want to know is, where'd he get the stuff to start the fire?" Jeff said. "Where'd he get butane?"

I started to explain but Zack cut me off. "I gave him the lighter." There was silence. "And I bought the butane with him, but it was *only* to be used inside the lighter, as fuel."

Jeff narrowed his eyes. "That was totally irresponsible."

"Listen, Jeff," I said, "if Gabriel wanted to start a fire, he didn't need Zack's lighter. Our house is full of matches."

"But this was in his pocket!" Jeff said.

Rose nodded. "Way too tempting."

"He's eleven, not five," Zack said. "I thought if I treated him like a man, he'd act thataway."

Jeff flinched at "thataway."

"This could have happened anywhere," I said. "The point is, what do we do now—"

"But it didn't happen anywhere. It happened at your house. It's the same old problem—you coddle them and they think they can get away with anything. I want them to live with me."

I went rigid.

"When you're away and I have them for a week or longer, I can make real progress. They act more polite, they behave more responsibly."

Fear was shooting through me. When Jeff said he wanted something, I immediately felt defensive and terrified he would get it. Zack shifted in his chair.

"It's clearly in their interest," Jeff said. "They need more structure and discipline."

"I don't agree," I said. "Sophie still isn't comfortable at your place—"

"Because she doesn't spend enough time here. And Gabriel absolutely needs to live with me. He needs a strong father in the house."

"Wait," Rose said, leaning toward Jeff. "We haven't discussed this."

"We're discussing it now."

"Jeffrey." She smiled and exaggerated her pronunciation. "If Gabriel lived here *all the time*—"

"He's my son."

"Of course, I understand. But he's rude to me, and you already spend more time with him than most of the dads I know."

"I want him under my roof," Jeff said.

Rose wasn't smiling now, and for once I was glad she was at the table. "That's a deal point I'm not sure I can accept."

"This is not a negotiation. These are my children."

"Let's not make any drastic changes," I said. "Gabriel showed poor judgment and was irresponsible, but he wasn't malicious. And he's going to have consequences. He's going to pay for repairing the fence, and he and Jason have to clean up the yard by themselves."

"It's gonna take quite a while," Zack said. "He's gonna learn something."

Jeff set his mouth and shook his head.

Two days later, I drove Gabriel and Jason out to a burn foundation in the valley where the director, a stately, silver-haired woman, had created a program for "juvenile fire starters." She sat the boys down in a conference room and told them a lighted match was more deadly than a loaded gun. "A bullet can kill only one person, but a single match can start a fire that kills hundreds, and it can't be controlled." She showed them blown-up photos of young people who'd been scarred and disfigured in fires. Gabriel and Jason folded their arms across their chests.

She explained how a third-degree burn destroys the deepest layer of skin, which houses the nerves, oil, and sweat glands. "Once it's destroyed, the skin can't ever grow back, and you won't survive unless something is done quickly," she said. The doctors first have to cut away all the dead, burned skin. "It's the most excruciating thing you could ever have to live through." Then the doctors attach a temporary skin—from a pig or a cadaver. A few days later, they start the long process of grafting: they shave a small piece of good skin from another area of the body, stretch it and put it through a meshing machine, and attach it to the raw flesh.

I felt nauseated, I wanted to double over as she described how the raw flesh is sanded so it will bleed and the red corpuscles will "grab onto the graft." The boys had unfolded their arms and were slumped in their chairs, staring at the director. She brought out a photo of a teenage boy wearing a "pressure garment," which made him look like the man in the iron mask: only his eyes, nostrils, and mouth poked through. She said the garment is like a heavy elastic bandage and must be worn after surgery so the grafted skin won't shrink and the scar tissue won't spread with ugly tendrils all over the body. The burn victim must live in the pressure garment for a year and a half.

If the burn victim is young, she said, he'll have many more surgeries as he gets older because the grafted skin won't grow. "He might have a hundred surgeries by the time he's twenty-one." She said the doctors can't replace features that burn. "If you lose your lips, you'll have a slit in your face the rest of your life."

The boys were visibly shaken as we walked out of the burn

center. I resolved to buy collapsible ladders for the upstairs bedrooms in our house so that in case of a fire, we'd have a means of escape. But days passed and I didn't get around to buying the ladders.

I had a difficult week at the ranch. A freelance writer we'd hired to do a special episode turned in the first act and nothing more because he'd been offered a job on a new series and didn't have time to finish our script. So we were thrown, once again, into crisis mode.

Josef and I holed up in the trailer all week and I didn't go down to the set. On Friday, I walked to the pavilion for lunch and scanned the tables for Zack, but he wasn't sitting with the extras or the wranglers. I asked Mike Riggins where he was.

"Didn't need him today."

I glanced down the table. Half a dozen riding extras were in costume, eating ice cream.

"We had a short call, so I'm spreading the work around," Mike said. "Everybody's gotta stay home a few days."

McCoy added, "Zack don't need to work. He's got you!" The whole table broke up.

When I drove home that night, I was determined that with every mile, I would put the conflicts and toxins of the ranch behind me so I could have a pleasant weekend with the children and Zack. On Friday nights, we celebrated Shabbat and I always asked Veronica to make a special meal—roast turkey breast with cranberries and mashed potatoes—and then I'd fix a Caesar salad. Zack would stop at Polly's and pick up a banberry pie: vanilla custard with bananas on the bottom and strawberries and whipped cream on top.

We gathered at the table and Sophie lit the candles, singing the prayer. She had a sweet, compelling voice, but the sight of the match set off a nervous association. Gabriel said the blessing over the wine, using grape soda, and we tore off pieces of challah and thanked God for causing grain to grow from the earth. As we passed the bowls of food, we discussed what we'd do the rest of the evening. Gabriel wanted to go see *The Crow*. "That'd be fine," Zack said, but Sophie said she was tired, it was too late for a movie. She wanted to play Monopoly.

"I hate Monopoly," Gabriel said.

I suggested we rent videos. Sophie agreed but Gabriel started ranting that we always did what Sophie wanted, never what he wanted. I told him this was my suggestion, a compromise.

"Sophie gets treated like a goddess and I get treated like crap."

"Don't talk like that. You won't rent a movie."

"Sor-ry," he said with sarcasm. "Sor-ry!"

We were driving home from the video store and Sophie was sitting in front. She reached over to change the radio station.

"Sophie, take your feet off the dashboard."

"In a minute."

"Now."

"Okay!" She jerked her feet down.

"I've told you this twenty times."

"I know, I know."

"Look. You left mud prints."

She swiped at the mud with her hand. "So? You care more

about your car than you do about me." She twisted in her seat to face Gabriel in back. "Stop kicking!"

I saw his leg hit the seat from the corner of my eye. "Gabriel, don't."

"What? I wasn't doing anything. You always listen to her. You never listen to me."

Sophie unwrapped a stick of gum and threw the paper on the floor. "Put your gum wrapper in the garbage bag. Not on the floor," I said.

"All right. All right!"

"It's not all right!" I was screaming as I hit the garage-door opener.

"You're a terrible mom," Sophie said. "All you do is yell at me. I'd rather have a rock for a mom than you. A rock would raise me better."

Zack was standing at the refrigerator, talking to Veronica, when I slammed into the house and told the kids to go to their rooms.

"No, Mom," Sophie said.

"Why? I didn't do anything!" Gabriel protested.

I yanked the videos from their hands. "Go up to your rooms right now or I'll get in my car and drive away. The hell with you."

They tramped up the stairs, Gabriel muttering that I was the strictest mom of anyone in school. "My mom is crazy. She's a lunatic."

Zack and Veronica exchanged a look. Zack had sensed, very early in his visits, how important Veronica was—what a vital link in the household. He took an interest in her, teased her. In the morning, they were usually the first ones up and drank coffee together in the breakfast nook. I'd hear Veronica giggling and being girlish in a way she never acted with anyone else. She told me, "I don't think you could find a better man."

Veronica excused herself to go watch her *novela*, a soap opera that ran every night on the Spanish-language station. Zack said, "I'm gonna go outside for a minute." He took the cigarette pack from his pocket and walked out into the shadows.

I banged around the kitchen, putting leftovers away and pouring myself a shot of T.Q. Hot tequila. Zack came back inside, gave me a hug, and nudged my face with his, trying to make me meet his lips.

"Mom!" Gabriel yelled.

I kissed Zack on the mouth.

"Mom!"

"Leave him be," Zack said.

"I'm bleeding!"

I broke away and hurried up the stairs. Gabriel was standing just inside the door of his bedroom. Blood was streaming down his right arm, his hand, his T-shirt.

I gasped, "What happened?" I took hold of his arm, looking for the cut.

I looked at his face. He smirked. "Nosebleed."

I dropped his arm. "Lie down. I'll get Kleenex . . . "

"I don't need your help."

"Then why'd you call me?"

"Because I want you to have a heart attack and die."

I walked to the bedroom where Zack was waiting and sank into the overstuffed chair. I wanted to lie down in the street and let the cars run over me. My children were setting fires, swearing, bleeding, running amok. They were uncivilized hellions. I was a failure. Jeff was asking for custody and I'd probably have to hire a lawyer and go to court and it was not going to look good. "They'll be sent to live with their dad," I said.

"Let 'em go," Zack said, "it might be the best thing for everyone. Let 'em see what it's like over there. And Jeff and Rose will get a bellyful and before you know it, they'll be back . . . "

Shut up, shut up. I wanted to scream, I'm losing my children!

There was banging on the door. Zack went to open it and I heard Gabriel say, "Where's Mom?"

"Busy."

"Sophie's destroying my room."

"Let's go see about it. You and me."

He and Gabriel walked down the hall and I went to the doorway and stopped. I could hear the children yelling about who'd done what first and who was at fault.

Zack said, "Sophie, you got no business barging into his room and messing with his things, and Gabriel, you got no business taking her CDMan from her. Let me have it."

After a moment, I heard Sophie say, "But it's mine."

"I'm gonna hold on to it until you both settle down and start acting like decent people."

"You can't do that," Sophie said. "I'm telling my dad."

"Go ahead. I want to talk to your dad about you. You're twelve but you act like a two-year-old." His voice was threatening. "Now stay in your rooms and quit bothering each other. If there's more trouble, I'll be back. And next time, I won't be this nice."

He walked back to the bedroom and stood staring at me. "I never did that before."

"I'm glad you did."

He started pacing. "Part of this is my fault. If I wasn't around, things wouldn't be so tough for them."

"I don't know about that," I said. I was not going to give up my private life and be celibate until they grew up. Some man would be here, getting what they wanted—my attention.

Zack sat down and took my hands. "Up until now, I haven't told you how I think you oughta raise your kids because I did a poor job with my own. I was way too strict. I choked each one of 'em at some point."

"Choked them?"

He nodded. "I kept my hands around their throats until they were about to black out and then I let go. They sat there and thought about it a good long time. I only had to do it once."

"You couldn't do that now. You'd get reported."

"They could have reported me then, but they knew better. What you don't realize is, you've got all the power. You just don't use it. You take away with one hand and give back with the other." I looked at him. "You told Gabriel he couldn't rent a video and then he rented one."

I was stung; it was true. I couldn't stand for the kids to feel disappointed or pained, for evenings to be ruined, for someone to get left at home when I'd bought tickets for a play. I gave them second chances. Third. When I did deliver a punishment, I agonized. I hated saying no to them and it wasn't just me, it was the single most common failure of baby boomers who were parents. We'd rebelled against rules, authority, the Establishment, and we didn't like ruling over our children. We wanted them to trust and admire us, to enjoy hanging out with us, to feel the opposite of what we'd felt for our own parents.

"Your kids are asking you to draw the wagons around 'em,"

Zack said. "Your daughter told you she wants a rock for a mother."

I nodded.

"If you want me to, I could help you get those kids in line."

"Would you?"

"Are you sure?"

I nodded. "Please."

He pursed his lips, pulled the curtains closed, and turned on the lamp he'd made from his old green boots. "Here's the plan. We're gonna sit 'em down and tell 'em that family's a two-way deal. I want you to make a list of all the things you do for them—driving them to school, taking them to soccer games, dance classes, buying them clothes—hell, you don't even think about half the stuff you do and they sure as hell don't. This is gonna bring it to their attention."

Okay, I thought, I could make lists.

"Then make a list of what you want them to do. Spell it all out and we'll put it on the refrigerator so they can't say they didn't know about it. Then we tell 'em: If they do their part, you're gonna do yours. If they don't, they get nothing from you. No rides to school. No dance lessons. No television or computer. No meals cooked for 'em or laundry done. No allowance. For a month."

"A month!"

Zack raised his hands.

"A week maybe," I said.

"If you do it for a week, you'll have to do it again because they're tougher than you. They can tolerate anything for a week. If you do it for a month, you won't have to do it again."

"What about school?"

"Let 'em ride their bikes or walk."

"It's a long way."

"Good. Let 'em start appreciating what they're taking for granted."

We sat down the next morning at the round kitchen table with the kids and Veronica. Sophie scooted her chair as far from Zack as she could. I'd printed out copies of the list I'd made of specific requirements: "Be respectful and courteous. Say hello when you come in the house and good-bye when you leave. Do your homework before watching TV. Clean up after eating." We were not asking them to get up at four and milk cows.

I read the list aloud and then gave them the list of their privileges: meals, rides, lessons, movies, computer games. Sophie began acting like a diligent student, raising her hand, asking what would happen if she did A but not B, would she still lose C and D? Gabriel cried and pounded his head on the table. "You're taking away my freedom. I'll have to wear a mask."

"Gabriel," I said, "These are not difficult things. Be courteous—"

"What if I'm in a bad mood?"

"You still have to be courteous."

"What if I forget one time? I lose everything."

"No, you'll get a warning. We want you to succeed. People make mistakes, and if you correct the infraction, there won't be a punishment."

Gabriel crumpled up the lists and threw them on the floor. "This is Zack's fault! I hate Zack!"

◆

Things were relatively quiet the rest of the weekend and on Sunday, we decided to go out for dinner and watch the sunset at Gladstone's 4 Fish. As we drove down Channel Road to the beach, Sophie blew her nose into a Kleenex, balled it up, and threw it at Zack. Gabriel burst out laughing. I turned around in my seat. "Hey!"

"I was throwing it out the window," Sophie said.

"She missed," Gabriel said.

Zack pulled over and stopped. "It's dangerous and you know better. We could've had a wreck."

"Sorry," Sophie said.

He started driving again. I heard the kids giggling and Gabriel whispering to Sophie. Then a marking pen went flying toward Zack's head. He screeched to a stop.

"It slipped out of my hand," Sophie said, trying not to laugh. "I was drawing and it just—"

"It just flew up," Gabriel said.

"We're not gonna buy you dinner, we're going home," Zack said.

"You don't buy anyway," Sophie said. "Mom does." Gabriel cracked up.

"You two can walk home," I said.

"Chill, Mom," Gabriel said.

"Get out of the car."

"No. Come on."

I stepped out of the car and went to open the back door but Gabriel pushed the lock down. I asked them two more times to get out. "If you don't get out, I'm going to suspend all your privileges for one week. Get out now."

They didn't move.

"You lost your privileges."

Zack stepped outside, opened the back door with his key, and reached in for Gabriel's arm.

"Don't touch me—that's child abuse."

"No, sir. I'm helping you out of the car because you won't get out on your own." He picked up the cell phone and thrust it at Gabriel. "Call the cops—call nine-one-one—let 'em come out here and tell you where they send kids who won't mind their parents."

Gabriel slid out of the car, followed by Sophie, and they huddled on the sidewalk. Zack and I got back inside. He started the motor and leaned out the window. "Go on—walk ahead of us."

Gabriel shook his head.

Zack looked at me. "It's about a mile to the house. It's not gonna kill 'em."

"What if they don't move?"

"They will." He switched on a Clint Black tape. "Sara, we've got to make them do this or we lose all ground."

I looked down in my lap. Gabriel was stubborn, he'd sleep on the sidewalk to make a point. Zack leaned over, took my face in his hands, and started kissing me. When we pulled apart, the children were plodding up the street, their heads down, like reluctant cattle.

We followed them, pulling over frequently, and when we returned to the house, I ordered dinner from Louise's for Zack and me and we ate by ourselves in the garden. Gabriel made popcorn. Sophie put a box of frozen macaroni and cheese in the microwave. I unplugged the TV and computer and told the kids they wouldn't be using them for a week.

Sophie cried, she said she was missing *The Simpsons*, all her favorite shows. "I'm sorry I threw things in the car. I already walked home, and I'm really sorry. I won't do it again. Please," she begged, "a week is so long."

I felt the impulse to relent, to reduce the sentence from a week to a day. Maybe I'd lowered the boom too quickly in the heat of the moment. "The decision stands," I said.

On Monday morning, the kids walked through the house in hostile silence, peering at me as if from the back of their skulls. They strapped on helmets and set off on their bikes for school. I stood in the driveway, watching them ride away. I was supposed to be writing at home but I couldn't concentrate. Zack said, "Let's drive up to Topanga."

It was a crisp October day and the leaves on the sycamore trees had turned yellow and were falling. We walked into the cabin and opened the doors to the deck. A breeze ruffled the rawhide strings that were dangling above Zack's table. He showed me the piece he'd been working on. It was a miniature bridle, and he'd just attached a tiny silver bit that had Lilliputian roses engraved on its sides. The rawhide, in its crude state, seemed a base match for the silver—the sow's ear to the silk purse—but when cut and braided finely, the blond cords brought out the detail and luster of the silver, which in turn cast its gleams back on the slender cords.

"I like it. Your fingers are so muscular and they do this delicate work."

"There's a lot of money in miniatures, I just can't figure out how to get hold of it."

"What about that show in Sun Valley?"

He shook his head. "I don't think they'd go for this."

"Why not?"

"It's not a serious piece, I'm just tinkering."

"It's beautiful, it's intricate, and it's something people could display in an office or at home. Send it to them."

"You really think I should?"

"Absolutely. What's the worst that could happen? It won't sell."

"Yeah, I'm real good at handling that."

He motioned me to the bed and had me lie down. He rubbed my neck, my jaws, which were sore from being clenched, and I was worrying about the children, had they made it to school all right? Would the new regime work and would I have the stamina for it? And then I was aware of Zack's lips moving down my spine to the small of my back.

We made love for hours and held each other and something began to shift, the scales were being reset. It seemed as if we were not merely touching skin and nerves but deeper places. We found our way beyond the children and the wranglers and the fires and summit meetings to a different realm, a private reserve where time was suspended and we were free, as Zack put it, "to frolic." In this realm, all was lush, mysterious, dappled with the light that shines through trees after a sudden spring rain. We lay silently with our chests pressed together, feeling the breath move in and out, and there was an exchange between his skin and mine, his ribs and mine, his heart and mine that filled our dry cells and made us whole.

In this realm, he was not a foreign being. I didn't see our union as strange or absurd. We were home, in protected waters, where the sun was warm and the sky was blue. This was a place I couldn't reach with anyone else, and I realized I'd come to crave it almost more than I craved the sexual bliss.

"This is the only time I'm really at peace," I said quietly.

He smiled. "You're my angel. My wild little angel."

12

Ah, but that peace, that heartfelt gratitude, that inrush of love for the world and its creatures is as hard to hold as a soap bubble. When we were alone in bed, Zack joked that we should make up bumper stickers, "Oneness Through Sex," but when we put on our clothes and drove off in the rusty red truck and the Mercedes wagon, we knew the bumper stickers would look, as we did, merely odd. Whatever existed between us did not carry into the world. At six in the morning, Zack was checking his saddle and facing down McCoy and I was steeling myself for the children's rage and pleas for leniency. I watched them slam the kitchen cabinets as they fixed their own lunches and then strapped on thirty-pound book bags and wobbled on their bikes toward school.

When they rode off, however, they called, "Good-bye, Mom," without prompting—something I'd been asking them to do for a year. As the week wore on, they became more resourceful. They washed their own clothes, they walked or rode their bikes to the library and to friends' houses, but Sophie had to miss all her dance classes because the studio was too far. She was worried that the other girls would move ahead of her. She broke down and cried that she was under so much stress—trying to do well in school, keep up her dancing, and take honors assignments that gave her hours of extra work. "And I've got all this pressure at home—two houses, two parents who've both got a boyfriend or girlfriend I'm forced to get along with." She cried so hard that her eyes turned red and I was bleeding inside.

At the ranch, we had a production meeting for a script about a female outlaw. When I walked into the conference room, the department heads were already seated at the large, oval table. I took my place beside the director. The first AD, Frank Martinez, opened a three-ring binder with the script inside. "Let's get started," Frank said. "Scene one. We're outside the saloon and Sully sees a stranger untie the horses and start rustling them out of town."

The costume designer raised her hand. "You want the outlaw dressed so we can't tell she's a woman, right?"

"Right," I said.

"What about her hair? Should we cut it short?"

"No, let's give her some kind of hat so she can tuck it up."

"How many horses are we talking about?" Vince Barsocchini said. He was the line producer and we called him "Mr. No."

"Ten," I said.

Vince shook his head. "Can't do it. Four."

"That won't make the statement we want. This girl is audacious."

"We gotta cut back on extras and stock," Vince said.

"Then let's do eight," I said. "This is the teaser and we want to start bold. We'll make cuts later."

Vince frowned. I glanced at Mike Riggins, sitting at the far end of the table. Every horse meant cash in his pocket and I'd just doubled his take.

"Scene two. Inside the general store . . . "

We moved on through the script, scene by scene, and when we'd finished, I followed Mike out the door. We started walking down the road toward the Western town.

"What's happening with Zack?" I said.

Mike looked at me sideways. "He's not much of a rider."

I startled. I thought Zack's riding ability was above question.

"But he's better than some. So it's not too bad."

"Is that why he's not working today?"

Mike gave his flinty smile. "Maybe he doesn't kiss enough ass." I stared at him. "A lot of these riders come out to my place on the weekends and work on my fences and things."

He took out a pack of Camels. "If Zack's with you, he'll work. If not . . ." He struck a match and lit a cigarette.

"He *is* with me," I said, "and let's get something straight. I'm the best friend you've got in that trailer, Mike, and you need a friend. I appreciate your giving Zack the job—I didn't ask for that—but now that he's here, I'm sure you'll find a way to keep him working." I turned and walked back to the trailer.

It was after ten when I heard Zack's boots coming down the hall to my bedroom. I'd fallen asleep in the overstuffed chair with a script in my hands. He flopped down in the opposite chair, his eyes slightly bloodshot. "Hello, baby."

"I tried calling you."

"Oh, I was out."

"Where?"

He gave a lopsided smile. "I went up to that bar by County Line." He leaned over to kiss me and there was the loamy smell of beer. "You look so sweet and pretty."

"Have a good time?"

He tipped his head from side to side. "Tolerable."

"I talked to Mike."

"Did you."

I'd debated whether to repeat the conversation to him and decided I'd better. He should know, and there was no point in waiting. As I'd feared, he went into a rage. "I ain't going back there because if I do, I'll punch that sucker out." He walked over to the window and jammed his boot up on the bench. "I trained my own horses for twenty years and I got 'em to work for me every day, twelve hours a day. I'd like to see Mike do that. He wouldn't last ten minutes at Red River."

"He's full of shit. But why is he doing this?"

Zack wheeled around. "He's like one of those bosses on the waterfront. You work. You don't. Kiss my ass."

"But I'm his biggest ally. I'm the one who fights for more horses and wagons. Last season, he was an inch away from being fired and I helped save his operation."

"He doesn't own me. He owns all the others."

I considered this. "Well, let's not forget, he's the one who brought you here."

"Yeah."

"Your call time Monday is six-eighteen."

Zack walked back to the chair and sat down. "I hate being a burden to you."

"You're not. I'm sorry you have to go through this."

He coughed. "There's something else."

I looked at him. He seemed to be fishing for words, pulling them up, hefting them and tossing them back. He stared at the floral throw rug, on which was woven a tree of life with plumed birds resting on its branches. "I'm sorta behind with my bills, and the rent's due. I was wondering . . . you think you could loan me some money?"

"How much?"

He fidgeted. "A thousand."

My mouth dropped. He only had to come up with two hundred for the rent, I was paying the rest.

"I had to get the transmission fixed on my truck. And I haven't been working that steady, as you know. I'll pay you back in a few weeks."

"A thousand."

"I know the tally's running up."

"Zack, what I've given you before was a gift, and I was happy to give it. But let's not talk about loans because we both know there's no chance of your paying them back."

"I had some bad luck. All right?"

"Luck?"

One of the neighbor's dogs, a basset hound, began to howl from his outdoor kennel. "You don't have to concern yourself with it," Zack said.

Had there been an accident, an emergency with his kids?

He picked up a vase that was sitting on the table and turned it in his hands. "McCoy and a lot of the guys from the set were at the bar. McCoy was all puffed up about some horse he'd bought, he said nobody could beat it. But Cal, you know, that young kid? He's won every race he's ever been in. Before we knew it, we were all driving out to Simi Valley, we were flying high and the pot had gotten quite large."

"No."

"Everybody was drunk. We were out in the dark with the headlights on from the trucks, having us a match race. It seemed like a sure thing. I had two hundred bucks. I figured I could double it. And I liked the idea of taking money from McCoy." He tapped his boot on the floor. "It just didn't work out thataway."

I put my face in my hands.

He leaned forward. "Baby, I try to take good care of you. I'd give my life for you. But I'm no good at bills. I'll pay 'em, but they're gonna be overdue."

He put his hand on my jeans, running his fingers up my thigh, but I moved his hand away.

"I'm sorry," I said, "you gamble money you can't afford to lose and then ask me to bail you out?"

His face went tight. "Never mind. Forget it. Sorry I asked." He pulled back in the chair. "I thought we were partners but I guess I was wrong about that."

"We are partners, but I'd like you to be able to at least take care of yourself."

"Why don't you go run off with Josef? Get it done with."

"What? What are you talking about."

"I know what's going on. I watch you with him."

I had the impulse to laugh. "We're friends. We work together."

"He's the man you oughta be with. Get yourself a better boy-friend."

The intercom buzzed and Sophie's voice came crackling into the room. "Mom, could you please put me to bed?"

"In a few minutes." I looked at Zack.

"Go ahead. This ain't a good time, but it rarely is. When you call my house, Sara, I could be having brain surgery and

I'll talk to you. But when I call here, I've got to make an appointment. There's only certain hours I can call, certain nights I can be here."

"Mom! When're you coming?"

I went to the phone and pressed the intercom. "I'm talking to Zack. Brush your teeth and put on your nightgown. I'll look in on you later." I turned to him. "I spend more time with you than with anybody else except my children."

"You see me when it suits you, and when it doesn't, I get sent to the bench. Well I'm sick of being sent to the bench. I didn't come all this way to sit on the bench. I've given you everything I have and you give me—"

"Nothing? Is that what you think?"

"If you want to cut to the bottom line, yes."

"I've given you a lot!"

"I'm not talking about money."

"Neither am I."

"I'm tired of being the entertainment! I'm tired of being some kind of plaything, a sex toy. You call me up when you want to be amused, like you're sending out for pizza and when you don't, never mind. I'm eating in tonight."

"That's not true. I've brought you into the place I work, into my home, my family. I've put myself on the line."

He picked up the Stetson from the table and set it purposefully on his head.

"Zack."

"You know how much I miss my son? My friends? I miss . . . God, I miss being able to ride out in the desert and get lost."

"I know it's been hard. You pulled up your roots. You had to make a much bigger sacrifice than I did."

"We both sacrificed what we could afford." He rose to his feet and stared at me. "It just turns out that I could afford a lot more than you."

So I brooded. Should I give him the thousand dollars or let him dig himself out? This was a hot fuse, an inflamed nerve, because I'm not someone who's free with money and I don't like this in myself. I count pennies, I check the bill in restaurants. When I was young and used to read comic books, I identified with Scrooge McDuck. I could see myself hugging that gold. I worry that I don't have enough in the bank or if I do, it will run out and then I won't have enough. I don't like to buy things. Shopping, for me, is not therapeutic, it's painful, and I trace this directly to the way my mother taught me to shop. When we set out to buy a dress for my graduation from grammar school, I fell in love with a pale lavender organza with a purple sash. I felt ravishing and powerful in that dress, but it cost about a third more than the other dresses we'd looked at. So we drove from store to store, working our way from one end of the city to the other, checking prices and comparing because, to my mother, it was a sin to buy something merely because you loved it, you had to be getting a deal (preferably discounted or on sale). If a garment was too expensive, we wrote down the manufacturer and style number and my mother called around to see if she could get it wholesale, but she struck out with the lavender dress. We ended up buying a white skirt and sweater that was half the cost and, my mother assured me, just as beautiful, but it wasn't. At my graduation dance, there was a shadow self who haunted me, shimmering in the lavender dress.

I have friends who're generous and easy with funds. Jodie, with whom I'd gone hiking in Colorado with our sons, is always the first to pick up the bill, to open her checkbook and make hefty contributions to charity or give needy friends money that she doesn't expect them to pay back. I wished I were like that but I wasn't. So my first assumption, after the clash with Zack, was that I was being—as was my vestigial proclivity—stingy. I had the money and he needed it, and he was exceedingly giving with his time, his care. Men support their partners, I told myself, why shouldn't women, particularly when they earn decent sums? I could see the rationale, but the prospect made me profoundly uncomfortable. He was forty years old, his children were grown, why couldn't he stand on his own? I'd paid for him to join SAG, I'd subsidized his rent, picked up the tab for our meals and entertainment and trips. Why wasn't he able to cover his basic expenses?

And what did it say about me, that I couldn't link myself with a man from my own social and economic stratum, I had to pull someone in from the fringe? Zack had told me once that he was three paychecks away from being homeless. He had no net—no savings, no insurance. When money came in, he bought Dom Perignon and ordered custom boots and sent presents to his children and bought silver for his rawhide pieces, but he had no concept of planning for upcoming bills. The young PAs at the set didn't earn any more than Zack, but they had credit cards, they had insurance on their cars, they went to the dentist for regular cleanings. Zack had none of this and it terrified me.

He was a time bomb. He wouldn't be able to hold on to this job if not for me, and what would happen when the series went off the air? He would sit in his room and braid horse gear for a microscopic audience. I'd been planning to leave *Dr. Quinn* after one more season to pursue my own projects, but I would be giving up a guaranteed paycheck for zero guaranteed. I didn't want to take on one more person to support. And I was angry. I saw two choices: I could bail him out or cut him loose, and if I bailed him out, I'd be giving him the message that he didn't have to be responsible.

"He understands me, he accepts me, he makes me laugh," I told Josef and Jeanne when I saw them in the writers' trailer. "But on the other side of the scale—"

"There's always another side of the scale," Jeanne said.

Josef added, "He doesn't look like he's one step away from the street."

"He starches his shirts! When I met him, he didn't own a bed but he had an ironing board."

"Maybe he just needs to learn some management skills?" Jeanne suggested.

I shook my head.

Josef smiled. "He's a cowboy."

I resolved to call Zack and tell him all that I was thinking. He usually responded well to the truth, even if it was difficult. But when I dialed his number, I heard three ascending beep tones and a cheerful female voice: "The number you have reached is no longer in service. If you feel you've reached this recording in error, please check the number and try your call again." I must have misdialed. I called again and heard the same recording. What the hell was going on? You have to not pay your bills for months and they send you multiple warnings in red envelopes before they shut off your phone!

◆

Gabriel was in the backyard, crouched on the cement, working on some kind of motor. He pulled the cord and the engine coughed, then sputtered and died. He pulled it again. Nothing. Odd-shaped pieces of metal, pipes, and cans of grease were spread around the driveway. In the shadows behind Gabriel, someone was standing at the workbench, running a power saw. I walked toward them. It was Zack.

"Hey, guys." I patted Gabriel's shoulder.

"Hi, Mom."

Zack switched off the saw and drew himself up. He was wearing a turquoise shirt and the turquoise boots with black stitching and when I looked in his eyes, my breath caught.

"How're *you*?" he said.

"I tried calling, but your phone . . . "

"It's resting," he said, and winked.

I watched him. "How're you doing?"

"Ready to move ahead now." He smiled. "Okay?"

I looked about the yard. "What's going on here?"

"We're building a go-cart," Gabriel said, "but we can't get it to run."

Zack said they'd been gathering parts at junkyards and garage sales and had acquired a go-cart skeleton, to which they'd attached an old car seat and a lawn mower engine. "The motor was frozen, so we took it apart and we've been soaking it in solvent."

"It's never gonna run," Gabriel said.

"Sure it is. It's like a puzzle. There's only so many pieces. We try one thing and if that doesn't click, we try the next."

"It's too much trouble," Gabriel complained.

"Come on, cowboy, we're closin' in. We know it's the carburetor. We've just got to get that right balance of gas and air going in so it doesn't flood."

I took Zack's arm and drew him aside. "Listen, we don't want another butane incident."

"And we're not gonna have one. Trust me." He held up his hand.

"But where's he going to drive this thing?"

"On a go-cart track. They've got one in the valley. It's a controlled deal. They inspect your vehicle, you can only go so fast, and you've got to wear a helmet."

I looked at Gabriel, pulling the cord, trying again to start the motor. "I'll have to clear this with Jeff."

"You do that. I'll talk to him if you want. Hell, this is good for Gabriel. He'll be driving in a few years and he oughta know how an engine works."

He leaned forward to kiss me. His lips left a sticky trail and I wiped my mouth as I turned and walked into the house.

I called them for dinner an hour later and avoided Zack's eyes as we ate barbecued chicken and rice. After we'd cleaned up the kitchen, I tested Sophie on her French vocabulary. Then I helped Gabriel write a science report on arthropods. After I'd put the kids to bed, I found Zack in the bedroom, sitting in his chair by the window. "I got some good news," he said, clicking off a rerun of *Star Trek*.

"What's that?" I took my chair facing him.

"You know that miniature you encouraged me to send to Sun Valley?"

"Yes."

He'd brought a bottle of Armagnac up from the kitchen and poured it into two small glasses. "The gal who runs the museum called me today, right before the phone died." He lifted his glass. "The piece is sold."

"Are you serious?"

"Someone bought it on opening night. The president of the local cattle association."

"So the tag has a red dot?"

"They're mailing me a check. Twelve hundred dollars."

"This is fantastic. Congratulations!"

He downed the Armagnac. "I've broken my record. I still can't believe it."

"Why didn't you tell me before? I would have bought champagne."

"We'll have lots of time to celebrate, baby. This is just the beginning. We're on the upswing."

I felt myself sinking. He handed me my glass and I stared at the rich, amber liquid. "It's getting late."

"You got somewhere you need to be?"

"No."

He leaned forward. "What is it?"

"Nothing. I'm just . . . thrilled for you."

"You look like you're a million miles away."

I put the brandy to my lips.

"I'm sorry about the other night. I hated having to come to you like that."

I took a breath. "I don't understand . . . how you could not pay your phone bill all these months."

Zack shrugged.

"What happened to the money you've been earning?"

"It came and went."

I set the brandy glass down on the table. "It feels like I'm being mean-spirited and petty but if you don't pay your bills and I'm always covering them, it just won't work."

He nodded. "If we founder on anything, it'll be this. It's not gonna be because of another man or woman. At least on my part."

I told him about the jumbled emotions—confused, pissed-off, guilty—I'd been having. "I've been thinking . . . I'd like some time by myself." I watched his face, expecting pain or rage or stony withdrawal because, in actuality, I was asking him to sit on the bench.

"Sweetheart, that's all right. Take as much time as you want."

Relief washed through me.

"I love you, Sara. I want to spend the rest of my days loving you, but the only way I want you is if you're here of your own free will. If you've got doubts. If your happiness is somewhere else . . . "

"There's no one else."

"Whatever it is."

"I just need time."

"I understand. And I give it to you. I won't be hard to find."

I didn't know what to say. At that moment I had no desire to be anywhere else. "This is not what I expected."

He smiled, and I could not see, or did not choose to see, the turmoil below the surface. I could not perceive what this was costing him. I looked in his eyes and he looked in mine and we held that point together until everything—sounds, colors, thoughts—blurred and dissolved.

I moved across the chair and into his arms.

"I never pretended to be anything but what I am."

"I know that," I whispered.

"Let me put you to sleep."

He helped me slip off my clothes. He pulled up the quilt with its purple roses and vines and tucked me in. He kissed my hand, turned off the lamp, and I heard the spurs—*ka-chink, ka-chink*—go down the hall.

13

Zack stayed in Topanga braiding for several days and his phone continued to "rest." Jeff flew to France for a cable-film convention, which gave the children an unexpected reprieve from the grind of moving continuously back and forth. They missed their father but reveled in the luxury of being free to settle in one place. We ate dinner at odd times. On Sunday, we decided to get in the car and drive up the coast with no particular destination, as we'd often done after the divorce and hadn't for some time.

They'd both earned back their privileges by now, but when I asked Gabriel to carry the picnic basket to the car, he said, "Jeez, I've got my backpack. Why don't you ask Sophie for a change!"

I put down the canvas bag I was holding and turned to walk upstairs.

"Mom, I'm sorry. I lost control," Gabriel said. "I'd be happy to help you." He affected a smile, picked up the basket, and carried it to the station wagon.

Sophie opened the driver's door for me and buckled my seat belt around me, performing the task Zack habitually did. "Thanks," I said, and she smiled, satisfied.

When we reached Ventura, we decided to catch the boat for Anacapa Island, a wildlife preserve that's a nesting ground for the Western gull. We'd been told that all the birds who're born there fly back every year to lay their eggs. At the time we arrived, the babies were six weeks old and thousands of them were clustered across the rocks—little balls of brown fur with white spots. On the boat ride over, Sophie had said she absolutely would not go on a nature walk. "You have to stop and talk about one little plant. Then you move two inches and talk about the new plant." When we docked, though, and a ranger named Debbie in a crisp green uniform started gathering people for a hike, Sophie shrugged and got in line.

We covered the island in forty minutes, watching the baby gulls trying to fly, jumping up and down and flapping their fuzzy arms. "We call it trampolining," Ranger Debbie said. "In a few more weeks they'll be able to stay in the air."

When the tour ended, we wandered off the trail and sat on a boulder to watch the sea lions sliding and sunning themselves on the rocks in the cove below. Sophie started to sing "Baby Beluga." The kids had loved the song when they were younger and now we all joined in, clowning and hamming, drawing out the notes of the chorus: "Baaaa-bee be-loooo-ga." Gabriel started drumming the rhythm on his thighs. Without warning, three large gulls came flapping and shrieking toward us. Sophie screamed. Gabriel started running back to the trail. The gulls began to dive at us, beating their wings and squawking so loudly it hurt the ears. I grabbed Sophie's hand as we raced toward the trail, hunching down, covering our heads and swatting at the air. This is insane, I thought, it's a goddamned scene from *The Birds*. When we reached the trail, the gulls fell away and circled back toward the spot where we'd been sitting. Sophie was shaken. I put my arm around her, patting her. "It's all right. We must have come too close to their nest and they were protecting their babies. They're gone now."

We followed the trail back to the boat dock and ate our lunch at picnic tables with the other passengers. The gulls around the dock seemed completely benign. Gabriel and Sophie grew bold again and wanted to throw them bits of bread. A large sign warned us not to feed the birds, but they started throwing scraps anyway. I told them if they didn't stop, they'd have their privileges revoked.

"There was nothing on that list about feeding birds," Gabriel said.

"How about doing what Mom asks you to do?"

"Yeah yeah yeah," Sophie said. "Look! That white one's gonna fly." We watched an albino baby gull that was trampolining, bouncing higher and higher until it seemed it was surely going to levitate but it dropped exhausted to the rocks. I handed Sophie a chicken leg and Gabriel an avocado sandwich. I was opening the fruit salad when we heard a high-pitched call. A gull flew straight down the center of the picnic table. The feathers and flapping blocked my view of Sophie, and when the gull swooped away, I saw the chicken leg was gone.

"Did he grab it right out of your hand?"

She nodded.

"The nerve!" Gabriel said.

"I felt something pulling and I let go." She covered her mouth and started laughing. We all laughed—that helpless laughter that makes you want to collapse in a ball and laugh harder and when it subsides, you feel cleansed and content.

On the crossing back to Ventura, the three of us stood at the prow, rising and plunging with the boat as it cut through the swells. Suddenly the boat stopped and the engines were shut off. We looked about, puzzled, rocking from side to side in the silence. "Dolphins!" someone shouted. In moments they were all around us—hundreds and hundreds. Passengers were cheering and rushing to the rail.

"Look!"

"I see!"

"Get the camera!"

I noticed, not for the first time, how the sight of dolphins can boost the spirit of even the grayest soul. It's like pulling the lever on a slot machine and getting a jackpot. The movement of the animals—arching and cresting, jumping in the air with an insouciant flick of the tail—suggests a wild delight as opposed to the jagged, cold-eyed purpose of the shark or the fat, indolent posture of the seal or the majestic hugeness of whales. We grabbed hold of the rope and leaned over the water as the dolphins swam right up and rotated on their sides so that one eye seemed to look straight at us.

"This is amazing," Gabriel said. "I can't believe it. I love this day!"

Sophie was stretching her arm toward the water as if she could touch their silvery skin. "We *have* to come back."

◆

At eight the next morning, I was standing in the "elephant stage," the old, tin-roofed barn that had been converted into a sound studio. I'd driven in early to watch the rehearsal of a romantic scene I'd written for Dr. Mike and Sully, just after they've returned from their honeymoon. In the scene, it's late at night, Sully's ready to go to bed but Mike is troubled about her fifteen-year-old daughter. As she tells Sully her concerns, he listens and offers advice but at the same time, he's unlacing her shoes. He slips off her stockings, massages her foot, then kisses her sole and she's not thinking about her daughter anymore.

The director, Bobby Roth, walked onto the set and gave me a hug. He was slim, wiry, with an aquiline nose and a head of curly dark hair that seemed a manifestation of the nervous coiled energy with which he worked. I was happy Bobby was directing this show. He was one of the most talented directors we'd used and had a knack for intimate moments.

"Let's rehearse this," Bobby said.

Jane Seymour and Joe Lando, wearing their street clothes, walked to the bed. She sat down with her back to the headboard and he sat at the foot. The tiny, cramped set began filling up with people, talking and laughing. Word had gotten out about this scene, and every crew member who had any reason to be on the set was there.

Zack was not at the ranch today because we were shooting interiors. The previous week, when he'd walked down the Western street, the wranglers and some of the camera and sound crew had called: "What's this about a foot massage? Kiss her feet?! Jesus, she's been sweating in boots all day!" But the young women who worked on hair and makeup began stealing looks at Zack, and Mike Riggins's girlfriend, Sue, a stunt double, said she liked the idea of a foot massage. This made the male crew madder. Now the girls would start expecting shit like this. Mike yelled at Zack in front of the riders, "You don't kiss a woman's ass and you sure as hell don't kiss their feet."

Zack raised both his hands as if admitting he shot the sheriff. "I did it. All right?"

"What kind of a man would do that?"

"One who pleases his woman."

They hooted and swore.

"Why do you think I'm here?" Zack said. "It's not because I can ride a fucking horse."

"Let's be adults," Bobby said. "Or I'm gonna have to clear the set." The room fell silent. Bobby made his way over equipment boxes and camera tracks to the bed, where he crouched beside Jane and Joe.

"I've shot a lot of love scenes," he said, "and I've found that when you see everything, it's not as exciting as when you don't see it all but you can imagine." He made a frame with his hands. "I'm gonna start out wide, when you're talking and Joe's taking off your shoes." He turned to Joe. "Then I want you to slide up closer." Joe edged forward so he was even with Jane's torso. "That's good. I'm gonna come in tight now, so I'll only have you from here up." He touched their shoulders. "We won't know what you're doing with your hands, Joe, but we'll see her face responding. Can we try that?"

Joe and Jane ran their lines, mechanically, blocking out how they'd move and where they'd be at key points of dialogue. Ozzie Smith, the director of photography, told his camera operators what lenses he wanted and what lights he needed to create the illusion of candlelight.

"Second team," the AD called. Jane and Joe were driven to their trailers to change into their costumes and have their makeup and hair done. The stand-ins took their places on the bed, so the crew could continue adjusting lights and checking meter readings and laying tracks for the camera.

I walked up the hill to the writers' trailer and collected my messages. Zack hadn't called but I didn't expect him to. I worked on the outline for a new episode and from time to time, my eye traveled to the pictures of Zack on the desk: one had been taken by Jeanne at Elko; one showed us both on horses at the feedlot in Casa Grande; one was from Topanga where I'd shot him on the deck, naked from the waist up, laughing.

My beeper went off; they were ready on the set. I walked back to the elephant stage just as Jane reappeared wearing a long Victorian dress and lace-up boots. She settled herself against the pillows on the bed while Joe stripped off his shirt and, wearing only deerskin pants, sat down by her feet. The room was tense. "Quiet, please!"

Jane and Joe had dated while they were shooting the pilot but they'd broken up before *Dr. Quinn* had made it to the air. During the first season, Jane had married the director James Keach and Joe had brought a succession of exceptionally beautiful young girlfriends to the ranch. So there was history, tension, and competition between them. Jane was the star of the show but Joe wanted equal treatment, which he didn't receive. They criticized each other and at times barely spoke off camera, but when asked to play a romantic scene, they did some of their strongest work.

They created a mood of love and sensual longing that was palpable, that came across as authentic. Josef used to say that

Joe turned on all the wattage for these scenes. "He fixes those electric blue eyes on her. He touches her like he means it, he really wants to fuck her and he makes her want it too. That's how he tortures her."

She wasn't protesting, though. She softened, she melted, she took fire and in that moment of ignition there was no one on the set but the two of them. Nothing else mattered, nothing else counted.

"Let's shoot one," Bobby said. The doors to the set were secured. A bell rang. I pulled a wooden box to a spot where I could watch and not be noticed.

"Action."

Jane ran a brush through her hair. "Colleen's been acting . . . differently. Haven't you noticed?"

"She's growing up," Joe said.

He unlaced her boot and I was struck by how quickly and gracefully he was able to slip it off. He reached up under her dress and took hold of the black stocking.

"She wants to go on a hayride and I said no. She has school in the morning."

Joe slid the stocking down her calf, over her ankle and her toes. Jane had beautiful feet, with a dancer's high arches.

"Didn't you ever go on a hayride?" he said.

"We didn't have them in Boston." She flinched. "My feet are cold."

"Won't be for long."

He looked in her eyes as he massaged her foot, then slipped off the other boot and stocking.

"She's so young . . . That feels nice."

He began massaging the sole of her other foot.

"I don't think she's . . . ready," Jane said.

"Can we talk about this some other time?"

"I don't want her to be hurt. She . . . knows so little."

"She's delivered a baby. Sewed up a bullet wound." Joe kissed the arch of her foot.

"With medicine, yes, she's competent beyond her years. But in other . . . areas . . . she's very naive."

He put his lips around her toe. That wasn't in the script. He was sucking her toe, for God's sake, and this was eight o'clock family television.

"As . . . I was," Jane whispered.

He had her now. She sank back against the pillows. He edged forward and pushed down the fabric of her dress. He ran his hand down her body, out of camera frame. She closed her eyes and her lips parted.

Bonnie, the script supervisor, made a knocking sound on the floor.

Jane and Joe startled. "Yes?" Jane called.

Bonnie read the lines that would be dubbed in later by the actor playing Jane's son: "I need you to help me with my essay."

Joe ran his lips up the side of her neck.

I squirmed in the darkness. It was eerie, uncomfortable, and thrilling to watch them enacting a scene taken straight from my bedroom. And I saw what, impossibly, I had not seen until this moment: the story I was writing every week was the story I was living, or was it the other way around? Jane was playing a doctor from a cultured family, educated in Boston, and Joe was a mountain man, unschooled but wise and possessed of sexual power.

"I'll help you in the morning," Jane called through the door to her son. "We're . . . rather tired now."

"But, Ma . . ."

Joe kissed her bare shoulder.

"In the morning. I'll wake you early and we'll . . . get it done. All right?"

"Oh, all right." Bonnie drummed her feet, making the sound of footsteps receding.

Joe called, "Good night, Brian." He smiled at Jane.

"You look pleased," she said.

"I am. When one of the kids knocks and you don't jump right up . . . I know I've got your attention."

She laughed softly. He leaned in for the kiss, she wrapped her arms around his neck, and they slid together down the bed and out of frame.

"Cut!" Bobby said. "Ozzie, talk to me."

"I lost Joe for a second on the push. But the light looks beauty-ful."

"Sound?" Bobby said.

"Good for me," the mixer said.

Bobby turned in my direction. "What'd you think?"

Jane, Joe, Ozzie, the crew—all were watching me.

"Great."

That night after the kids went to bed, I took a bath and flipped through an issue of *New York* magazine. Out of curiosity, I scanned the personals. Almost every periodical from the *Los Angeles Times* to the *Jewish Journal* now carried personal ads, but those in *New York* were reputed to be the most discriminating.

"Mozart, Monet, and Margaux. Successful attorney, handsome, witty, 50 but looks 40, likes fine wine, classical music,

CNN." I imagined sipping Chateau Lafitte with him on leather couches, listening to string quartets on a state-of-the-art sound system. I don't think so.

"Accomplished, wealthy, spiritual vegetarian, not afraid to laugh laugh laugh!" I imagined eating tofu and geranium petals with him on china plates. Ha ha ha.

"Physician and publisher, good-looking, many cultural interests, lives on large estate with two modern guest wings." This was sounding interesting. "Seeks tall—5'7" or above . . ." That was me. ". . . slender, passionate, educated woman, no children at home." I was out.

I read on: There was the upbeat Jewish veterinarian; the athletic venture capitalist who volunteers with underprivileged kids; the TV journalist, Ivy grad, "who's a jeans guy on the weekends with an intermittent tux for fund-raisers." They wanted to walk on the beach and sit by the fireplace and see foreign movies and ski in the Rockies and play Scrabble and golf. "If you like Vermont leaves, van Gogh landscapes, lobster in Maine, daffodils in Central Park . . ." Who the hell doesn't, I thought, tossing *New York* on the floor and stepping out of the bath.

In the days that followed I took the case to my friends: was Zack the man I should be with and if not, who was? If someone voted for him, I pointed out the obvious warning signs and when someone voted no, I argued in his favor. Nora, a writer in Chicago who'd been having an on-and-off romance with another writer, Jake, for years, said no. "I can't bear it when someone isn't like me. Jake and I are such a match—in sentiments, humor, taste. When I feel it's not a match I get irritated and grumpy. So I couldn't conceive of being with a person like Zack."

"But we are a match in the deepest sense," I said, "and he's there one hundred percent. I can be in the clutches of an anxiety attack, struggling to breathe, and he holds me and listens and makes love to me and in a short while, the pain is gone. Just gone."

"Well, that's the thing," Nora admitted. "Jake is not there. He adds to my anxiety."

Other friends said Zack was a train wreck and this was the time to jump. But Jeanne said I was crazy not to hold on. "You have fabulous sex, he respects your need for solitude, and he adores you." Jeanne nodded. "I'd say that's worth a thousand dollars."

I found, as I talked, that there was a notion that still gripped me with an almost preternatural power: the notion of an equal relationship, where both partners have work they love, both contribute financially, and both take care of one another and nurture each other's talent. There were a few, very few couples who seemed to have attained this kind of union. I stress *seemed* because there were rude shocks, as when the fabled writing couple, Michael Dorris and Louise Erdrich, filed for divorce and he later committed suicide. My own experience, when I'd been involved with a supposed equal, was that at the end of a long day, we needed a wife and we also needed a mistress: someone to draw the bath, light candles, rub our shoulders, and lead us into the garden because we both were too exhausted.

I took note when I read about strong and accomplished women who'd married men who looked after them. Jane Smiley, whose novels I admired, was quoted in an interview as saying that her husband's job was "managing me." Roseanne had divorced her comedian husband, Tom Arnold, and married her bodyguard. Valerie Harper had married her personal trainer, whom she helped become a producer. Then there were the New York women writers and intellectuals—Elaine May, Anne Roiphe, Lois Gould, Barbara Lazear Ascher—who'd married psychiatrists and, I imagined, had live-in therapy. But the truth, and I knew it, was that no one takes care of you, even if it seems that person may.

In the middle of the week, during lunch, we had a cast read-through for a two-hour special about a cattle drive. The actors sat around the conference table and we took chairs behind them, making notes. It was our chance to hear what the story sounded like on its feet: what was funny, what was moving, what fell flat. I was having trouble concentrating and leaned over to Josef. "Could you cover this?"

"Sure. You all right?"

"Just need some air."

I left the trailer and walked down the road to the Western town. I saw Mike Riggins and, on impulse, asked if I could borrow a horse to ride.

He gave me his flinty stare. "By yourself?"

"Yes."

He nodded. There were three horses tied to the hitching post, one of whom was Solomon, who'd bucked me off when the saddlebag on his back had come loose. I hesitated. There was no bag on him today. I walked over and undid his reins.

"How long you plan on staying out?" Mike said.

"Not sure."

I swung up into the saddle and headed for the trail to Malibu Creek State Park. It had rained the past few days so the air was dramatically clear and crisp. The colors of the landscape were more brilliant than I'd seen in months: the sky was the bluest blue, the clouds were fluffy white. I glanced at Solomon's head and he flipped his ears back. I tensed. He dropped his neck and I gave a sharp jerk up with one rein. "Easy, Solomon." He threw his head up and down, trying to yank the reins from my hand. I jerked again, keeping my arm stiff and ready while an anxious pulse was beating in my throat. After a few minutes, he relaxed his neck and walked ahead steadily. I loosened my grip.

We came to the tall rock face by Malibu Creek where the stunt boy had leaped thirty feet onto cardboard boxes. I got off and tied Solomon to a tree. I sat down on a log. Because of the rains, the water was high and swift as it coursed over rocks and fallen tree trunks. I sat there, idly plucking grass, watching the shadows of the sycamores and the dark red mountains reflected in the stream. And then there was a moment when I knew, with sureness, what I had not known before: there were two roads I could take. I could walk ahead with Zack or I could walk on by myself, and either way I was going to be all right. Either way I would survive, and more than that, I would have a life rich with adventure, challenge, grief, reward. I felt a sudden lightness. It was like choosing left or right, blue or red. I had a preference—and at this moment I saw what it was— but it had nothing to do with logic or arguments or the consequences of my choice.

I began to take deep, slow breaths. I had the impulse to call up all the friends I'd known and tell them I loved them. I was thirteen again, walking nude through my family's house in the early morning darkness when everyone else was still sleeping, just to feel the joy of moving with the air on my skin.

◆

It was six and the sun had set when I drove up the dirt road to Zack's cabin. His truck wasn't there. I knocked on the door and when I heard no answer, took the key from its hiding place in a eucalyptus tree. I opened the door. "Zack?" I switched on a lamp. Maybe he'd gone out for a beer. I walked through the cabin to the kitchen. There was a half-filled cup of coffee on the table and an ashtray overflowing with butts. He couldn't have gone far, I thought, but something made me turn and look at his work table: the rawhide strings and tools were gone. I hurried to the closet. His clothes and boots were gone. There were no hats hanging on the cow skull.

I rushed outside and up the path to Alice's house. She answered the door in a faded pink bathrobe. "Have you seen Zack?" I asked. She looked at me with myopic puzzlement.

"He left."

14

I drove down the canyon, cutting sharply around the curves, using the cell phone to check my answering machine. Nothing. I dialed Phoenix.

"Hello?"

"Hi, Nathan, it's Sara."

"Hey! How ya doing?" His voice had its tail-wagging eagerness.

"Is your father there?"

"My dad?"

"He seems to have left his place in Topanga." I paused. "He told his landlady he had to leave and didn't know when he'd be back."

"He ain't here."

"Nathan," I said gently, "I'm worried. Please tell me if you've heard from him."

"I talked to him, let's see . . . Sunday, I think."

"He didn't mention this?"

"Nope. He sure didn't."

"If he calls or shows up, would you let me know?" I gave him my number and explained how to place a collect call. I told him he could do this even though he couldn't dial long distance from his phone.

"All right."

When I pulled up to the house, Sophie came out the front door, raising her hands to stop me in the driveway. "Mom, don't pull into the garage."

"Why not?"

She was grinning, expectant. "Just get out now, okay? Don't worry, it's not bad. Come with me, you'll see."

Her eyes flitted to the yard and back. She was nearly bursting with some secret. Could Zack be there?

"Trust me." She opened the car door and motioned me to walk up the driveway with her. I heard mischievous giggling. I scanned the yard. The outdoor lights were on, casting circles of brassy yellow on the cement. I heard an engine sputter to life and Gabriel came roaring out of the garage driving the go-cart. The engine was running, it was thrumming, the cart was moving right along and he gave a triumphal wave as he drove past me wearing his helmet. Sophie ran after him and I followed. He steered down the driveway, up the sidewalk and into our neighbor's circular drive where he veered around and came back to the house, cutting his speed and stopping in the yard.

"How'd you get it to run?" I said.

He was climbing out of the cart. "The float finally came. We ordered it from a catalog and it just got here today."

"You put it in yourself?"

He nodded, taking off his helmet. "I tried calling Zack, but his phone's dead or something. So I opened it up, and it looked just

like the one we'd taken out. I screwed it in, pulled the cord, and
the motor started! I can't wait to show Zack. Is he coming for
dinner?"

"No."

"When's he coming then?"

"Not . . . for a while."

Gabriel looked puzzled.

"He had to go out of town."

"No! When's he coming back?"

"I'm not sure. Maybe in a few days."

"But he said he'd take me to the track this weekend. That's
not fair!"

I looked at the go-cart with the old car seat bolted onto the
metal skeleton from the junkyard, then at Gabriel. "I'll take
you to the track."

The next morning, I started shaking before I was fully awake
and could remember why. I reached for the phone and called
Nathan. I tried coming at him from a different angle, explaining that Zack and I had had, not a fight but . . . a discussion
that might have upset him. I wanted a chance to straighten
things out.

"Mmm-hmm," Nathan said.

"I'm sure he'll call you sooner or later."

"I don't know about that. When he and my mom were
splitting up, he just took off. It was a year before I saw him."

"A year."

I won't be hard to find.

"Aw, it probably won't be that long."

"Nathan, please, would you . . . tell him I love him?"

"If I get a chance, you bet I will."

I drove to the ranch knowing we had a full call—twenty riding extras—hoping blindly that somehow he'd be there. I walked to the blacksmith shop where the riders sit around between takes. "Where the hell's Zack at?" Mike Riggins called.

"He had an emergency. Family problem. I was supposed to tell you."

"How long is he gonna be out?"

I hesitated, and Mike gave a smug grin. You dropped him. Finally came to your senses.

"I'll let you know."

I went back to the office and threw myself into work, writing revisions for "Cattle Drive," consulting my notes on what Beth wanted, what the network wanted. When the phone rang, I jumped for it but it wasn't Zack. It was my agent; it was Veronica; it was the doctor at the Smithsonian who checked our scripts for historical accuracy.

The following days passed in a blur of story conferences and rewrites and shepherding the children through their hectic schedules—dance, soccer, Hebrew school, dentist appointments. As I drove to and from the ranch, I rehearsed what I'd say when he did call: I was sorry, I was upset, I was relieved. But after a week passed with no word, I berated him for bailing out so abruptly, for not having the decency to tell me he was going and at least say good-bye to the children.

"Is he all right?" Gabriel asked.

"Yes, I think he is."

"He's mad at me," Sophie said, "that's why he left. I said mean things, like, he smells."

"No, that's not the reason."

I was to blame, I thought as I headed down the Pacific Coast Highway. I'd tried to domesticate him, which I never should have done, and if I'd succeeded I wouldn't have liked the result. And I'd kept him on the margins, making him fit and bend around my custody schedule, my work schedule.

But he'd said he understood, he'd said it was all right. *Take as much time as you want.* And the kids—Gabriel felt betrayed and Sophie felt responsible and guilty. Hadn't he thought about them? Maybe it was better that he'd left. Yes, it was the best thing, we'd known all along, it couldn't go on. I was prepared to walk ahead on my own, it was time to detach myself and then I had to pull off the road and double over in agony.

At home, the kids were buzzing over a chain letter Gabriel had just received. "It says if I send copies to ten people and a dollar to the person at the top of the list, in fourteen days I'll get a hundred and eighty dollars! I can buy those cymbals I want—Zildjian hi-hats."

I told him I'd sent dozens of chain letters, mailing postcards, jewelry, and dollar bills to the first name on the list with the promise that in fourteen days I'd be the first name and I'd receive a bounty. "But in all my years, I've never received one thing from a chain."

"But this one works," Gabriel said. "And it's bad luck to break it. One guy had his house burn down, exactly fourteen days after he broke it."

"Well, okay, if you want to copy the letter ten times and address envelopes and buy stamps . . . "

"I'll help you," Sophie said. "We'll copy it on Mom's

machine and deliver them in the neighborhood."

"Brilliant," Gabriel said.

They made Xerox copies of the letter and stuffed them into envelopes, addressing them to "Current Resident." I stood on the balcony and smiled, watching them hurry across the lawns as if they were on a stealth mission, drop the letters into mailboxes, and dash back to the sidewalk.

That weekend I took them to see a revival of *Carousel* at the music center. I'd seen the movie with Shirley Jones when I was young and listened to the album until I knew every song by heart. I remembered it now as high schmaltz, but at the first notes of the overture and the sight of a dozen fresh-faced young women sitting in a row, shoulders bent, working at the loom in the mill, I started tearing up. By the time the play was over, Sophie was crying and I was sobbing so hard I had wads of wet Kleenex in my lap and couldn't breathe through my nose. Julie Jordan had married the carnival barker, Billy Bigelow, when everyone warned her not to and then he'd been shot, leaving her stranded with a baby and outcast. Gabriel pretended to be unmoved. "How come you guys were crying so much?"

"Come on, Gabriel," Sophie said, "when the father came down from heaven and tried to talk to his daughter, I saw you wiping your eyes."

He shrugged.

"I felt sad for the daughter," Sophie said. "The kids in town made fun of her and she had no friends."

I was crying, I told them, because of the choices we're asked to make in life between the conventional, safe prospect and the romantic long shot, and sometimes following your heart can lead to pain and ruin. "Life is a storm you have to walk through with your head up and then the sun comes out."

The three of us held hands, as we almost never did, while we walked up the stairs and made our way across the theater plaza and into the parking structure.

In the morning, I dropped them at school and was taking my automatic route to the ranch when I turned, instead, onto the ramp for the San Diego Freeway. I called the office on the cell phone and asked for Beth, but she was at a meeting with CBS executives. I asked for Josef.

"I have to go out of town for a few days," I said.

"When?"

"Now."

"Are you serious?"

"Something's come up."

"Really? What's wrong?"

"Nothing. It's . . . personal."

"But 'Cattle Drive' starts today, right?"

"Yes." The entire cast, crew, and truckloads of equipment were being moved to Simi Valley to a cattle ranch we'd leased for the episode.

"I think you need to be there, Sara. God knows what kind of problems they're gonna run into."

"Any chance you could drive out?"

"Not really. We've got the production meeting for 'Fathers and Sons' this morning, and casting in the afternoon. Could you put it off a day, till we get this episode rolling?"

"No. I'm sorry."

He paused, and I could hear the concern and irritation in his voice. "Okay. I'll let Beth know."

I caught the nine-thirty flight to Phoenix, rented a Pontiac

Grand Am, and drove through the old part of the city to the Coronado section with its overgrown yards and chain-link fences. I pressed a switch that triggered a four-way click, locking the doors. I had no plan. I pulled up to the house and there was no red truck. Nathan was coming out the door with his web-footed glide, carrying a backpack that seemed to weigh as much as he did.

When I called his name he turned, disoriented, and squinted in my direction through the bottle-thick glasses.

"It's Sara."

"Cool! What're you doing here?"

"Can I come in?" I stepped out of the Grand Am.

He shifted his weight. "I was just gonna catch the bus to school."

"I'll drive you there."

"Smokin' deal."

He turned around, felt for the keyhole, and unlocked the door. I followed him inside and was stopped by the smell of stale beer, old food, cigarettes.

"He's not here," Nathan said.

"But he's been here." As soon as I said it, I knew. I looked at my watch. "Let me take you out to lunch, Nathan. Then I'll drop you at the college."

We drove to the Lone Star Steak House where Zack and I had eaten in a booth on New Year's Eve. I ordered Nathan a Corona. "I know your dad's going to stay in touch with you. If nothing else, to send you money for art supplies."

"Yeah, he might do that."

The waitress brought our salads and Nathan ate holding the fork with his fist, the way he held his brushes.

"I'm sure he made you promise not to tell me. But you know your dad. He's stubborn."

"That's true. But you're a darn good match for him." He waved the fork. "Comin' all this way." He took a drink of beer.

"Your dad wants me to find him, Nathan."

He threw his head back and laughed. "You're real persuasive."

Our steaks came and he let out an appreciative "Ooooh." He bent his head over the plate so he could see what he was cutting and I thought, He's nervous. We talked about his classes and where he wanted to study after Phoenix College. There was a Native American art school in New Mexico, and he was also applying to the San Francisco Art Institute.

"Are you worried about him?"

He mashed butter into his baked potato. "Kind of."

"Is he in trouble?"

He took a bite of potato and chewed.

"Whatever's going on, he should be with people who love him."

He started nodding. "Mmm-hmm. I think you're right about that." He finished his beer.

"Would you like another?"

He nodded and I signaled the waitress.

"He can't breathe good."

"What?"

"He's got lung . . . "

I felt the room light up and gray over.

"Cancer?"

"No. Chronic lung disease. It's real bad. It's destroying his lungs."

"How long has he known this?"

The waitress brought another Corona and he took a swallow. "He came down here a day or so after you called. He was sleeping on the couch that night and he got to coughing so hard he couldn't breathe, he was all red and choking. I called his buddy Ray, and we hauled him over to the emergency hospital."

Nathan wiped his mouth with his hand.

"And then?" I said gingerly.

"They gave him a breathing treatment. He'll kill me if he knows I told you this."

I wasn't hearing all the words. "Treatment?"

"He had to sit and breathe some medicine mixed with, I don't know, warm vapors I think, from a tube for a few hours, and then he was all right."

"But . . . does he need more treatment?"

Nathan shook his head. "He needs to stop smoking. If he does, the doctors think there's a good chance his lungs could heal up." He adjusted the glasses behind his ears. "He says he's gonna quit. But if he doesn't—"

"Where is he?"

"That's what I ain't sure of. He went down south to see his maestro."

"Joe Pintero?"

"Yep. Joe retired a few years back and all my dad knows is, he's living in a line shack on a big ranch down by the border. He doesn't have a phone, and I can't tell you how to get there. If you do find the place and my dad's there, I don't know what shape he'll be in. If he's not there, don't even bother with Joe. He won't tell you nothing."

I dropped Nathan at Phoenix College and made several wrong turns before finding my way onto Interstate 10. Martina McBride was on the radio singing "Independence Day." As I drove south, the gas stations and minimalls gave way to stretches of sand and groves of saguaro cactus—that archetypal desert plant that never fails to excite me. The saguaros stand as tall as a two- or three-story building, with great green arms pointing, reaching, drooping, entwining with each other. I spotted a cluster that made me pull over to the shoulder and stare. Five giant saguaros had five black turkey vultures perched on their tops, etched against the inky blue sky. The birds' wings were extended so they looked like bats with red gobbler heads, but they weren't bats, they were carrion eaters.

I pulled off the interstate in Tucson to buy gas and bottled water. A few hours later, I passed Benson and picked up the two-lane road for Douglas and Agua Prieta. The sun was setting now and the sky was turning lambent gold with puffs of lavender and rose, enveloping me like Surround Sound. Zack had often talked about Arizona sunsets: he said they had to be female, they were so damn sensuous. I noticed the countryside was changing. The sand and spiky vegetation had receded and in its place were grassy hills with herds of cattle on the slopes. The road curved and made switchbacks around pine and oak trees, on one of whose trunks was nailed a hand-lettered sign: "Drive Slowly, No M.D. Around."

At an intersection of two dirt roads, I stopped at an old adobe grocery store with a gas pump in front. I bought a bag of peanut M&M's and asked the lady sitting on a stool behind the register, "Can you tell me how to get to the Mule Shoe Ranch?"

She had wispy orange hair she'd obviously dyed herself. "Honey, there isn't any sign. It starts about five miles down, but it's thirty thousand acres. You want the main ranch house?"

"I'm looking for the line shack."

"They got lots."

"The place where Joe Pintero's staying."

She stubbed out a cigarette in a can that had once held stewed tomatoes. "That's over by Patagonia."

"I have a map in the car." I turned and opened the screen door. "It's raining."

"Yep. It's been doin' that every day 'bout this time. It won't last too long."

I found the word "Patagonia" on the map next to a small dot, but no solid lines leading up to it, only a faint dotted one. I showed it to the woman and she shook her head.

"Just go down the road about twenty-four miles and there's a big iron gate on the right. You turn in there. In about a mile, you'll come to a cattle guard and then a fork. Bear left and left again at the Y. Take that, let's see, about four miles. Then, well, just keep to the left, and you'll run into it."

I asked her to repeat the directions and wrote them down. "Thanks."

"You might want to wait till daylight," she said. "I got blankets. You could sleep in the store."

"That's very kind, but I'd rather go on."

By the time I found the iron gate, the sky was pitch black and it was still raining. I didn't mind, sometimes it was easier to drive in the dark, I could focus on what was right before me in the headlights and not be distracted by what was on either side. There were ruts and rocks but I was doing all right.

I felt the wheels bump over metal—the cattle guard. Then the fork, as promised. I took the left road and came to the Y. Nothing could stop me. I turned left again with the rain still beating and the wipers swishing but after five minutes, I was back at the same Y. I looked at my notes. She'd said left but maybe she'd forgotten about this Y. Or had I missed a turn? I tried taking the road to the right but in no time, the rocks were so big I had to steer around them and then I hit a boulder and was bounced and thrown sideways into a rut. I jammed on the brakes but the car was fishtailing, I had no traction, the nose dropped and I was falling, oh God—I put my arms out and braced. I was sliding down a hill or cliff, this was stupid, it was harebrained, I was going to pay and then the car thudded to a stop with the front end buried in mud.

I shoved at the door. Something was blocking it—dirt. I pulled the door back in and pushed again, and again. It heaved open. I climbed out, slipping and sinking to my ankles and grabbing the door handle. I looked around—all was black except for the car's dulled headlamps under the dirt. I had no flashlight, I was drenched with rain. I had no cell phone and even if I did it wouldn't work here. I hadn't seen a car or light of any kind in twenty miles.

I climbed back in and honked the horn. Cows bellowed back from what seemed close range. In moments I heard them grunting and snuffling around the car. I rolled down the window and yelled, "Get on! Hee-yah!" They stared at me, then turned and retreated clumsily up the ravine.

I crawled into the backseat, stretched out, and tried to sleep, which was impossible. It was only eight P.M., a long wait until daybreak. I switched on the radio and turned the dial—nothing but static and a Spanish-language station playing mariachi music with trumpet flourishes. Was it Mexico? Arizona? I don't know where the fuck I am!

◆

It started getting light around six. The rain had stopped, so I slung my purse over my shoulder and picked up the water bottle. But where should I walk? There were hills rolling away in all directions and no sign of human life. I decided to follow the pocked, muddy road I'd taken the night before. It must lead somewhere.

I walked a mile, picking my way around pools of rainwater and rocks, then walked another mile. The sun was rising and I turned toward it. This was east, which meant I'd been walking west. Was that right? This could be the stretch where immigrants trying to cross the border get lost and die of thirst and exposure. I took off my jacket and wrapped it around my waist. I scanned the horizon. Something was moving on a plateau about a half mile away. It was coming in my direction but as I kept walking, we didn't seem to be getting nearer to each other. I drank some water and kept walking. Then I saw it was a rider. I stopped and shielded my eyes. He was wearing a dark hat, riding a sorrel horse. Not Zack. But whoever it was probably knew Joe Pintero. Maybe it was Joe. I looked around at the deserted hills, the empty roads. It could be anyone.

I watched the rider. He dropped into a gully and disappeared. A pulse started knocking in my chest, out of rhythm—like an irregular heartbeat when you want to panic and tell yourself to just wait and breathe.

The rider came up out of the gully and trotted straight toward me, his legs hanging loose, his seat not moving from the saddle. I recognized the posture—elegant, relaxed—and hugged myself with relief. I started to smooth my hair but it was useless. My eyes were red, my clothes damp and wrinkled.

He stopped his horse five yards away, stepped down, and

dropped the reins in the dirt. "What the hell are you doing out here?" He came striding toward me.

"I tried to drive in last night. My car went over a ravine and got stuck in the mud."

He nodded. I could not help noticing that he looked good—color in his skin, alertness in his green eyes. New black Stetson. "We heard something," he said. "Thought it was one of those goddamned tourists we have to haul out of trouble."

"How're you feeling?"

He stared at me. "All right."

"Why did you run off?"

"I didn't run off. I got dismissed."

"You said you'd give me time."

"For what? I know I'm not the guy you always wanted. But where is he? Am I supposed to just hang around till he shows up or you get bored or fed up with me and then I'll be dismissed?"

"Zack, I came here to tell you . . ." I started again. "I care about you more than I care about anyone except my children, and they're growing up, they'll move on."

"Nice words."

"Words?"

"The party's over. We had a good time."

"What are you saying? I just left my job—I took off cold with nobody to cover for me—and flew down here, I rented a car that I've wrecked and I'm gonna have to pay for, and I spent the night in a goddamn ditch in a rainstorm with cows, scared out of my mind. Doesn't that tell you anything?"

"Yeah. You're a stubborn woman who'll go to any extreme to have her way."

"And you're not stubborn?" I pummeled his arm. "You're the most bullheaded, obstinate, mulish, pigheaded, stiff-necked jerk."

"See, your first impression was not that wrong. You thought I was a fucking jerk. But I got your attention."

"Is that what this is about?"

"Sweetheart, I told you . . ." He broke into a smile. "You gotta be tough to run with me."

We were in each other's arms. He was kissing my cheeks, my eyelids. "You look beautiful."

"No."

"Yes, you do." He started nudging me toward the sorrel horse. "Let's go see Joe. You'll like him. He makes good tortillas. Think you can ride?"

"Maybe."

He grasped the stirrup as I climbed up into the saddle. Then he swung up behind me so he was sitting on the horse's bare back. He made a clicking sound with his tongue and we started walking through the mud.

"Old Joe's been giving me quite a talking to."

"Has he?"

"He doesn't like me smoking any better than you do. And he told me, 'Son, if you must be beat up in life, it's best that it be done by a woman.'"

I laughed.

"I love to hear you laugh."

"I love you."

I relaxed back against him, breathing in the smell of horse and rain-wet grass.

"You're supposed to." He had one hand on the reins, the other around me and he was unbuttoning my shirt. Then his fingers were on my skin, talking to me with every footfall, as he urged the sorrel animal up the hill and toward the line shack.

EPILOGUE

It's been five years since Zack and I met in Elko, Nevada. Kurt Vonnegut once wrote that "peculiar travel suggestions are dancing lessons from God." If a wrangler at *Dr. Quinn* hadn't suggested I go to the cowboy poetry festival, if I hadn't blindly jumped on a plane, if Zack hadn't taken a ride with a silversmith who'd urged him to venture to a place he'd never been and to which he's never returned, we would have lived out our days and our orbits would not have intersected.

Yet here we are. What once seemed ludicrous and impossible has become the norm, although, as Zack puts it, "normal's a relative term." At times, I ask myself, how did this happen? How did I steer so far from the conventional track? I've always been something of a nonconformist but when I was younger, so many people were behaving in wild, flamboyant ways that my own eccentricity was masked. Now it's in full view.

We live in separate places, which suits us. Zack's cabin in Topanga was torn down two years ago and we found him a studio ten minutes from my house. We both crave solitude and look forward to seeing each other, three or four times a week. Yet it's been a while since we've had one of our lost weekends. We're no longer starved, we're well-fed and sated, though we retain a keen memory of that state and no wish to revisit it.

Sophie and Gabriel have made their peace with Zack. In their fashion. They've come to grasp that he won't harm them and he's not going away. The last time I went to Sophie's school for a conference, her French teacher asked, "Is there really a cowboy? Because sometimes you wonder if kids are exaggerating."

"There is," I said.

"Well, she certainly gets a lot of mileage out of it."

"How do you mean?"

"Telling stories about him, making people laugh."

Gabriel still likes to work with Zack on projects. Most recently, they installed a security system in Gabriel's rehearsal room, so his band can store their amps and equipment inside. Both kids are moving off on their own and far less interested in spending time with me. Gabriel just got his learner's permit to drive and Sophie's looking at colleges on the Internet.

The future is as uncertain today as it was when we met. *Dr. Quinn* was canceled last May by CBS. Zack has continued to sell more of his pieces—enough to buy a new truck and retire Willie. But each headstall he braids seems to be more challenging, complex, and time-consuming than the last. Money is always an issue. At this moment, neither Zack nor I knows what our next course of work will be.

But this afternoon, at four, we took off in his truck for Malibu and rode the horses we lease on Chumash Indian trails. Because of the El Niño rains, the hills were a glorious drunken green, and the wildflowers! There were floating clouds of yellow mustard, purple lupine, scarlet paintbrush. If you grabbed a handful of wild fennel and passed it under your nose, it was bracing, like the bite of fresh horseradish.

On the way home, we stopped at Gladstone's and ate steamed lobsters that had been flown in from Maine. Zack asked why the lobsters can't be raised in Pacific waters.

"I don't know. It's not their habitat," I said.

"It's not mine either, but I've adapted."

We went home and soaked in the tub, climbed into bed, and made our way to that private reserve, that peaceful cove where we can laugh and be silly and feel loved and all else seems to fade. That's the thing. After five years, we can still find the way. Sometimes it takes longer, but we do arrive. Trust the heart.

—July 1998
Santa Monica, California

Listen to
COWBOY
as read by the author
SARA DAVIDSON

While working on the television series *Dr. Quinn, Medicine Woman*, critically acclaimed author Sara Davidson has a chance meeting with an attractive, green-eyed cowboy from Arizona. At first she dismisses him as an "insolent yokel," but months later, feeling at loose ends, she calls and invites him to visit for a weekend—a weekend which alters the course of both their lives . . .

"A fascinating, intricate, complex love story that cuts across class lines, defying social expectations. Davidson's relationship with Zack is full of complications and negotiations, terrible and wonderful. If we accept that love is a mystery, this mystery holds you until the last page and beyond."
—Whitney Otto, author of *How to Make an American Quilt*

ISBN 0-694-52135-3 • $18.00 ($26.50 Can.)
3 hours/2 cassettes
Abridged

Available at bookstores everywhere, or call 1-800-331-3761 to order.

HarperAudio
A Division of HarperCollinsPublishers
www.harperaudio.com